THE UNBREAKABLE
HEART
OF
OLIVA
DENARO

THE UNBREAKABLE HEART

OF

OLIVA DENARO

a novel

VIOLA ARDONE

Translated from the Italian by Clarissa Botsford

 HarperVia

An Imprint of HarperCollins*Publishers*

Excerpt from "Nessuno." Lyrics by Antonietta De Simone, music by Edilio Capotosti and Vittorio Mascheroni. © 1959 by Sugarmusic S.p.a. Tutti.

Excerpt from "Non arrossire." Lyrics by Maria Monti and Giulio Rapetti Mogol, music by Giorgio Gaberscik and Davide Pennati. © 1960 by Universal Music Publishing Ricordi S.r.l.

Excerpts from the poem "Lettera a una madre" by Alba de Céspedes, from *Le ragazze di maggio* (Milan: Mondadori, 1970), © 2015, Mondadori Libri S.p.A., Milano.

Excerpt from *Anne of Green Gables* by Lucy Maud Montgomery.

Excerpt from "Renato" by Alberto Testa and Alberto Cortez.

Excerpt from "Donatella." Lyrics by Donatella Rettore and music by Claudio Rego. © 1981 by Universal Music Publishing Ricordi S.r.l. / Senso Unico S.n.c.

Excerpt from the poem "L'addio del grembiulino bianco" by Michele Antonucci.

HarperCollins books may be purchased for educational, business, or sales promotional use. For information, please email the Special Markets Department at SPsales@harpercollins.com.

Originally published as *Oliva Denaro* in Italy in 2021 by Einaudi.

FIRST HARPERVIA EDITION PUBLISHED IN 2023

Designed by Janet Evans Scanlon
Part opener art: © pilipphoto/stock.adobe.com, © Olga Moonlight/stock.adobe.com

Library of Congress Cataloging-in-Publication Data is available upon request.

ISBN 978-0-06-327687-1
ISBN 978-0-06-327688-8 (Library Edition)

23 24 25 26 27 LBC 5 4 3 2 1

For Carolina and Enzo, my parents

CONTENTS

PART ONE

1960

1

A girl is a jug: you break her, you take her. That's what Mother says.

I would have been happier as a boy like Cosimino but when they made me nobody asked me what I wanted. We were together and the same in the belly but after we came out, we were different: me dressed in pink, him in blue, me with a rag doll, him, a wooden sword, me in a flowery dress and him in stripy shorts. At nine, he learned to whistle, with and without his fingers, while I could tie my hair in a high or a low ponytail. Now that we're going on fifteen, he's four inches taller than me and allowed to do far more: walk around town night and day, wear shorts or long pants on holidays, talk to girls and boys of all ages, drink watered-down wine on Sunday, swear, spit, and, in summer, race down to the beach and have a swim in his trunks. I'm in favor of bathing in the sea.

Between the two of us, Cosimino is Mother's favorite because he's fair-skinned and blond like Father, whereas I'm raven-haired. He isn't a jug. He won't break. And even if he does, he'll be put back together again.

I was always good at school and Cosimino couldn't be bothered. Mother was never upset by this. She said he should roll up his sleeves and get a good job so his life doesn't wind up like Father's. Watching Father pore over the tomato plants in the vegetable garden made me think he'd never given a thought to how things would wind up. He's for starting new projects from scratch. Like when he managed to buy some chickens with the money that he made selling snails we'd harvested after a heavy shower. He said I could choose their names and, since I like colors, I went for Rosina, Celestina, Verdina, Violetta, and Nerina . . . Then he wanted to build a chicken coop with wooden boards and I passed him the nails, and then a trough for the chicken feed, and I passed him the saw. When everything was ready, I said, "Pà, shall we paint it yellow?"

Mother weighed in, "Do you think those bird-brained animals care whether it's yellow or black? Don't waste any paint."

"They'd be happier if it was yellow," I meekly ventured, "and when they're happy they lay more eggs."

"Really? Did they whisper that in your ear?" Mother retorted. Then she spun on her heel and marched back into the house, muttering in the Cosentino-Calabrian dialect she grew up with, which is different from Sicilian. That's what she always speaks when her nerves are jangled, so that we can't understand when she complains about coming down south.

Father picked up a paintbrush, dipped it in yellow, then drew it out, the paint dripping down the pot the same hue as beaten eggs ready for an omelet, which I could practically smell. I'm all in favor of omelets.

We painted the coop together and our fresh brush-strokes gleamed in the sun.

"Salvo Denaro, you're as stubborn as a mule and your daughter's no better," Mother shouted as she came back into the yard. Whenever she was angry, she addressed us by our full names like a schoolteacher.

"Never once do you two listen to me. And look at you, wearing your good skirt to work in. God forbid you get it dirty! Go and get changed, and keep yourself clean," she ordered, yanking the paintbrush out of my hands.

Glaring at Father, she reproached, "I gave you a male heir." She summoned Cosimino, who slunk into the yard, reluctantly picking up a brush, but ten minutes later his hand started hurting and he sidled away hoping no one would notice. In the meantime, I'd put on the apron I use when I do my chores and returned to working with Father until sunset, when the chickens went to roost happily in their little yellow hutch.

The next morning, one of them was dead as a doornail: it was Celestina. The stink of paint, Mother yelled in Calabrian. Chicken fever, Father whispered in my ear. I didn't know who to believe: she talks and talks and never stops spouting lists of rules, and that's why it's so easy to disobey her. Father, on the other hand, usually chooses silence, and that's why I can never work out how to make him love me. Whatever the cause, we buried the hen behind the vegetable garden and Father drew the sign of the cross in the air before him, his index and middle fingers bunched together.

"Rest in peace," he murmured, and we went back into the house. Even animals have a hard life, I thought to myself.

2

After that day, I never painted with Father again. Mother says it's his fault that I haven't had a visit from the marquis yet because he brought me up as a tomboy. I'm not at all in favor of the marquis. I've only glimpsed him once and it was frightening. After breakfast one day, I went into the bathroom and saw a washbowl with red-stained rags looking like a dead animal floating in rust-colored water. Mother walked in.

"What are you looking at?"

I inched away from the basin without answering.

"It's the marquis," she told me, unfazed. Then she emptied the dirty water out and started scrubbing the rags with soapstone until they were white again.

"It'll be your turn soon," she added, and I started praying that day would never come.

The rules of the marquis are: keep your eyes down, toe the line, and stay home. Until my turn comes, I can work in the vegetable garden, go to market with Father to sell herbs, frogs, or snails, shoot stones at the boys with my sling when they tease my friend Saro, who has a crooked leg, run down the big road with Cosimino, and come home all sweaty with dirty knees. The marquis has already come for my other friends. As soon as he did, the hems of their skirts came down, spots blemished their faces, and breasts sprouted under their blouses. Crocefissa has even grown a few hairs on her chin and the boys have taken to calling her "brigando Musolino," like the famous whiskered bandit. She doesn't mind. She goes around looking distressed, her hands pressed against her belly as if she were having a baby, and asks the same thing every time she meets her friends, as if she'd won a prize: "My blood has come, has yours?"

The marquis doesn't visit boys, ever. They're not like us: they grow up in stages, not all in one day.

There's always a relative waiting outside school to walk my friends home, whereas they used to be allowed to go back on their own. If they cross paths with any boys on their way, they lower their eyes even though they know the boys stare right where their blouses gape, which is why they look down but walk upright so that the buttons look fit to burst at any moment. Strutting like that, they look like Father's hens.

My sister is four years older than me, and she used to strut before she got married. She's light-skinned and blond like Father, and whenever she left the house, all the boys used to stare: the more they stared, the more she strutted, and the more they stared. I know because I was supposed to keep an eye on her since Cosimino was always out and about. Her name is Fortunata, but she's not so fortunate now. One stare today, another stare tomorrow, one stare too many, and lo and behold there was a baby in her belly. It turned out that the mayor's nephew, Gerò Musciacco, had been the one to put it there. I heard because after supper they would all huddle in the kitchen—Fortunata, Mother, and Father—talking in hushed tones. It was no secret, given that the whole town of Martorana knew about it.

Gerò Musciacco's father didn't want his son to marry her because we're poor. My sister cried, Mother banged her fists on the table, cursing everyone in her dialect. "God forbid you should be dishonored," she moaned. Father chose silence. I'm all in favor of silence. "The rifle! Go talk to Musciacco with your rifle!" Mother prodded. He poured himself a glass of water, downed it slowly, dabbing at his mouth with a napkin, rose from the table, and said, "I wouldn't prefer that," before returning to work in the vegetable garden. From that day on, nobody spoke for a month except my brother, who was a young lad and didn't bother about much in general.

I thought it was my fault because, instead of chaperoning Fortunata that afternoon, I had gone to Saro's house to eat anchovy pasta, a special dish his mother, Nardina, cooked just for me. I'm in favor of special dishes. That must have been when the man took advantage and stuck a baby in her belly.

One morning, Mother left the house in her Sunday best and didn't come back until after dark. The following day, Fortunata woke up early and started crocheting little white booties. Father watched her working. "Are you happy to marry this man?" he asked. She cast her eyes down and continued to wind the wool around the crochet hook. Two months later, the wedding took place, and I got our room all to myself.

The rules of a wedding are: wear a white dress, walk down the aisle to the priest, and say yes. At the wedding banquet, Mrs. Scibetta, who lives in a nice house where Mother and I go to card woolen mattresses every year and for whom we do some sewing jobs, told everyone that Gerò Musciacco's father had accepted the match only because he'd been persuaded by his cousin, Baroness Careri, who'd been contacted by the priest, Don Ignazio, who had received a petition from his housekeeper, Nellina, who had been Fortunata's godmother, and who had been convinced by Mother the day she'd departed early in her Sunday best.

Fortunata pretended to ignore the gossip, but she had changed: she stopped strutting and her wedding dress looked as if it had been let out, not for her breasts but for the nice ripe watermelon poking out between its folds. After the wedding, she left to live in Musciacco's house. We didn't see her for three months, and then Nellina found her in the vestry looking distraught with no belly. The baby had gone, and she had dark blotches on her arms and face. She said she had fallen down the front steps. The housekeeper told the baroness, who complained to her cousin, who berated his son for being careless with his wife. Fortunata went back to her husband's house, started dressing in black, and has worn mourning ever since. She never receives any visits and never goes out, so at least there's no risk she'll fall again. Her husband, on the other hand, has a fine time of it, alone or in company, as if he were still a bachelor. When he strolls down the road, he stares at all the young girls as if he wanted to stick babies in their bellies, too.

3

There's no one waiting for me outside school. There's one girl in my class who is also allowed to go home on her own. Her name is Liliana but she's different because her father, Mr. Calò, is the town Communist. His wife, Fina, goes out to work as if she were a man and he doesn't care if people say he can't feed his own family.

Calò has a beard and small glasses, which gives him the air of a scholar, but deep down he's a bumpkin, Mother says. Mark my words, she says, I bet he hardly made it through eighth grade. He loves talking to people, and on the second Thursday of every month holds a town meeting in an old fishing hut in the lower town near the sea to discuss Martorana's problems, as if anything might come of it. That is how the world is, was, and always will be, Mother says. You can knead words for as long as you like but you'll never make bread.

Her father being a Communist gives Liliana only advantages: she can go out without a chaperone, wear long pants like men, and read photo-novels and advice columns in magazines filled with pictures of movie stars. I've never been to the movies because Mother says they put crickets in your head, which means I make do with billboards and secretly sketching the faces of stars in my notebook. Liliana speaks to people as equals, and I'm not supposed to be friends with her because she's not proper, but since she and I are the only girls without chaperones, we walk part of the way home together after school. To begin with, I didn't speak to her. Then one day she showed me a magazine with a photo of Handsome Antonio, the one in the movie. I asked if I could take a quick peek because every time I see that actor, I get a languorous feeling in my stomach. She didn't wait for me to ask twice. Right away she handed it to me, saying that communism teaches us that nice things should be shared. I'm all in favor of communism now.

I slipped the magazine under my blouse and, once I got home, I hid it beneath a loose bed slat beside a little bag with a stub of old lipstick I'd found in the bathroom at school and my notebook filled with pencil portraits of movie stars.

When we were at elementary school, Liliana and I were Miss Rosaria's pets: she was a champion at multiplication tables, but I beat her in grammar. The teacher would pin stars to the white smocks of her most diligent pupils. The rules for getting stars were: read without sounding out the letters, write without smudging the page, add in your head without using your fingers. Liliana and I were equals but she knew quite a few words from politics that she'd heard at her father's meetings, and she was always showing them off. I decided I would learn some more words, too. The teacher had brought some books from her house, placing them on a shelf at the back of the classroom so that we could read them whenever we wanted. They had smooth white pages that slipped through your fingers, colored pictures, and lots of animals that talked like humans. I'm not in favor of that because the best thing about animals is they choose silence, like Father.

I loved the dictionary: inside there were lots of words I didn't know that could be used to express the kinds of thoughts you have in your head but don't know how to say. One morning, I'd forgotten to bring my arithmetic homework. I stood up and said, "Miss, I'm sorry but I *obliviated* my workbook today," to try out the new word. Instead of punishing me, she rewarded me with an extra star. She said that culture saves us and can take us great distances. I didn't want to go anywhere. I just liked the sound of that fancy verb.

When Miss Rosaria left at the end of fourth grade, the picture books were packed into a box and taken away and the dictionary vanished with them, along with all the words inside. Luckily, I'd already copied lots of them into my exercise book and I could run through them whenever I liked. When I used them, people were intimidated, as if I was superior to them. Mother wasn't. When she asked me what the teacher who'd taken Miss Rosaria's place was like, I said, "He's pretty tedious," and got a slap and a telling-off in Calabrian. "God forbid words like that come out of a girl's mouth! It's not proper."

4

The new teacher was already old when he arrived. He was called Mr. Scialò, and he rode in on a bus from the city every morning. Only a few years to go before his retirement, so he'd come back to Sicily after teaching for years on the continent, in Rome. He told us he'd eaten minestrone with none other than the minister of education, and since he repeated it at least once a day, we started to call him "Mr. Minestrone."

Mr. Minestrone's lessons were nothing like Miss Rosaria's. On the first day, he took out a little book with gray pages from a worn-out leather briefcase.

"Write, children," he said, and started to dictate a nursery rhyme entitled "Adieu Little White Pinafore." A friend of his had written it, and he liked it so much that he was determined to make us learn it by heart for the end-of-year exam.

What a sad day, oh my delight,
when you abandon me!
You feel a different plight
A pang in my heart
that will never restart.

Bent over our desks, we transcribed the verses of the poem into our notebooks. It was supposed to be the little white pinafore talking: saying how sorry it was to abandon the young girl who would be going into middle school and replacing it with a black pinafore. Before leaving her, it gave her some advice:

I tremble, little girl,
as you are about to reach
a dangerous age!

I'm not in favor of advice. Advice reminds me of those fables with talking animals. Mr. Minestrone cleared his throat and went on dictating, looking at us one by one as if he were issuing a timely warning about the dangers that were about to befall each of us girls.

Keep yourself virtuous;
Let none speak ill,
And never thrill
In bad company.
Throw away
Those evil magazines:
What, pray, is the worth of science
when you have lost your innocence?

"Maestro, shouldn't *science* rhyme with *innocence*?" Rosalina asked from the back of the class. Liliana and I exchanged a look of horror from one end of the classroom to the other. "Should I spell it '*s-c-e-n-c-e*'?" Rosalina asked again, after the teacher had already explained it once.

"Don't worry, Rosalina, you'll never lose your *innocence* with your lack of '*s-c-e-n-c-e*,' *sense*," I scoffed. All my classmates laughed; Mr. Minestrone stopped dictating and walked up to my desk. Before he could open his mouth, I tried to get back into his good graces with my usual big-word trick. "Maestro, please excuse my facetiousness."

"A well-brought-up girl doesn't need to learn new words. A trained parrot would be just as useful. This is the result of certain bad teaching methods," he said, looking pointedly at the empty shelf where Miss Rosaria's books used to sit. Then he returned to his dictation.

> *Be serious in your studies,*
> *set aside your comics,*
> *and your histrionics.*

When I finished elementary school, my white pinafore was torn up into rags to buff up the few pieces of silver tableware Mother had brought with her from Calabria. When it's time for the once-a-week polish and I see the scraps, I can hear Mr. Minestrone's voice: "Keep yourself virtuous, let none speak ill, and never thrill . . ."

Over the summer, Mother took my shoulder, waist, and hip measurements and cut a pattern out of black cloth to make my new school pinafore. When it was ready, I tried it on. She got on her knees and asked me turn around to see whether the hem was straight. Then she got up, pinched my chin between her thumb and index finger, and said, "It's perfect. Don't forget, keep yourself clean."

The pinafore lasted the whole three years because I took good care of it and because she'd made it nice and big to begin with.

After my middle school leaving certificate, I asked if I could go on to high school, but she shook her head.

"What's she going to be? A scientist?" she said to Father. He said nothing and went out to work in the garden. A week later, he showed her a sheet of paper with his big, sloping signature at the bottom: he'd enrolled me in the teacher training institute.

"It's thanks to me that your eldest daughter's honor was restored," she yelled.

"When she gets her certificate in four years," Father answered, "she can be an elementary school teacher and become independent."

"Independent of who?" she snarled.

"Of her family, of a husband . . ." he explained.

"And how's she going to find a husband with her head in her books all the time?" she snapped.

Father chose silence and went out to feed the chickens. She followed him out the door, yelling in dialect, "What kind of man won't protect his womenfolk? You'll need more than a rifle! You're no better than a sheep. Baa!"

We found out that Mrs. Scibetta had also enrolled her

youngest daughter, Mena, so the next day Mother let out the hem of my pinafore, unfolding the extra material she'd hidden inside, and hemmed it again. I saw the black cotton unfurl from that hidden pocket. Maybe she'd planned for me to carry on at school all along. Or maybe she was just very sensible.

5

When I was little, Father used to go out to the countryside on his own to harvest snails. I would wait for him to come home until I could see his towhead glinting in the sunlight from a distance. He looked as big and strong as a giant. One morning, I woke up at dawn while everyone else was still asleep and asked if I could go with him. From that moment on, I was his helper. We walked side by side inspecting leaves, and if he spotted any snails, he would squeeze my hand lightly twice. Every now and again, I'd bend down and pick daisies in the middle of the fields. I'd close my eyes and move my lips without making a sound: he loves me he loves me not he loves me he loves me not he loves me.

A month ago, just as we were preparing to go out in our rubber boots, buckets in hand, Mother stared at me as if she were seeing me for the first time. "That skirt is immodest, it pulls up behind," she said. "Give it here so I can fix it for you. You can't go around like that."

It wasn't true: the skirt hung straight down because my body was as spindly as a boy's, but she couldn't accept the fact that I hadn't changed one bit.

"We're going out for snails, not the patron saint festival," I protested. I smoothed the scratchy fiber down with my hands to demonstrate that the skirt fit me but of course I had to go into the bathroom and take it off. I slipped on an old misshapen one that covered my knobby knees. Father was waiting for me with his canvas bag and a knife in hand. Sometimes, instead of snails we'd catch frogs, which is more difficult. Snails sit there in their shells glued to a rock as good as gold, while frogs hop about here, there, and everywhere. They must have crickets in their heads, too.

"When I was your age, I was already wearing a bra and stockings," Mother said as I joined Father at the door. "But we were more restrained in our day. Our parents didn't let us do what we liked, not like nowadays. There were quite a few young lads who had their eyes on me anyway . . ."

I was so shocked I dropped the bucket I was holding: I'd always imagined Mother as an obedient snail, but it seems she'd once been a sprightly frog.

"I always kept myself clean," she clarified. "I didn't need a chaperone to follow my every step. And in my family, if you said one word too many you'd be struck dumb forever. Things are different now. There's too much freedom: the radio, the movies, dances. When I was growing up, these things would have been unimaginable. People like nothing better than to embroider and then unpick the stitches with their gossip. They could easily come and tell you things people have done before they've even happened. That's why at a certain age we need to keep our daughters home. These days, a boy is a scoundrel and a girl is a jug: you break her, you take her."

I started rocking with impatience, shifting my weight from one leg to the other. The more time passed, the fewer snails we'd find. They come out into the open early.

"Cosimino, would you accept a broken jug?" she asked my twin, still in his pajamas, his hair tousled from sleep. He smiled because he knew the rules of being a brother: keep an eye on your sister, make sure people respect her, threaten anyone who doesn't. And maybe he was ashamed of having a sister who still went around wearing skirts above her knees and clogs and resembled a boy gone wrong. Amalia and Salvo's ugly daughter, people probably whispered: sharp-edged and spindly, eyes as black as olives, a slit of a mouth in a round, dark face, raven hair. I bet she'll bring us bad luck, wreck our homes. A solitary, disheveled creature she is, wandering around on her own, with only Don Vito Musumeci's crippled boy Saro for company. The mother embroiders wedding trousseaux, but the daughter will end up a spinster.

When she took me with her to ladies' houses to deliver her sewing work, she would show them how good I was at embroidery, and they would give me a cookie or a slice of bread with a thin layer of jam and a reassuring pat because they thought I'd spend the rest of my life embroidering the wedding linen for other girls.

"Leave her be, Mà," Cosimino said, rubbing his eyes. "Leave her be. Who's going to take this jug anyway?"

"Who takes her, takes her," Mother answered. "As long

as she's in one piece. He'll have time to regret it once they're married."

I'm not sure I'm in favor of marriage. I don't want to end up like Fortunata, who let Musciacco get her pregnant while I dug into my anchovy pasta at Nardina's house. That's why I always run down the road: boys breathing down your neck are like a pair of bellows with hands that can grab you. I run to be invisible, I run with my boy's body and my girl's heart, I run for all the times I won't be allowed to anymore, I run for my girlfriends who already have to wear proper shoes and long skirts and who can only take slow little steps, and I also run for my sister, who has been buried alive at home as if she were already dead.

"Relax, Oliva," Mother said. "From now on, your brother will be the one going out to collect snails and frogs. It's not a job for girls."

She yanked me by the arm and made me sit.

"Cosimino has no experience," Father muttered, looking down at his shoes.

"What are you doing about that, then? You can't even teach him to collect snails, not that you know how to catch anything else."

Cosimino sloped away reluctantly to get ready, picked up my bag, and joined Father outside the house. I watched them from the window as they vanished from view into the fields under the rising sun without saying a word to each other.

6

"Oliva! What are you staring at? Flies?"

Mother called from the kitchen. I was at the window waiting for Cosimino to come back so I could run out and count the snails. I was scared he might have found more than I usually did.

"Did you change the water?" she asked, scouring the tiles. "Yes," I said. I dragged the bucket into my room and bent over to peer at my reflection.

"Vanity is the daughter of the devil," she hissed. I lifted my gaze from the water and felt ashamed. She was on all fours, scrubbing with the coarse cloth. "I was vain, too, when I was your age, whatever you may think. I used to look at myself all the time, but there comes a point when you get over it," she said with a raspy cough that is her way of laughing. "You turn into a beauty, the lads start looking at you in the street, you get a husband, have children, and it's all over."

I wrung out the cloth and got down on my knees next to her to clean the floor. She was still a beauty in my eyes, while my face reflected in the round bucket was the same color as the water: a dirty gray.

She went to empty the bucket in the vegetable garden behind the house, drying her forehead with her forearm.

"My mother had four more children after me: all girls," she went on. "A boy never came. My father wanted to keep trying for one but my mother didn't. 'We'll have five of them to marry off, Mimmo. Five,' she would say, opening her hand in front of his face with her five fingers splayed out. I thought I was the most beautiful of them all: vanity was my ruin."

I started scrubbing the floor with more elbow grease. Her confiding in me like that was embarrassing. "I was sent to clean a notary's office in the hope that one day I would marry not the notary himself but someone who happened to be there, a trainee, a lawyer, someone with a sizable estate . . . Instead, I set my heart on a young Sicilian who'd come to sign away his rights. An uncle of his from Calabria had died leaving only debts. He was towheaded with green eyes, he spoke very little, and seemed kind. My mother said, 'Do you want to ruin your life for ten inches of face?'"

Mother gave another of her raspy laughs that sounded just like a cough.

"I didn't listen to her and we ran away. We organized a *fuitina*, eloping by crossing the Strait of Messina at night when the sea was rough. Some honeymoon: the only orange blossom I saw was in the ferry bathroom with my stomach upturned."

She held her belly as if she could still feel the discomfort.

"She was right, my dearly departed mother was. She died giving birth to her last child, the boy my father had been waiting for. They both left this world together, may their souls rest in peace. You should heed your mother, unlike me. My eyes follow you wherever you go. I'm watching you even when you can't see me. Vanity is the daughter of the devil."

I'm not at all in favor of the devil. So I went outside to throw the water away and when I saw Father arrive, followed by Cosimino holding the bucket, I didn't dare count the snails to find out whether he'd missed me.

7

Liliana's not like me: she's beautiful, but has no intention of getting married. She says a woman needs a man like a sheep needs a Sunday outfit.

"What kind of life will you have?" I asked her one day as we walked home from school. "A vagabond's life? A woman who never gives birth will get ill with nerves, Mother says."

Liliana handed me a new magazine, which I hid in my book bag, and smiled. "I'm going to go and work on the continent."

"You want to spend your whole life cleaning for someone?"

"That's not the only job women can do! I'm going to be a deputy in the parliament, like Nilde Iotti."

"Who's that? A friend of your father's?"

Liliana raised her eyebrows with an air of superiority, like when she won a star at elementary school and I didn't. I felt a stab of envy: I had no idea who this Nilde woman was and I didn't even know that the word *deputata* existed in the feminine. Miss Rosaria's dictionary didn't gender any of the jobs in anything but masculine forms—if you were a minister, mayor, judge, doctor, or notary, you were by definition male.

"My father says change has to come from us women in

the South because they've taught us for centuries to keep quiet and now we have to learn to make some noise," Liliana explained, as if she were talking to someone much younger than her.

"A girl who makes noise is not proper," I answered, because that's what Mother always said. Liliana made no comment and carried on walking. Then she stopped short, held my hand, and smiled.

"Why don't you come to a meeting in the hut sometime?"

"It wouldn't be proper. There are Communists there!" I immediately replied without thinking, suddenly embarrassed.

"Lots of people join in. You won't guess who," she tempted with an air of mystery.

"Did Mrs. Scibetta ever come?" I asked, eyes wide open.

"Your father's come more than once."

I felt my pulse race and quickly changed the subject. I didn't want to know whether it was true or not.

"If you change your mind, I'll give you all the magazines I have at home."

Under the bed slat, I kept the notebooks where I would sketch faces and divide them into categories according to the different movie plots: "unlucky brunettes," "frivolous blonds," "scandalous redheads" (the only example I had was Rita Hayworth). Actresses were "daughters of the devil" and actors were either "good and brave," "ugly and evil," "star-crossed lovers," or "handsome and dangerous." Handsome Antonio had a whole section to himself.

If Liliana gave me all her back issues, I'd be able to fill two whole notebooks, I thought to myself, as Mother's voice grew fainter in the back of my head.

"Including the inserts?" I asked, just to be sure.

Liliana lowered her chin, which meant yes.

When we reached the junction with the big road, I took the dirt track and started running home. Then I stopped and shouted back at her, "I'll come, then," and started running again.

8

didn't go. But one day Liliana invited me to her house after school to help with some portraits and I accepted so that I could show off how good I was at drawing. I expected to find paper and colored pencils but she showed me into a dark storage room with washing lines strung from one side to the other.

"With all that sun outside, why do you have to hang your washing in here?" I asked. I stepped a little farther inside and saw that there were photographs hanging from the pegs, not clothes.

"Come," she said, leading me by the hand to one of the sheets hanging from the line. "What can you see?"

I stared at the paper rectangle and saw nothing. "I don't know. It's dark in here," I said defensively.

"There's no hurry. Looking is one thing, seeing is another. It's a skill you can learn."

It was like being back at elementary school when I always wanted to be top of the class, even though in high school I was better than her at reciting Latin declensions with Mrs. Terlizzi. I narrowed my eyes like I do when I thread a needle. Maybe it was the effort but it looked as though something was slowly materializing on the white paper.

Liliana was smiling because she'd already played this

game. I stared so long that my eyes welled with tears and I was no longer able to distinguish the shapes on the paper from the shadow cast by my damp eyelashes. I closed them and rubbed for a second. By the time I opened my eyes again, a figure had appeared before them: a shadowy young girl with jutting bones and unruly hair. I had that languorous feeling in the pit of my stomach and a warm rush spread from just below my belly through my whole body.

"You took it on the sly!"

I lowered my eyes. I didn't like looking at a face that had not known it was being observed. And anyway, if God made me ugly it wasn't my fault, was it? Liliana rifled through more brown strips that curled up like snake skin.

"Don't you like the photo?"

"I don't know."

"Do you think it's badly done?"

"I think it's well done and that's why I don't like it."

The girl who had just snatched a ball from a boy who had been teasing Saro because of his crippled walk, the girl who had run like crazy without looking back, the girl who would stop a moment later, pick up a stone, and shoot it with her sling: that raggedy black monkey was none other than me.

Liliana smiled softly but I was unhappy. "It's the first time I've seen a picture of myself, and in any case, looking at yourself is not proper: a beauty may admire her life but a plain girl makes a better wife. That's what Mother says."

I turned my back on her and looked more closely at the paper with my face on it.

Liliana opened a drawer and started rummaging for something. She took out a hand mirror with a wooden handle. On the back, there was the face of a rag doll with brown woolen braids.

"Take it," she said. I pushed it away but she insisted. So I looked.

Full lips, not as plump as Liliana's but no longer those of a young girl, eyes like long, slanted leaves, with two black olives in the middle, a small, straight nose, and thick eyebrows. Mother had lied: I wasn't plain.

"I need to go," I said.

"It's a present," Liliana said, as she continued to unroll the film. I furtively tucked the mirror under the waistband of my skirt as if Mother were watching. I took two steps toward the door but then turned back again to look at the image that stared at me as it hung from the peg. It didn't feel as alien as before.

"Why did you take a picture of me, of all people?"

Liliana grabbed my hand with her delicate fingers, which were so different from my dark, bony ones that were as knotted as magnolia roots.

"Come and see," she said, guiding me into a dark, windowless study. Hanging on the wall, and piled up in cardboard boxes cluttering the floor, there were more photos: Liliana playing with a blond doll, Geppino the knife-sharpener at the butcher's, three dirty ragamuffins with a blowgun aiming at a woman leaning over her balcony, the priest disrobing, two girls walking with their heads down while a young man purses his lips in a wolf whistle. Me and her walking home from school unaccompanied. In one picture I thought I saw Father, though it may just have been a farmhand walking into the distance toward the sunset. "My father took them," she said. "Sometimes he sends them to the papers and they pay him something per picture."

"There are thousands of faces around here," I answered. "What's so special about them?"

Among pictures of peasants with broken shoes and women with black scarves tied around their faces, there was one of a man lying on the road, a white sheet covering everything but his shoes, a dark stain spreading. It looked black because there weren't any colors in the photographs, so you had to imagine them. Then another: a piazza with three dead people, no sheets, black blood everywhere. I covered my eyes with my hands.

"Taking pictures of the dead is evil," I said.

"My father shoots life and that includes everything, even what you don't want to see."

"I need to go," I said. It was too hot in that room. Vanity is the daughter of the devil, the voice in my head rang.

9

When I got back home, Mother wasn't there. She'd gone to our neighbor's house for a wake: Pietro Pinna had died at eighty-five. The rules for funerals are: dress in black, pay your respects, and shed real tears. Whenever someone in town died, they always invited her to the wake because she was good at keening even when she didn't know the deceased. She would always come back looking relaxed, as if the tears had washed her cheeks clean.

I went into my room, closing the door, and lifted the loose bed slat so that I could hide Liliana's mirror. But first, I rolled the tube of lipstick in my hand. I opened it and twisted the base, pushing up the last residue of brilliant red. I put my ear against the door to make sure nobody would catch me in the act. Looking at my reflection, I pouted and sucked my cheeks in like the movie stars on the billboards. I applied it to my lips, which were instantly stained red. I put on another coat: the waxy paste tickled my skin and gave me that languid feeling in my stomach. My lips now dominated the dark oval of my face, as if they had bled my other features dry. Was I that mouth? Was I that face at the center of the wooden frame? I lifted my chin, closed my eyes, and rested my lips on the surface. The cold glass stuck to my mouth and I pulled away in shame. There was a slightly blurred, heart-shaped red stain on the mirror. At that moment, I felt a stab of pain in my belly, radiating out to my back, as if something were churning in my guts. I thought it must be the devil's punishment. Maybe a baby had crept in and I was pregnant like Fortunata, which meant they would be handing me over to someone quickly before it began to show.

I ran into the bathroom and scrubbed my mouth until my lips burned.

At dinner, Mother didn't notice that I hadn't kept myself clean. As she rinsed the dishes, she looked happy: keening at the wake had left her with a smile. It wasn't true, then, that her eyes could see me at all times.

10

The hut was dark and stank of fish. Liliana was sitting in the front row with a notebook open on her lap and a pen in her hand. The meeting had already started, so I stood in the back by the door. Antonino Calò was in the middle of the room. He didn't say much but he looked every single person in the eye, which is not proper, Mother always said, especially with women. Luckily, I was hidden behind a pile of old fishing nets so his eyes didn't catch mine. The only women there were widows who could do what they liked since their husbands had died, God bless their souls. I'm in favor of widows, because they belong only to themselves.

Calò's voice was as gentle as a woman's. He was kind to everyone and never contradicted anyone. The meeting was boring and I couldn't understand why Mother had forbade me from going, but by that point I couldn't move. I was trapped behind the tangle of nets. Calò asked lots of questions. Easy questions: What do women do? What do men do? What are their qualities? Things even kids at elementary school know: women are women and stay at home, men are men and bring home the bacon. Everyone gave an answer and Liliana wrote everything down in her notebook like when she takes notes during Mrs. Terlizzi's lessons. When two people disagreed and started arguing, Calò stepped in with that soft voice of his and said there was no need to fight, we were there to discuss our views and come to an understanding. What was the point of saying what we thought if nobody would say what was right or wrong, then? Miss Rosaria, for example, would tell us when we gave her the wrong answer. We might have been upset by it but at least we learned. Once, when we were parsing sentences, she dictated the phrase "A woman is equal to a man and has the same rights." We all bent our heads over our notebooks and started working on the exercise: "woman = feminine singular noun." I didn't like the sound of it.

"Miss, the exercise must be wrong," I said, plucking up courage. My teacher touched the bouncy red curls that she never tied up.

"What do you mean, Oliva? I don't understand."

"Woman is never in the singular," I explained.

She counted on her fingers: "A woman, singular, women, plural. What's the problem?"

But I wasn't satisfied. "A woman is never by herself: when she's home, she's with the kids; when she goes out to market, or church, or to a funeral, she's always with other people. And if there aren't any women to chaperone her, a man has to accompany her."

My teacher raised a finger in the air, the nail varnished

bright red, and scrunched up her nose as she always did when she was thinking.

"I've never seen it in the singular," I repeated timidly.

Miss Rosaria sighed and went on to dictate another sentence for us to parse, and the whole class leaned over their books once again to tackle the exercise in our round cursive. I thought I must have said something so stupid it didn't even deserve a response, but when the bell rang and everyone filed out of class, she called me to her desk. From close up, her hair gave off a smell that made my stomach lurch with that sickly languor and I thought that boys must follow her on the street to sniff up that perfume.

"Maybe you're right, Oliva," she explained. "But grammar can also be determined by the lives we choose to lead."

"What do you mean?" I asked, mortified because I was struggling to understand.

"That it depends on us. Being a feminine singular noun depends on you, too."

She caressed my face. Her fingers were like peach skin. Outside school, everyone was heading off in different directions: me, running as usual, her, making her way past the men's gazes.

At the end of the year, the head teacher came into class to tell us that Miss Rosaria had transferred to another school and that we would be getting a new teacher. Rumormongers began their idle work, saying everything and its opposite: that she had taken a lover, more than one, in fact; that she'd been seen being affectionate to a boy who was younger than her; that she had been pregnant and gotten rid of the baby on the sly; that she'd been having an affair with the head teacher and been forced to leave Martorana. Though the head teacher still had his job.

Who knows? Maybe she had gone to the fishing hut, too, and sat in the front row next to Liliana, speaking in public and shaking her sweet-smelling curls. Without the slightest shame.

"What do you think of women who take up jobs?" Calò asked at a certain juncture. He wasn't speaking in dialect. He enunciated every syllable carefully, like Claudio Villa does when he's singing "Mamma sono tanto felice." Every time he asked a new question, there would be silence to begin with. All you could hear was a soft babbling like a brook: the subdued clamor of snide comments. Some poked their neighbors with their elbows and snickered, the few women present looked down at the ground, Liliana raised her pen and waited. Then someone would throw a wisecrack into the mix, just to make everyone laugh.

"A woman, Calò? What kind of job would a woman like to do?" asked a short, squat man who from behind looked like Ciccio the haberdasher.

"A sniper?" a lanky man in the corner quipped, winking at the man seated beside him.

"I don't know," Antonino Calò continued without altering his tone of voice. "What do you all think? Are there any more suitable jobs?"

Nobody uttered a word, as if they were contemplating something never before taken seriously.

"Domestic service," a young man in a sugar-paper blue jacket ventured.

"Seamstress. Hairdresser. Jobs that can be done at home," another man from the opposite end of the room added.

"Are you saying that women can only work in the home?" Antonino Calò probed, keeping his cards close. He let people talk and then they started questioning themselves, the chuckling subsiding.

"There are some jobs that are not suitable. Any with a position of responsibility like, say, a judge. Can you imagine a woman with a gown over her dress?" said the man who looked like Ciccio.

"The world would be topsy-turvy," a neighbor remarked.

"Well, don't you think that the law could change? They could open the judgeship to women," Liliana intervened.

"It's not just a matter of the law," replied a young man with black curly hair and a sprig of jasmine behind his ear. I didn't remember seeing him before. "It's feminine nature that's particular. Women are fickle, subject to the cycles of the moon. There are days when their reason is clouded. What if a female judge had to deliver a verdict on one of *those* days? Would she send an innocent man to jail in the felon's place?"

"Women teach," Liliana countered. "And if they can teach in elementary school, a job with great responsibility, then they can also practice other professions."

"An elementary school teacher?" the young man with curly hair teased. "You mean like that redhead who was friendly with all the men in town?" He winked and started tossing an orange, flinging it up in the air before catching it. The men around him were laughing and my cheeks burned, as if he'd slapped me.

"She was disgraceful," a woman next to me shrieked.

I couldn't hold back any longer and hissed through my teeth, "You're just jealous."

"Jealous? Jealous of who?" she screeched.

"The only thing you can do is sow lies about someone you don't even know," I answered, my voice quavering with anger.

"Since when did young minxes like you have the right to speak?"

"If old spinsters have . . ."

Everyone turned to look at me. Liliana whispered something in her father's ear, and then he spotted me in my hiding place.

"Carry on, Oliva. We're listening."

"I have nothing to say . . ." I stammered in embarrassment.

From the other end of the room, Liliana coaxed me on with a gesture of her hand.

"Miss Rosaria . . ." I started to say, but lost my nerve immediately.

"Was she your teacher?" Calò asked, taking a few steps toward me.

I nodded.

"You knew her well, then?"

"She was my teacher for four years. Then she had to . . . leave."

I looked over at the men to see who was still in the mood for a laugh and who wasn't. Calò waited for me to go on, in no hurry.

"She was a good teacher, Miss Rosaria was, and she wasn't disgraceful. She taught us our multiplication tables, verbs, sentence parsing, the Ancient Romans, and all the names of the provinces."

Nobody said a word. Calò was still looking at me, expecting me to continue.

"She taught us that a man and a woman are equal," I said, "and that women should have the same freedom as men."

"Then she *is* disgraceful!" the curly-haired man sneered, pocketing the orange. When he stared my way, I recognized him: he was the son of the pastry chef. When I was little, I would go into the family pastry shop and he, who was a little older than me, would smile from behind the counter, sink a knife into a mound of ricotta and sugar, and hold it out for me to lick. The sweet mixture melted on my tongue and that languorous feeling invaded my stomach. Then, almost overnight, he was gone and I never saw him again. My favorites became marzipan cakes.

"Please be kind enough to speak in turn and ask for the floor," Calò said calmly. "Do go on, Oliva."

"If Miss Rosaria had no shame it was not because of what you're implying," I said, marshaling courage, "but because she had nothing at all to be ashamed of. She never did anyone harm. You're the ones who did her wrong."

The young man with the orange sneered and motioned applause. The men in the fishing hut started muttering and the old woman next to me wrapped herself in her shawl and got up to leave. The meeting was over but nobody else moved. They were waiting for Calò.

"Well, perhaps today we can conclude with Oliva's words. She has reminded us that we should only feel shame if we have hurt somebody, done something wrong, or committed a crime. And one more thing, if I have understood correctly: we should not judge someone if we do not know them, simply on the basis of hearsay. Isn't that right, Oliva?"

The question echoed as I pushed my way through the crowd toward the exit. *Isn't that right, Oliva?* I kept asking myself as I ran home. I didn't know whether it was right or wrong. Nor did I know why I, of all people—someone who had always tried to make themselves invisible in the presence of adults—had spoken so brashly in front of every-one. Was it because of Liliana's magazines? Because Father had been to the hut once? Or to test whether Mother really could see me wherever I went? As I raced home, I felt dis-graceful, too.

11

I was out of breath by the time I arrived at the end of the dirt track. The chickens were pecking freely outside our door, like bored schoolyard kids, whiling away the time before class resumed.

"Shoo! Shoo!" I yelled as I clapped my hands but they took no notice, challenging me with a blank expression. "Who let you out? . . . Cosimino?" I yelled. "The hens are out of the coop."

Cosimino was nowhere to be found. He was always gallivanting about and nobody ever told him off for it. Mother wasn't home, either. She'd gone to deliver some sewing to Mrs. Jannuzzo, who'd lost a daughter my age to a lung infection. "I'll go on my own," she said whenever she had to deliver some work, "out of respect for Mrs. Jannuzzo." As if it were disrespectful to have a daughter who was still alive. But I was happy because it meant I had some time on my own. If it hadn't been for Mrs. Jannuzzo, I'd never have been able to go to the fishing hut.

"Shoo! Shoo!" I shouted again, herding the hens toward the coop. Rosina, Verdina, Violetta, Nerina . . . I counted them and, luckily, they were all there. "Good little hens, you didn't run away."

I ushered them all into the pen and shut the gate: they

strutted around happily, almost relieved their escape had been unsuccessful. "Good little hens," I said again. "Good little idiots, you really do have bird brains, don't you? You love a cage more than your freedom." The chickens peered up at me, their heads bobbing back and forth in dumb little lurches: What could they know about freedom when they'd been born and bred in a cage? The thought turned my anger to pity. If you've spent your whole life in prison, you can't even appreciate what you've lost. "Isn't that right, Violetta? Nerina?"

And anyway, what kind of life would a free hen have? Miss Rosaria came to mind, again. Where did she go when she had to leave our school and this town? What did she do once the gate was open?

"The life of a disgraced woman." The phrase rang in my head. I hadn't invented it. They were someone else's words. It had been those men in the hut who had laughed coarsely and who had probably given her wolf whistles every time she crossed the piazza. Or one of those women who only have wicked things to say about others: the scissor tongues. I'm different, I thought, but they are all inside me. I'm Oliva Denaro but I'm also them: the toothless spinster seated next to me in the hut, the town gossips gathered in black to recite the Rosary, the girls at school with long skirts and downcast eyes, Crocefissa who boasts about the marquis paying her a visit. I'm my mother, too, and one day I'll be just like her and I won't even have had the time to notice.

We women in our cages are no better than these hens. And I'm not in favor of cages.

"It serves you right! You should have run!" I yelled, opening the gate again and making the poor scared creatures flap their wings and skedaddle around the yard as I chased them.

"They're hens, not jailbirds," a voice behind me called out, making me jump.

I whipped around, my heart in my throat. Liliana appeared out of the shadows and took a couple of steps toward me.

"Have you come to take a few more pictures of me on the sly? I told you I don't like having my picture taken. It's not proper."

"I'm glad you came to the meeting."

Liliana smiled and stared at me just as I had stared at the chickens minutes ago. "I brought you the magazines I promised, and this, too."

She handed me a stack of magazines with a yellow envelope on top. I picked it up between my finger and my thumb. Nobody in my family had ever received a letter.

"It's the photo you saw at my house. You said you liked it."

"All I said was that it looked like me."

"Can you accept a present from a friend? Is it proper?"

I didn't have time to respond before I saw the silhouette of Mother at the end of the dirt track. She walked with her chin digging into her chest, as if someone were dragging her

by the bridle and every step was painful. Everything is painful for her: the light in the morning when it filters through
the half-open shutters, Father lying next to her snoring, my
spindly shapelessness, work in the fields, the lack of rain,
the baby my sister never had, the eye of the needle that gets
narrower and narrower as she grows older, Cosimino's lazi-
ness, silence, chaos, her mother, rest her soul, who told her
quite rightly not to run off with a young towhead without
talent or skill, modern times, the old days, life passing, idle
chatter, the cold, the heat, the tittle-tattle. They were all accomplices in her downfall.

"Oliva, Olì! What are you doing in the yard? Who are
you talking to? Come into the house. It's getting dark, God
forbid someone should see you!"

I stuck the envelope under the waistband of my skirt
and stepped back.

"Good evening, Signora Denaro," Liliana said politely.

"Good evening," Mother answered without even a glance
as she disappeared behind the door. Liliana stood there
holding the magazines and didn't say a word. I turned away
and went into the house, like a hen into her coop.

12

I n the name of the Father, the Son, and the Holy Spirit. Amen."

"Amen."

Mrs. Scibetta had invited me to recite the Rosary on the first Friday of the month. The rules of the Rosary are: hold the beads, repeat the prayers, wait for it to finish.

I would have preferred to go to school that morning but I was unable to get out of this engagement because May is the month of Mary and, anyway, I had to pay my penance for Liliana's visit. I had stuffed the envelope with my photo in it alongside the mirror, lipstick, and my sketches of movie stars under the loose bed slat.

". . . died and was buried and the third day he rose again according to the Scripture . . ."

That evening Mother had told me that Communists were godless, that Liliana was an unsuitable classmate, and that if it were up to her she'd have taken me out of school because it's not proper for a girl to know too much.

". . . forgive us our trespasses, as we forgive those who trespass against us . . ."

"Are we supposed to end up on everybody's tongues?" she had asked me once we were inside.

"Why would they talk about me, Mà? I'm too young," I had answered.

"Marquis or not, it doesn't matter anymore. They see you now."

Life in Martorana is made of gazes, I thought: it is all about seeing and being seen. And everyone would like to look better than they really are in the eyes of others.

"*. . . now and at the hour of our death. Amen.*"
"*Amen.*"

Mrs. Scibetta's daughters, Nora the fat one and Mena the skinny one, were sitting on either side of their mother like the wings of a crow. She and her husband had been looking for suitable boys for more than a year but despite their best efforts they had found none. The Randazzo widow had also been invited to recite the Rosary. She had given birth to a son before her husband died of syphilis, a sinful disease, Mother said, though the widow insisted it was a weakness in the lung that had killed him. The son's name was Egidio. He was short and bald but Mrs. Scibetta had her sights on him for one of her daughters, maybe the skinny one, Mother said. They were seated, Mrs. Scibetta and her daughters, on a brown sofa and they looked just like the pious women at the Crucifixion. On the other side of the room, there was Mother, me, and Miluzza, a friend of mine from elementary school who had been orphaned very young and taken in by Mrs. Scibetta as a lady's companion. She was more of a companion for the pots and pans in the kitchen and the broom in the closet, as far as I could tell. Mrs. Scibetta had set her to work as a scullery maid and would keep her there for life. That's what Mother said. Miluzza and I were sitting on hard, knotted-wood benches.

"As it was in the beginning, is now, and ever shall be. World without end. Amen."
"Amen."

Every now and again, Mrs. Scibetta's fat daughter gave a sigh and wiped away the drops of sweat that trickled down her forehead, dropped onto her neck and descended between her breasts, which were as big as winter melons. Gray-haired Mrs. Scibetta, with her long, mousy face, led the Rosary while we responded. She and her husband had been forced into marriage because her father, bless his soul, had once seen them talking behind the cowshed. He'd been a good-looking young man back then and had at first refused. But then her father, whose surname was Buttafuoco like Mrs. Scibetta's maiden name, used both the carrot and the stick to persuade him, Mother said. Nevertheless, the marriage had been a success: her husband had given her his surname and old Buttafuoco had provided the money. Both sides had decided it was in their best interest.

"The First Sorrowful Mystery . . ."

Mrs. Scibetta raised her hands in the air and began chanting the Agony of Jesus in the Garden, followed by the Lord's Prayer and ten Hail Marys. The voices soon fell out of sync and shortly everyone was at a different point in the prayer. The Scibetta sisters took advantage of the situation to spread the latest gossip. The Randazzo widow, between Hail Marys, managed to interrupt one sister or the other with a quick question: "And how was that?" "Who do you mean? Cirinnà's daughter?" Mrs. Scibetta pretended not to hear and carried on muttering a litany of incomprehensible words, her palms pressed together in prayer. Everyone was chanting their own version.

"The Second Sorrowful Mystery . . ."

The voices stopped all at once and Mrs. Scibetta started reciting the Scourging at the Pillar. As soon as she went back to the Hail Marys, the gossip machine started up again.

"Five knife stabs she managed to inflict on her husband's bit on the side," the widow announced, raising five fingers.

"It was no secret that Agatina's husband had a second family in the city. Even the strays knew it," Nora commented idly.

"We found out that he had given the kids the same names, between one family and the other, to make things easier for him. When they told Agatina, she saw red, caught the bus with a knife hidden in her bra, and stabbed the other woman in broad daylight in front of everyone," the widow went on.

"Jesus! Did they send her to prison?" Mena screamed, holding her hands over her face. Mrs. Scibetta looked sternly at her and she lowered her voice.

"What happened to the woman?"

The widow murmured a few prayers softly to whet their appetites with the wait. "The bit on the side survived, and so did Agatina," she eventually said.

Miluzza, who was farther away, tried to read the widow's lips. "It was an honor killing," the widow concluded. "The law was on her side."

They all launched into gossip, exchanging takes on the subject, and Mother began reciting her prayers even louder to cover their voices. Mrs. Scibetta droned on without a care in the world because she already knew everything there was to know about everybody.

"The Third Sorrowful Mystery . . ."

As we moved on to the next bead, the fat Scibetta girl glared at me and elbowed her skinny sister. "She was seen in the hut with the Communists," she said loud enough for Mother to hear. She paid no heed and continued chanting her prayers. "Who? Oliva?" the skinny sister gasped, sounding out my name clearly. In the pause between prayers, all eyes were on me. Including Mother's. I felt my cheeks burn and the blood quiver in my veins. The chanting started again but everyone now focused on what the fat sister had to say. In order to raise the stakes, she lingered in silence, drying the drop of sweat that was sliding down her right nostril.

"The Fourth Sorrowful Mystery . . ." their mother intoned with her palms raised to the heavens.

"Well, well, even pips squeak," the Randazzo widow opined, clearing her throat to attract Mother's attention.

"If you sleep with dogs you end up with fleas . . ." the skinny sister said.

"Speaking of dogs and fleas, at least in the old days she only associated with Musumeci's cripple. Now she's hobnobbing with Communists."

"They heard her defending that disgraceful woman."

"She's dabbling in politics now, is she?"

"Come on. She's young enough to be suckling milk."

"She was . . . but no longer."

They weren't even bothering to whisper anymore, looking around to gauge our reactions. Now I knew why we'd been invited to recite the Rosary.

Mother turned a deaf ear but her hands were so tightly knit in prayer that her knuckles were white. The bones looked as though they were about to pierce her skin and crumble from the pressure.

Miluzza kept her eyes on the ground and didn't say a word. She must have witnessed these little performances routinely enough: the Scibetta sisters sitting on the brown sofa tearing reputations to shreds, with all the girls in town on the hot seat, like those poor Christians in the Colosseum facing the lions.

"The Fifth Sorrowful Mystery: Jesus is crucified and dies on the cross." Mrs. Scibetta was forced to raise her voice in order to he heard over the sniping.

After a moment's silence, another string of Hail Marys started. I uncrossed my hands and rested them on my lap. Words burned on my tongue. These people were nothing like me. I didn't know why I had accepted their invitation. It was a mistake. I wanted to tell these bigots off but my jaw had locked, as if the top set of my teeth had been screwed to the bottom.

"Christ have mercy," Mrs. Scibetta exclaimed.

"Christ have mercy," the others confirmed in chorus.

"God have mercy," she insisted.

"God have mercy," they responded.

Mrs. and Misses Scibetta have mercy, I said in my head. I'm not disgraceful and you're not going to force me out of Martorana like you did Miss Rosaria. What have I done that's so wrong? If I'd stabbed a woman five times as Agatina had done I would have been absolved by both the courts and the people sitting here in this living room.

"Holy Mary, pray for us."

"Holy Mother of God, pray for us."

"Holy Virgin, Queen of Virgins, pray for us."

Mother was invoking the Holy Virgin as if she were inviting her to come down to earth and immediately sort out this business.

"Mother most pure, pray for us."
"Mother most chaste, pray for us."
"Mother ever a virgin, pray for us."

I joined in the chorus: Mother, listen to me! I'm like you. I'm Oliva, the little girl who runs around town in wooden clogs. What do I know about all this man-and-woman stuff? About who should go out and work and who shouldn't? Who should bring home the money? Who has to stay home and who is allowed to go out?

"Virgin most prudent, pray for us."
"Virgin most honorable, pray for us."
"Virgin most blessed, pray for us."

They pursed their lips every time they said "Virgin." It felt like they were addressing me.

"Virgin most mighty, pray for us."
"Virgin most clement, pray for us."
"Virgin most faithful, pray for us."

The prayer was a rhythmic slap. Suddenly, the bench felt so uncomfortable that I could no longer sit there and

I leaped to my feet. The chanting ceased for a moment. Everyone was staring, even Mrs. Scibetta. I don't know about Mother because I was turning away from her. I could see her in my mind's eye, her eyes narrowed and the bulging green vein that beats in her temples when she's furious.

"I'm not a broken jug," I yelled. I couldn't say anything else, there was no air in that room. I turned to Mother and Miluzza then back to the Scibettas. Their faces looked identical. All the girls in Martorana look the same, I thought: same clothes, same hairstyle, same way of walking close to the wall, same eyes reduced to twin slits after spending so much time holed up at home in the dark.

I made my way slowly to the door, opened it, and felt the sun strike me in the face. The supplicating voices behind me went back to their tuneless chanting.

"Queen of the family, pray for us."
"Queen of peace, pray for us."

"Pray for us," I muttered under my breath, making the sign of the cross. I slammed the door and started running. As fast as I possibly could.

13

I heard voices around me as my clogs clattered on the flagstones. My hair was flying and my skirt was hitched up over my knees as usual, except that this time I wasn't fleeing from boys and their slingshots. I was escaping the gossip, the shame, Mother. My body didn't want to mature into a woman's but the outside world already saw me as such. I was no longer invisible: I could be watched and judged.

There were certain words I had only ever overheard. I had never bothered to listen to the chanting. But now these words were being used to sting me. For years, they had been background noise to my childhood games but now they were a swarm of wasps attacking me. Miss Rosaria was right, words were weapons. Not just long ones. Even everyday words can be hurtful when they rattle around in the mouths of the ignorant.

For Mrs. Scibetta and her daughters, they were my initiation and that was why I was running so fast, because the sting hurts more if you stay still. Miss Rosaria must have run so fast. She must have gone so far away. I imagined her crossing the street in a big city surrounded by trams and buses, her loose hair bouncing at her shoulders, her mouth painted red like a movie star. In my fantasy she was finally walking on her own: there were no men stopping to point at her or give a wolf whistle. I wonder whether her wasp stings still itch.

I ran as far as the sea but the beach was empty and I was so scared I went back up the road toward town, ending up, without even realizing it, at Saro's house. His father, Don Vito Musumeci, had been one of the most handsome young men in Martorana, dark-skinned with blue eyes. The girls used to swoon over him. He could have pointed his finger and chosen any one of them but he chose Nardina, who had nothing to her name except him. People started to say that he'd gone for a plain wife because he was all talk and no action, that there was something wrong with him, that the marriage would not be blessed with children. And then Saro came along and everyone agreed from day one that the boy bore no resemblance to him. That's what Mother said. Saro had red hair and brown eyes and a birthmark on his left cheek. My schoolmates found the mark creepy but to me it looked like a ripe strawberry and I wanted to brush my lips against it to see what it tasted like.

He limped toward me from his father's carpentry workshop.

"What happened?" he asked.

"Nothing. Why do you think something happened?"

"With that face there must be something."

I dried the sweat from my forehead and plopped down on our bench. We had grown up together in this yard: we used to play at changing the color of our hair with wood chips. He chose walnut and rubbed the sawdust over his head to make his hair as dark as his father's. I chose spruce so I could be as blond as my sister. We also used to run until we were out of breath and then collapse in the yard, our arms and legs splayed, pretending to fly. We would lie there and look at the clouds. Saro would point at a cloud in the sky and say, "Look! Can you see? It's a sheep!" "No, it's not a sheep. It's a dog." "No way is that a dog." The cloud in the meantime would be transfigured by the wind. "It's a stag. Look at its antlers . . ." Another gust of wind and the white fluff would stretch out. "No, no, it's a snake," Saro would correct himself. "It's neither a sheep nor a stag, nor a serpent," I decreed. "Well, what is it, then?" "A marfoyle!" I said, dead serious. "What's that?" "A marfoyle," I repeated convincingly. "That's not fair. They don't exist!" But he wasn't certain because he had left school at eleven. "Can't you see it has two horns?" I asked, trying to get him to catch me out. "In fact, it's a two-horned marfoyle." "Really? And what does this two-horned marfoyle look like, then?" "Come on! Can't you see it?" It looks like a cloud," I said, giggling.

He sat down next to me. I wanted to tell him about the wasp stings, the Rosary, and the Sorrowful Mysteries, but words failed me. I ran my hand through his hair to comb out the residual wood shavings but said nothing. Nardina came out.

"Saro, come inside. It's ready."

I saw myself in her eyes and attempted to flatten down my frizzy hair.

"Oliva, you're here? I've just made the anchovy pasta you love so much. What luck!"

I didn't say anything about reciting the Rosary at the Scibettas even though she would have understood. She must have had more than her fair share of wasp stings to deal with.

14

After lunch, Nardina and Don Vito closed the shutters against the heat of the day and lay down for a rest. Saro wanted to stay in the yard for a bit but I was eager to get home, so I left. The town was bathed in yellow sunlight, everything was scorching hot. I hugged the wall to make the most of the meager shade it offered. It felt like the world had been emptied out.

I saw him at the end of the road before the turn for the piazza. He walked up to the water fountain and doused his head under the jet. As he straightened up, the water dripped off his black curls and trickled down his face. He ran both his hands through his hair, pulling it back from his forehead, and tucked a fresh twig of jasmine behind his right ear. He was dressed in white. When he saw me on the other side of the square, he gave a slight bow. I walked in his direction fast without daring to look him in the face. He put his hand in his pocket, pulled out an orange, and started peeling it. He sank his fingers into the segments and split the fruit in two, revealing the bloody flesh.

"Try it. It's sweet," he offered, stretching his arm out toward me as if he were about to grab me. I turned around but there was no one else on the street. Just him and me.

He brought the orange up to his face. "It refreshes your whole mouth, see? Like this."

He sank his teeth and tongue into the half-orange and sucked at it until all that was left was white pith on peel.

"This is for you," he said, handing me the other half. "Let's see if you like it as much as you did the ricotta beaten with sugar when you were little."

I took the orange and held it in my hand: it was still warm from his fingers and oozing with juice. The acid tang pierced my nostrils. It nauseated me but, at the same time, sent a twinge coursing through my belly.

I pursed my lips so that he wouldn't be able to read anything in my expression. A girl who smiles has already said yes, Mother's voice rang in my head. He was looking at me as if something beautiful was set within the dark angular face I had grown used to instead of my beady black eyes, and this scared me. In order to ward off my discomfort, I started reciting the first declension in Latin: *rosa, rosae, rosae.* I'd repeated it so many times before sleep to learn it by heart that it had become a prayer. *Rosa, rosae, rosae, rosam, rosa, rosa,* I went on chanting in my head until he took one more step toward me, coming so close that I could smell the jasmine behind his ear. "*Rosae, rosarum, rosis,*" I yelled so loudly that it sounded like a curse, and I thrust the hand holding the orange out to keep it at a distance. Then I pulled my arm back behind my head and lobbed it hard, like when I used to shoot stones with my slingshot when I was little. The half-sphere landed on his thigh, the blood-red pulp dripping down his white trouser leg. He took his hands out of his pockets and I flinched, thinking he was about to hit me. Instead, he started rubbing his leg and laughed. I took a few steps back and started running for my life without looking back. I ran across the piazza and all the way down the big road, pursued by the echo of his laugh. Just as I reached the turning for the dirt track, I tripped on a loose stone and lost my balance. My clogs flew off and I ended up sprawled on the ground, my knees in the dirt.

15

hat have you been up to now?" Mother shrieked when I got home.

"I fell and there was a bit of blood."

She checked my legs and I looked, too: there were abrasions on both knees but no cuts. I bent over and inspected my ankles, then I went up my legs to my thighs, following the bloodstain as far as the elastic of my underpants. I pulled my hand away and saw that it was as red as the juice of the blood orange. Thick, dark juice that didn't smell like citrus. I thought to myself: I stopped and spoke to that man and I got sick. I glanced at Mother to get a measure of how serious a sin I'd committed and how harsh my punishment would be. But she didn't tell me off. She took my hand and led me into the bathroom.

"The time has come for you, too. I told you it would, didn't I?" she said in a different register, the one she used with townswomen she was friendly with. She finally had proof that I, too, was female, that thanks to that trickle of blood she and I had more in common than we imagined.

"Come. I'll show you what you have to do."

It's all my fault, I thought to myself. It was that orange, that head with its shiny wet hair fresh from the water fountain, those eyes burrowing into me and stripping me naked, that voice talking to me. It was him that made it happen.

"You need to wash carefully, several times a day."

I stood there paralyzed in front of the washbowl that was filling with water. "You'll get used to it," she added, handing me some white rags folded into four. She laughed with her raspy little cough and sized me up, taking a step back as if she hadn't seen me in ages. She wore that contented smile she usually had after a funeral wake, and she seemed to have forgotten the business with the Rosary.

I ran my hand over my breasts. They were still flat and my blouse still tightly buttoned. My skirt fell straight over my hips without so much as a curve. Nothing has changed, I said to myself. The blood has come and left me exactly the same.

Like when they took me to get my ears pierced, the day before confirmation. Mother and Fortunata held my hands and it felt as if the closer we got to the clergy house, where Nellina the housekeeper was waiting to carry out the procedure, the tighter they gripped on to me. To begin with, I had been happy. All my friends at school had already done it. They had put on a show, flaunting the gold studs embedded in their flesh, so of course I'd wanted my own. But as soon as I reached the front door, I got cold feet.

"I've changed my mind, Mà. I don't want to do it anymore," I protested.

"What do you mean? How will that make us look with Nellina?" Mother was getting flustered.

I dug my heels in and refused to take one more step, imploring Fortunata to come to my aid. She fingered the two gold rings hanging from her earlobes.

"All girls have their ears pierced. Do you want people to take you for a boy?" She smiled. "You should be happy," she added. "Today, you become a grown-up."

I'm not at all in favor of growing up, I thought to myself.

Nellina ordered me to sit on the brown chair with stuffed arms and asked me to lean my head back. "Don't move for any reason in the world," she warned, as Mother clamped her hand on my forehead to restrain me. "You won't feel a thing."

It wasn't true. After holding a cube of ice to my lobe to numb it, she put a piece of cork behind it so that the needle wouldn't go through my neck after piercing the earlobe. I had decided to be good and sit still. I closed my eyes and the strong whiff of disinfectant upset my stomach. I tried concentrating on a nice memory so I could resist the pain. I remembered being treated to sugared ricotta at the pastry shop when I was little, after being awarded a star at school. But as soon as the tip of the needle started pushing into my flesh, I let out a scream and shook my head violently to free it from Mother's grip. A few drops of blood spotted my white blouse.

"Now look at the mess," Mother scolded me. "What

now?" she asked Nellina, embarrassed. "We need to wait for the wound to heal" was her verdict as she looked at the small gash on my right earlobe. Mother begged the housekeeper's forgiveness as if we'd offended her.

"She isn't ready yet," Nellina concluded, wiping my ear with a wad of cotton wool soaked in alcohol. "Bring her back in a while and we'll see whether we can fix the situation."

"And if we can't?" Mother asked, disheartened.

"If we can't, she'll have one hole higher than the other. And she'll have a reminder that you can't always do what you want in life."

On the way home, the wound was burning and my earlobe was pulsating like crazy, as if it were a second heartbeat, but I marched without complaining. Mother, on the other hand, did nothing but grumble the whole way. "Everything is hard with you. Things that are easy for other girls are complicated for you."

———

Piercing my ears was supposed to make me grow up but I had stayed exactly the same. Like with the marquis.

Mother went on giving me instructions on how to fold the linen rags properly so as not to stain my skirt, but I wasn't listening. I was thinking about the morning of my confirmation when I had ended up the only girl without pierced ears. I rubbed the scar on my right earlobe, where I could still feel a hard little bump. I'd never gone back to

Nellina to complete the operation. I'd remained an imperfect female specimen.

I took the rags from her hands and slipped my skirt off. She scrubbed the stain off with salt, which melts everything. Then she looked up at me. "You're getting pretty," she remarked, as if out of all the possible turns of events this was one she had least expected.

All of a sudden, I stopped feeling as though there was something wrong with me. If Mother thought I would be beautiful, then I would be. If Mother saw me, the whole world would see me. I had crossed the threshold of invisibility. I had become a woman like her.

As she rinsed out my skirt, I took advantage of our newfound intimacy and asked her point-blank, "What was it like the first time you saw Papà?"

She wasn't shocked by my question. She closed her eyes and smiled. "He made me feel special," she said. "But I was just young."

She stopped, as if she were grappling with a memory that was still hard to grasp.

"It all went too fast," she admitted finally. "Your father had come to Calabria to get his inheritance and came back home with me. A bargain!" She laughed, but without her usual raspy cough. Maybe that was the way she used to laugh when she was a girl.

"Did you love him?"

She rinsed the skirt out once more under running water and held it up to the light to make sure it was clean.

"Love or not . . . it's set in stone. Now you need to be careful," she said, all businesslike again, looking sideways at me.

"Careful about what?"

"Not to fall again."

I followed her into the yard without asking anything else. I'm not at all in favor of falling. She spread the skirt out with her hands, making sure all the seams were lined up, then turned away from me to peg it to the line as Liliana had done with her pictures. In the meantime, she listed the rules of the marquis even though I already knew them. Don't go out alone. Don't wear your skirt above your knee. Never talk face-to-face with a man.

"Not even with Saro?"

"Isn't Saro a man? What is he, then? A woman?"

"We've known each other since we were tiny."

"Well, now you've both grown up. If Saro has something to say to you, he can come and say it to your father. And to me."

I was speechless. I looked at where the stain on my skirt had been, afraid there would still be a ring.

"The rest is all superstition," she went on. "They say when the marquis comes you shouldn't touch meat or it'll go rotten, you shouldn't pick flowers or they'll wither, you shouldn't wash your hair or the curls won't hold. They're old wives' tales. You just need to do what you've always done: toe the line and don't ever surrender your honor, or you'll end up like your sister. It was thanks to me that Musciacco married her."

I thought of Fortunata's face the last time I saw her. She had told me to stay outside because she was washing the floors, she said. Her hair looked gray instead of blond, her face was covered in scratches that were visible from two floors below. Was that thanks to Mother, too?

"Am I allowed to run?" I asked, just to be sure.

"Do your friends run around? No. So you shouldn't run, either."

"Liliana..."

"The Communist's daughter doesn't count. She has too many crickets in her head."

Mother went up on tiptoes, checking every inch of my skirt hanging out to dry. "It's as good as new," she informed me, turning away. "Now it's up to you to keep it clean."

16

Since becoming a woman, I feel like I've been huddled under an awning during a storm: I don't venture out in case I get wet. I can't go to Saro's house. I can't go to the market. I can't go to Liliana's.

Every now and again I pull the photograph out from under the bed slat and see myself as I used to be, my hair plastered with sweat and my knees dirty. It feels like another lifetime. Cosimino takes me to school every morning and comes to fetch me in the afternoon. Soon, when the summer vacation comes, I'll be stuck at home all day embroidering other girls' trousseaux and waiting for someone to ask for my hand.

Before the school bell rings, Liliana says, "Are you coming to the meeting at the hut this afternoon?" although she knows perfectly well that I won't be coming this time, either. We leave the classroom and our paths diverge. She veers off on her own and I go to meet Cosimino. We walk toward the main road, and when we reach the pharmacy, I inhale deeply. As soon as we turn the corner, I hold my breath, cast my eyes down, and start counting the flagstones. I tell myself that if I manage to hold my breath as far as the next turning, Cosimino won't notice a thing. My bet has paid off so far. Two hundred and forty-two, two hundred and forty-three, two hundred and forty-four, two hundred and forty-five.

He stands there, on the corner of Don Ciccio's haberdashery, as he has every day since I stained his white trousers with the blood orange. Rain or shine, wind or scorching heat, he stands there and stares until I turn the corner and take the dirt road home. My skirt is clean now, but when he looks at me, it feels as if the stains are still there.

I count two hundred and forty-five steps in my head, step as lightly as I can, and try to make myself invisible. But under his gaze I become flesh. Like Liliana's photos that appear on the glossy paper, my body materializes when he looks at it. For two hundred and forty-five steps, my thighs, arms, mouth, hair, hips take on a life of their own under my clothes. I stoop, trying to hide, as if I were tying myself in a knot. The whole of life is a knot.

17

omeone's ears are ringing," Mother grumbles. I stop milking the goat and wait for the whistling to fade until the only thing I hear in the pen is my own breath mingling with the goat's. Only then can I start milking again, even though my hands are still trembling, which makes me squeeze too tight. Bianchina starts bleating in pain. I hear Father's steps come toward me. "You need to be gentle, Oliva. That's what girls like," he says, patting her back.

He goes back to the house. His voice is as quiet as rustling straw. Is he speaking for the goat or for me? At least when Mother opens her mouth, I know what is what. Her tongue is like a lick of fire but the burn soon heals. I dip my hands in the bucket and they come out as white as milk. I wish I were that pure.

She sits in the sun, bowed over the length of cotton. She's sewing me a dress for this year's patron saint festival. Until last year, the priest had me up onstage with the little ones and asked me to sing the solos. Mother would sew a pair of little archangel wings onto my shoulders and all the other mothers would praise her handiwork. This year I won't be singing with the others. I'll be wearing a white debutante's dress and everyone will know I'm not a girl anymore.

"Are you enjoying the little concert?" Mother says without taking her eyes off the cloth. "You encouraged the man and now he's out on the street whistling for you."

"He's not whistling for me . . ."

"Salvo, did you hear that? The young man with the curls is whistling for me!" she sneers.

I sit next to her and help her thread the needle.

"I've never said a word to him."

"You don't need words! All it takes is a look, a smile. A girl who smiles has already said yes."

My flesh crawls. Her eyes never stray from her sewing. I've never seen her without something to do in her hands. Needle and thread, mop and floorcloth, saucepan and ladle. Her hands never rest as she spits out flecks of truth and poison.

"Olì, do you realize who Pino Paternò is?" she says, pricking her finger as she says his name. A drop of blood wells into a tiny pool on the tip of her index finger, hanging there, suspended.

"No!" I yell, to the name and the dress. The debutante's dress is supposed to be pure white. White as a lily the dress, white as a lily the daughter, that's what she taught me. She holds her hand up to my face. I close my lips around her finger and suck the drop dry, just in time, before it dribbles onto the cotton and ruins it. The prick has gone and so has the red spot, the bitter iron of her blood dissolved in my mouth.

She pulls her hand away and rubs it on the rough fabric of her apron. "He's been coming here every single day for the past month with his warbling," she says, more tenderly than before. Maybe she's flattered by the idea that someone might be interested in me. "He hasn't come forward to make a request, which means his intentions are not serious. If he had his sights on you, he'd have come inside to discuss the matter. You whistle to a dog, not a woman!"

I thought that I wouldn't see him again once school came to an end, that I would go back to being as invisible as before. Instead, a few days later, the whistling began. At first, nobody noticed but I knew right away that it was him. My body knew: my lips, hips, thighs, bones, and neck came alive when they heard the sound, just as they had done under his gaze. I didn't even need to go to the window to see the outline of his shiny black curls, his lips curled into Cupid's bow as they channeled the air. I stood holding my breath behind the closed shutters, wondering whether he could see my silhouette.

"Paternò has property and we have nothing," she says loud enough for Father to hear from the end of the yard where he is stooped over the vegetables. "And since coming back to Martorana, he's set his eyes on you of all people. He must be having a ball defying the family, since he could have as many beauties as he wants . . ."

I plug my ears with my fingers to block out the serenade. I ask myself: Is it my fault if God made me ugly? When I unplug them, the serenade trumpets louder and my shame echoes down the entire street.

"Can't you say something?" she hisses at Father through her teeth. "Can't you do something?"

He rubs the dirt off his pants and loads the herbs into a basket. "What am I supposed to say? The man is happy and likes to whistle. Good for him."

"What about everyone else? God forbid we become the laughingstock of the town!"

Father starts whistling himself as he comes into the house. Mother yells at him in Calabrian before slumping back into her chair. "I give up. There's nothing to be gained from this man. Salvo Denaro, your blood is no better than a bedbug's." She peeks through the shutters, half-closed against the heat. "My mother was right, bless her soul. This man doesn't have the head for anything useful."

From the kitchen we can hear Father's whistling blending with the other tune rising from the street. "I'll go and talk to him," Cosimino yells, grabbing his jacket.

"Sit down, son. This is not your battle to fight. In this house, swords are nailed to the wall and empty scabbards go to war."

————

Mother folds the unfinished dress into the sewing basket and, turning to Father, says, "You don't even care about your son. Do you really hear and see nothing?"

Father doesn't stop whistling until the other man's goes silent and all you can hear on the street are receding steps.

When he stops, there is silence again. I'm not sure whether I'm still in favor of silence.

18

The piazza is crisscrossed with fairy lights and crowded with fair stalls: some are selling seeds, others roasted chickpeas, still others candy figurines or carob pods. The little girls with wings on their backs are clambering onto the stage. My replacement looks nothing like me: she's blond and fair-skinned. When she starts singing the solo, surrounded by the other girls in the choir, I feel as if my voice has been stolen.

I make my way to the square in my white dress and the new shoes Mother bought me with a loan from Mrs. Scibetta and which are close-toed and even have a low heel. I've always worn clogs and these shoes pinch my feet everywhere. Mother and Cosimino flank me. Father, wearing a hat, trails one step behind us with his hands in his pockets. I look over at the stalls selling lamb gut and rice balls to see whether my sister, Fortunata, is there. When we were little, we used to wander around the stalls together gaping at the sword swallower, who would bend impossibly backward as if the sword were actually penetrating his body and then extract the shiny blade whole without shedding a drop of blood. Since she got married, though, she hasn't been back to celebrate our patron saint. Come to think of it, what would she possibly want to celebrate?

Mrs. Scibetta and her daughters are parading the new dresses Mother and I made for them. They're accessorized with every piece of jewelry they own and, from a distance, they resemble three martyred saints ready for the procession. I can't see Fortunata but I can see her husband, Gerò Musciacco, sporting a fine suit and a greased mustache like a movie star on a billboard, coming from the main road. On his arm is a woman in a dress with a low neck and a hemline high above her knees. As soon as he sees us, he nods imperceptibly in a hint of greeting and immediately turns his head the other way, placing his arm around the woman, and kissing her in front of everyone. Mother mutters something in Calabrian but paints a smile on her face because there mustn't be any talk. Father and Cosimino are following the raffle to crosscheck the numbers as they are chosen. They have bought two tickets and hope to win first prize, which is a full meal with a first, second, and third course, wine, and dessert. The judge raises his hand in the air, then dips it into the bag of numbers. Every time he pulls a number out and reads it, the small crowd whoops with joy or disappointment.

The farther we go into the square, the more I feel everyone's eyes on me: I'm desperate to go home and slip back into the clogs I left by my bed. Luckily, Liliana comes along. She's wearing a tight-fitting flowery dress like the ones singers wear on TV and she has back-brushed her hair. "Come and dance, Oliva!" she says, yanking me by the elbow.

"My daughter doesn't dance," Mother says bluntly.

"It's just us girlfriends, there's nothing wrong . . ."

"My daughter doesn't have girlfriends," Mother hisses between her teeth.

At precisely that moment, the Scibetta sisters decide to hold hands and push their way through to the middle of the square, right in front of the stage. They're tapping their feet out of time with the music, while their mother looks on, contentedly clapping her hands. Looking pointedly in our direction, she waves her arms in front of her as if to say, "Go on, girls, go on." Being alone on the dance floor is enough to make her daughters look like clowns. But if they don't dance no one will notice them, condemning both to yet another year of spinsterhood before being eventually deemed unfit for marriage.

Mother gives me a little shove on the shoulder. "Off you go, you can dance. Girls partner with girls!"

The rules of dancing are: stay away from the boys, don't sing out loud, don't wiggle your hips as if you were possessed by the devil.

Liliana clearly doesn't know the rules since she's doing exactly the opposite of what Mother has always taught me. She twirls her wrists like the singer Mina. She snaps her fingers in time to the music, holding her arms out in front of her, and yells the lyrics out at the top of her voice: "*Nessuno, ti giuro, nessuno . . .*" My new shoes are hurting so much I have to shift my weight from one foot to the other like a tightrope walker. Liliana tosses her head, arches her back, and gyrates her hips. She's so beautiful it gives me that languorous feeling in my stomach. *"Nemmeno il destino ci può separare . . ."* the Scibetta sisters sing timidly, without swaying their hips. *"Tutto il mio mondo comincia con te, finisce con te,"* Liliana shouts just as some boys walk past. I turn to look over at Mother but, luckily, she's distracted and chatting to Nardina. Don Vito is standing in front of the café with a group of men, commenting on the women's dresses while their husbands are out of earshot. I can see him laughing, He has a nice mouth and eyes the color of the sea but his cheeks betray his displeasure. I think he must feel he has to put on an act so as not to give satisfaction to the gossips who call him "half a man" behind his back. They suffer as much as we do: male honor depends on the woman they choose, whereas female honor depends on their own flesh. Everyone defends what they have, just as everyone has their place in the patron saint procession.

We young women are dancing in the middle of the square, while the young men are standing around smoking and making comments. The Scibetta sisters, their feet still tapping completely offbeat, put their bejeweled heads together and jut their lips out to gasp, *"Perché questo amore si illuminerà d'eternità . . ."* Their attempts to attract the boys' attention are fruitless: all eyes are on Liliana, dancing with her head thrust back and her eyes closed.

Cosimino joins the onlookers together with Father, who is holding a new hat, the consolation prize from the raffle. My brother approaches us, taking a few dance steps, as the skinny Scibetta sister devours him with her eyes. Next to the boiled octopus and shellfish stand, there's a boy in long pants with red hair combed back with gel. He's standing apart from the others and he's not smoking. My first impression is that he is from out of town, but when he turns around, I see it is Saro. Until just a few months ago, we were allowed to hang out in front of his father's workshop: him, with his unkempt hair filled with sawdust, and me, sitting cross-legged on the grass. He's grown up, too. Now he's with the men, and when our eyes meet, we are both embarrassed.

Liliana grabs my hands and lifts them up in the air. I bring them back down: it's not proper for a girl to lift her arms higher than her shoulders, Mother says. They are now playing a slow Neapolitan song about a lover under the window of a married woman at night. The woman stands behind the shutters but doesn't lean out, her husband sleeps through the whole thing. The lover weeps on the street while the woman goes back to bed but can't sleep. Suddenly, I recognize the tune and fold my arms over my belly: it's the song I hear being whistled every day in front of my house.

The Scibetta sisters clasp each other for the slow dance, as they must have seen on TV.

"Neapolitan music makes me sad," I say to Liliana, dragging her away through the crowd. Through all the pushing and shoving, I smell the pungent scent of jasmine. Then a hand grips my wrist tight and yanks me. "May your sweetheart have this dance?"

I lose sight of Liliana in the crowd and try to wrest my hand free but his grip is like a vise.

"This is our song, remember?"

"I don't remember anything and I don't know you."

Paternò wraps his left arm around my waist and flattens my right palm against his. It's warm but not clammy. He brings his cheek to mine and the acrid scent of his musk mingles with the jasmine behind his ear, going right through me.

"'*Rosa fresca aulentissima . . .*' You went to school, so you know this poem, right?"

"I don't know anything. Let me go! Let's not give people anything to talk about."

"People will talk about whatever I want them to. Do you remember how it ends for the two lovers in the poem? They keep at it until their steely resolve melts."

The Neapolitan song comes to an end and the band onstage launches into a fast piece. I turn my head to see whether Liliana is with the others, dancing in couples. Paternò pulls me closer and starts twirling me through the crowd. I'm terrified of meeting Mother's gaze but at the same time I'm seeking it out, to beg her for help, to explain that none of this was my doing. He clasps me close and spins me until my feet almost lift off the ground. My shoes come off, locks of hair start pulling loose from my tight bun and falling onto my shoulders. All I can feel is his hand on my back, the scent of jasmine, and the smell of his skin. The heat coming off his body permeates mine, which feels alien to me, endowed with its own thoughts and its own will. I feel my belly turn to liquid and a terror I've never felt before rises to my throat.

"Let me go," I say quietly. "I don't want you. I don't want you. I don't want you!" I repeat it louder and louder each time, until I'm yelling it.

"You're a good girl," he says. "Proper girls aren't supposed to give in right away. They're supposed to play hard to get," he adds, brushing my chin with two fingers.

"The young lady doesn't want to dance. Didn't you hear her?" Saro had placed a hand on Paternò's shoulder. His voice was different: another thing that had changed since we stopped spending time together.

"Why wouldn't she? She's not a cripple like you."

Saro lunges at Paternò, his face so flushed with blood that his birthmark becomes almost invisible. He strikes blindly, never managing to hit him, and ends up grabbing a fistful of hair and yanking as hard as he can. His opponent raises his arm but doesn't fight back.

"I'm a gentleman. I'm not going to brawl with a boy who fights like a girl, specially not one already punished by God."

Saro's lips tremble. "You're no gentleman, only a loan shark," he yells, the tears cracking his voice. "You and your father have half the town under your thumb!"

A small crowd has formed around us and the band has stopped playing. Saro continues to show his fists and somebody intervenes, separating the two men. In the midst of the crowd, I see Father walking slowly toward me holding his new hat. I look at him but his expression gives nothing away. It's the same face he would make if he were gathering herbs in the fields.

"Salvo, for God's sake," I hear Mother screaming from behind me. Anyone else would think she is trying to stop him but I know perfectly well that she is inciting him. Salvo, for God's sake, do something, is what she's trying to say. For once show the town that you're a man. Show your worth, Salvo, for God's sake!

Mother's words hit him like a sledgehammer. He narrows his eyes, reaches out, and takes my hand.

"Won't this gracious father grant me the honor of a dance with his pretty daughter?" Paternò says, teasing him.

Father opens his mouth, pauses for a moment, and mutters, "I wouldn't prefer it," as he leads me away, my dress torn and my feet bare. Before turning onto a little side street, I look back and see Paternò standing alone in the middle of the piazza. Smiling.

"*Rosa!*" he shouts from the distance, so that everyone can hear him. "*Rosa fresca aulentissima . . .*"

19

When we get home, Father hangs his new hat in the entrance, changes into his work clothes, and disappears into the tool shed. After a while, he emerges with a wooden shelf and a pot of paint and sets both onto a table in the yard. For a few seconds he closes his eyes and presses down on his left arm as if he were stemming a wound, then he pulls a handkerchief out of his pocket and wipes his brow. When he opens his eyes again, he dips the brush into the red liquid and starts painting, first in one direction, then in the other, keeping up a steady rhythm. Mother joins him and starts grumbling, "Father and son squander what little money we managed to set aside at the raffle while daughter plays the prima ballerina in front of the whole town."

The swishing of brushstrokes on the rough wooden grain is his only answer.

"What are this man's intentions toward our daughter? Did you ask him? You wanted her to go to school, and that's fine, but now we need to start thinking about getting her settled."

"You need to be gentle with girls," he says, like with the goat.

I sit in a corner biting my nails as they talk about me in the same way they would about breeding an animal.

"I've already set up one of your daughters for you. You have me to thank for the fact that Fortunata is living the life of a lady in a house with servants."

I think of my sister's sunken eyes last time I saw her looking out her window and I'd like my eyes to sink, too, never again to see or be seen.

"Cosimino is still a boy. You need to do your bit. What does a decent husband and father do? He brings food to the table and takes care of the women of his household. Did you see the way that man looked at your daughter? If I prick you with a pin, you know what will come out, don't you? The blood of a bedbug. You're no better than a bedbug, you!"

Father stirs the paint with a wooden stick to test its consistency. He pours a little water into the pot and stirs again. Then he removes the dripping brush and hands it to my brother, turns on his heel, and calmly goes back into the house, where he dons his new hat, puts his shoes on again, and sets off toward the dirt track.

"Cosimino, son, carry on, will you? I've just remembered an urgent errand: I have to restore the family's honor before dinner."

My brother stands there with the brush in his hand, a puddle of red paint pooling at his feet. I feel faint, too feeble to get up. Mother watches the drops as they collect on the ground.

"Don't worry, Amalia," Father turns back to say. "It's paint, not blood. It'll wash away with water. The stain of that man, on the other hand, will never go away however hard you scrub." Then he walks off, leaving bright red footprints on the road.

I'm scared to stay at home and scared to follow the crimson signs on the road. I get up slowly, go into my room, and take off my dress. It's still as white as when we embroidered it but there's a long tear down the side. I slip back into my house clothes, put my clogs back on, hide my new dress in an old leather bag I used to use for school, and go out into the yard. There's a shovel leaning against the wall of the house. I pick it up and dig a hole at the foot of the olive tree. I dig it as deep as I can, throw the satchel with the dress in it, and cover it with earth until it vanishes from view. I cover everything over and go to watch Father walking farther and farther away into the dark.

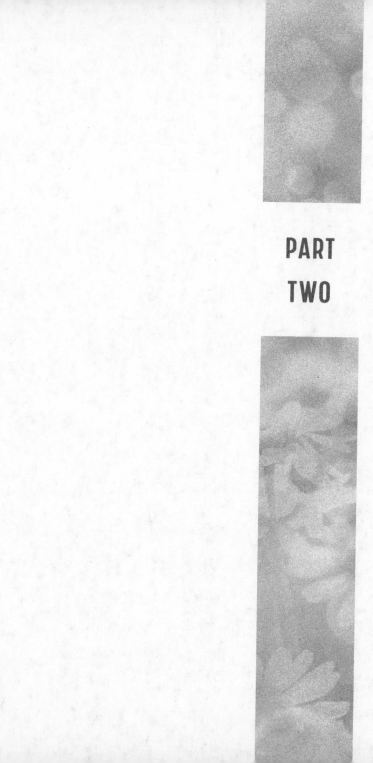

PART
TWO

20

They found him on the street. He had keeled over–his hat fallen off, his shirt gaping open–and he was holding his arm. In town, people whispered that he had been on his way to reclaim his honor from Paternò but that he had not been carrying any weapons. Dr. Provenzano said they had caught him just in time and we should thank the Virgin Mary for her miracles. I'm all in favor of miracles.

When Mother saw him in the hospital bed, she shook her head. "Don't do it again," she pleaded, running her hand through his hair. I'd never seen her touch any part of his body and understood he was about to die.

By mid-autumn, however, he was still in bed. He didn't speak much, as usual, and spent his days gazing out the window toward the fields, while Cosimino and I took care of the chickens, the goat, and the vegetables. I harvested the snails while my brother went out to catch frogs. When he came back, we would move the chairs into Father's room to keep him company, and Mother, Cosimino, and I would sit around the bucket with our knives. Cosimino started by cutting off the frog's head, which was the worst job, one Father always used to take on before his heart attack. Lots of blood spilled into the bucket. Then my brother passed the torso on to me and I did the less squeamish job of snipping off the tips of its four legs as swiftly as I could, before handing it over to Mother, who would turn out its guts. The work was tiring but worth it because ready-to-cook frogs sold much better at market. To get us all laughing, Cosimino would start telling us a story about a trial he said he had heard at the bar. We were the accused and the judge was meting out a sentence to each of us. I would only get a year because I had just cut off their feet. Mother would get fifteen years for inflicting serious injury, while he would receive a life sentence for delivering the death blow to the poor creatures. In the end, the judge ruled we had acted in self-defense and acquitted us all: if we didn't kill frogs, hunger would kill us. We all laughed as the red guts and webbed feet piled up in the bucket. Cosimino looked at Father out of the corner of his eye to see whether he was entertained but Father's attention was elsewhere: his gaze wandered from the pile of body parts to the window and beyond, landing on the very spot where I'd buried my dress. At least, that's what I thought.

My brother was the one to go to market, and when he returned, he left the money in a wicker basket on Father's bedside table. He was still the head of the family, after all.

Dr. Provenzano came for a checkup once a week and gave him some syrup. I'm in favor of syrup. When I was little, I had bronchitis and they gave me some that tasted of cherries. It was so good that I got up in the night and drank the whole bottle. I had such a bad stomachache afterward that they forced me to vomit to get it out of my system.

One day, the doctor said Father was better and if he wasn't getting up it was because his will was "defective."

"What does that mean?" Mother asked suspiciously.

"After a heart attack, there can be a kind of weariness of the spirit. You need to be patient," he answered.

"He's never had any will at all," Mother said. "How long will it take for him to go back to normal?"

Dr. Provenzano took off his glasses and rubbed his eyes with his knuckles as if he wanted to erase them.

"You need to be patient," he said again, and that was his last visit.

21

In the early weeks, there had been a line outside the door with one person coming in and another one leaving. Don Ignazio, Nellina, neighbors, busybodies who wanted to know what had happened. "Weak heart," Mother repeated, and they nodded dolefully but shot a glance at me. With her permission, I escaped to my room, opening my school books and pretending to study for a Latin test the next day even though I no longer attended school. After his heart attack, I'd been taken out.

"A respectable girl doesn't need a high school diploma," Mother had said, putting my black pinafore away.

It doesn't matter, I thought to myself. It was getting a bit tight, anyway.

Honesta puella laetitia familiae est I read in the first-year textbook, leafing through the dictionary to block out the chatter in the kitchen. "An honest girl is the joy of the family," I wrote in my notebook. They were right, I was the one responsible for Father's weak heart.

Only the skinny Scibetta sister, Mena, came to visit. She apologized on behalf of her mother: she and her sister had just gotten over a bad cold and they didn't want to risk a relapse. On her own, the skinny sister looked less slight than she did when she was next to the others. She wasn't much older than me but her mother's fear that she would never find a husband had turned her into a spinster. It's the same for all of us: we end up becoming what our mothers think of us.

"Isn't Cosimino here?" she asked, pinning her hair back.

"Don't worry, he's at the market," I answered, imagining she was being shy. "Take a seat, Mena," I said, smoothing my apron down over my hips. "Would you like some coffee, water, or mint syrup?"

"Thanks, Oliva, but you mustn't go to any trouble," she answered, becoming friendlier than she had ever been before. "Come and sit here with me."

When I had been invited to their house to recite the Rosary, I'd never been allowed to sit on the sofa. It was as if we belonged to different spheres: me, Mother, and Miluzza to one, the three of them to another. I sat down next to her. Mena took my hand and placed it on her lap.

"So, how did it happen?"

My fingers brushed the nap of her skirt, with its beautiful embroidery that I had helped sew only a year ago. I'd worked so hard on it but it didn't belong to me and I was embarrassed to touch it.

"It was a heart attack," I said. "It was Cosimino who found him on the main road . . ."

"You can tell me, Oliva," she interrupted. "We could be sisters and it's normal to share secrets."

I realized that I'd never held hands with my own sister, Fortunata.

"I don't know, Mena. What can I say?"

Mena flushed, which made her look skinny again. Her eyes glittered as if they were about to well up with tears but she didn't seem to be in any pain.

"The kiss," she whispered.

"What kiss, Mena?" I asked, confused.

"You can tell me, Oliva. It'll stay between the two of us."

I pulled back my hand, feeling the cloth slide between my fingers like when I'd embroidered it stitch after stitch.

"You're engaged and now you're acting all superior. I've always been your friend!" Mena pouted, wringing her hands. Real tears were beginning to flow.

"There has been no kiss and there's no engagement," I replied. "He's not someone we know, neither I nor my family."

Mena looked disappointed but at the same time a little relieved. She soon resumed her usual haughty expression, pulled her chair back, and gave me a spiteful look.

"He left town a boy and returned a man. Everyone says he's good-looking. Don't you think he is?"

I felt a tightening in my chest, looked over at Mother to see whether she was eavesdropping, and folded my arms over my apron.

"I've seen him no more than twice, if that, and I've never thought about it."

"He invited you to dance."

"He mistook me for someone else," I said, cutting her short.

"My mother says he's been living in the city with an

uncle all these years and that he runs a thriving business there because life in this town doesn't give him any satisfaction."

"Good for him," I muttered.

Mena leaned over and started whispering in my ear again. "They say he was forced to flee suddenly because of a matter of honor," she said heatedly. I stood up so brusquely that my chair tipped over backward. Mena got up, too, and Mother stuck her head in the door to see what was going on.

"It's nothing, Donna Amalia. I'm leaving, that's all," Mena stammered as she rushed to the door. "Mamma will be expecting you Friday for the Rosary."

"Thank you, Mena," Mother said, "but as you can see, I can't leave the house with my husband in this condition."

I breathed a sigh of relief. The last time I was there, I had run out of their house as if I had been caught stealing. It all came back to me: the sun beating down, the empty piazza, the blood-red juice of the orange staining the white trousers, and the blood trickling down my legs.

Mena sent her regards to Father and left. Mother and I were left in the kitchen getting supper ready and keeping our distance like two people who didn't want to catch a disease from each other.

22

I'm going to Mass alone this morning because Mother is delivering embroidered sheets for the wedding of Nellina's niece, Tindara, who is a year older than me and has had an advantageous match made for her. The rules of going to church are: stand up when the priest says "stand," sit down when he says "sit," and don't dislodge the wafer from the roof of your mouth with your tongue after taking communion.

I go into the church with my white veil on, cross myself, and join the others in the pews. Tindara is there with her new shoes and her hair pulled up high on her head. At sixteen, she already looks married. When the service is over, we all gather around her and Crocefissa, firing off a barrage of questions.

"What's your fiancé like? Which actor does he look like?"

Tindara wraps her arms around herself. "I don't know . . ."

"You don't know whether he's handsome or ugly?" Crocefissa pries.

She lowers her gaze in embarrassment and doesn't answer right away.

"I haven't seen my future husband yet. My aunt arranged the whole thing," she finally confesses.

We girls are perplexed. We thought arranged marriages were a thing of the past.

"My purity is my gift to him," Tindara justifies herself, "and he will provide me with a position," she continues, parroting the exact words her aunt must have taught her. "That is the basis of a happy marriage."

We don't know how to respond. Crocefissa is the only one of us impulsive enough to blurt out the words we all had on the tip of our tongues: "You don't even know what he looks like?"

"Of course I do. What do you think? He sent me a full-body portrait," Tindara says with a tremor in her voice. "I checked and there are no parts missing."

"So, what is this, then? Love at first correspondence?" Crocefissa jokes.

"Is he rich, at least?" Rosalina asks, rubbing her thumb and index finger together as if she were counting money.

"He's a sales representative," Tindara boasts. "He's solid," she informs us, striking the back of her left hand on the palm of her right, to indicate his substance.

"What happens," I ask timidly, "if when you see him in person, you don't feel anything, if there isn't any joy in your heart? In a week, you're going to have to live in the same house as him, day and night . . ."

Tindara's expression darkens and her eyes become narrow slits. "Look who's talking! We're not like you, you know!" The girls around me go quiet. "You get to choose your fiancé out on the street, you get him to serenade you outside your house, you let him kiss you in public, and ruin your father's health while you're about it! My future husband is an honorable man and in order to avoid any gossip, he thought it best not even to meet me so that my purity would be apparent to all."

"I didn't mean . . ."

"You're on everyone's lips. Everyone in town knows Pino Paternò."

When I hear his name, I feel his hand lingering on my hips, I smell the scent of his skin, and I'm consumed by shame.

The girls form a circle, like men betting on a cockfight: the gamecocks in the middle of the yard while the men watch the bloody spectacle. Except that Tindara and I are the ones in the middle of the square in front of the church, two hens in a coop.

"Her sister disgraced herself and so has she," Tindara hisses between her teeth before leaving, followed by Rosalina and Crocefissa. I'm left alone in the piazza like an odd button and start running home as fast as I can, even though I'm not supposed to any longer. My legs pump of their own accord as I recite *Rosa, rosae, rosae* . . . This is the only thing that works against the scissor tongues: running fast and chanting Latin.

When I get home, I look in on Father. He's not there. The bed is empty, the sheets perfectly smooth and tucked in at the corners.

"Pà," I call, quietly to begin with and then increasingly loud. I wander through the house, go back into his room, and sit on his bed, my balled-up hands on my lap. I'd like to run out and look for him but suddenly I feel tired, as if I had inherited Father's defective will. I lie down, rest my head on the pillow where his head has been resting for months, and breathe in his smell. Then, with a huge effort, I get up and go outside into the yard. In the mulch at the foot of the olive tree, I see a man stooping over the plants, his cap pulled down over his brow, channeling well water to the seedlings. I run toward him and throw my arms around his neck, clinging to him like unripe olives cling to a branch.

"I saw from the window a plant that needed some support," he explained simply, "so I got up."

23

After months of inactivity, his hands are as uncalloused as a child's. He ties the sapling to a twig planted in the ground, pulls up a few weeds that are robbing it of nutrients, and runs the young leaves through his fingers.

"I've been in the house too long," he muses as he pulls himself up onto one knee. "Come, let's go."

"Where?" I ask, perplexed.

"Put on your good dress."

My good dress is in my old leather satchel buried under the olive tree a few feet away but I don't have the courage to tell him. He turns back toward the house. The sun is high and it feels more like spring than fall. Half an hour later, he reemerges in his Sunday best, his hair brushed and his beard freshly trimmed, looking every bit as big and strong as the Greek gods Miss Rosario used to show us. He tucks his trouser legs up over his knees as he sits on the bench by the front door waiting. I run to my room and pull out of the wardrobe a yellow skirt that mother has adjusted for me and that I have never worn. When I get to the door, he stands and takes me by the arm.

We walk down the dirt track to the big road. Father walks with his head high and greets every person we meet as if he'd returned wealthy and happy from a long trip rather than a heart attack. The piazza is full of people. The women with their heads covered come out of church after the second Mass and hurry home to get lunch ready. Their husbands move in a herd and go to sit at the tables outside the bar to drink wine and play cards. Father says *buongiorno* to everyone, and people greet us in response. It is only once we walk past them that the buzz of gossip starts. I grab the sleeve of his jacket and stop in my tracks. I want to go back.

"Where are we going, Pà?"

"Today's Sunday, isn't it? On Sunday, we buy cakes," he said, without slowing down. I look at the ground and start counting the flagstones. I wish there really were an infinite number of them, like in the story of Achilles and the Tortoise that Mrs. Terlizzi taught us at school, but the slabs are not infinite. The glass door of the pastry shop is bright with reflected sunlight, which makes it impossible for me to see inside. I would like to pray to the Virgin Mary for the miracle that he not be there but, instead of the Rosary, I start chanting declensions. First declension singular: *Rosa, rosae, rosae, rosam, rosa, rosa.* If I get to the fifth declension without making a mistake, he won't be at the cash register. First declension plural: *rosae, rosarum, rosis, rosas, rosae, rosis.* My feet are like ants advancing so slowly that they multiply the number of their steps. Second declension singular: *lupus, lupi, lupum* . . . Father is propping me up as if he were bearing my whole weight on his shoulders. I go on: *lupum, lupe, lupo.* The people on the street watch us walk by: a father risen from the dead and his disgraced daughter out in town on a Sunday morning to purchase pastries from the very man who offended her honor. Third declension singular: *consul, consulis, consulem, consul, consule* . . . The third is more difficult, which makes it worth more. If I don't get the third declension wrong, there'll be an assistant behind the counter, my arm will feel lighter, my ant-steps will become giraffe-strides like the game Saro and I used to play when we were kids at his father's workshop, and we'll be able to retreat home out of everyone's sight to celebrate Sunday and Father's recovery. Third declension plural: *consules* and then? The letters get jumbled up in my mind. I've already forgotten everything and whatever I learn now is no use to me anymore. Mrs. Terlizzi glares at me from behind her desk, Miss Rosaria strips me of a star, Mother metes out a punishment.

The glass door opens and I hear Father's voice.

"Good day." I stare at the blue floor tiles and run through my memory in search of the genitive plural without finding it. My mind is blank.

"Good?" answers a man's voice. "Before you walked in, it was good. Now that I've seen you, it's excellent."

His laugh clashes with Father's silence.

"What can I do for you?" the man asks politely.

"We came to buy some cakes to celebrate my recovery." I'm so close to Father, I can feel the words vibrating in his chest before they are even uttered.

"In that case, I can't help you," he says, dropping the tongs and taking a couple of steps toward us. I can smell the jasmine in the air.

Father stiffens for a moment but then his body relaxes again.

"I can't *sell* you a cake to celebrate with," the man says. "I'd like to *give* you one."

I look up, and when I see the man's face I feel as out of breath as I was when we were dancing, except that I'm standing still.

"A nice cassata, then? The young lady will love it." He winks at me as he used to do when I was little and he would hold out the knife full of sugared ricotta for me to lick.

"Thank you, but I wouldn't prefer that," Father answers. His voice is calm, with no inflection, like when my mother asks him if he wants another helping of *aneletti* with his eggplant. I let go of his arm and start torturing my hands.

"You'll be offending me if you don't accept," the man said.

"My daughter has her own tastes," Father answered. "Don't you, Oliva? Look around. Which one would you like?"

I look at all the pastries with different colored frostings and all I see are the hands that girded my waist at the patron saint festival.

"You speak like a modern man," he said. "Someone who doesn't follow tradition. You say you want your daughter to be free to choose, but daughters don't usually tell their fathers what they like and what they don't like. Maybe respect for their parents stops them from expressing what they really want."

"There are no secrets between me and my daughter," Father insists. "Whatever she decides is right."

Paternò removes a cake from behind the glass: it is big and milky white, like the dress I buried underground, and glittering with candied fruit. I don't know whether I want it or not. I don't know whether there are secrets between me and Father. I know the most difficult words in the dictionary, I know how to embroider the most delicate cloth without making holes, I know a bit of Latin, even though I always get mixed up with the third declension, I know how to gut frogs. But I don't know anything about myself.

"Sir," the man continues impatiently, "do you really want to ruin your Sunday? I'm offering your daughter a gift and, believe me, it's a good deal for you, too. I don't even need a thank-you. Unfortunately, there are always ungrateful people around. So, take my advice: accept the cake and enjoy your Sunday."

Paternò wraps the cassata in blue paper with the name of the store printed in gold on it. He pulls out a length of ribbon, takes the scissors, and snips, lifting his eyes every now and again to stare at me so that I have to lower mine. As he cuts the ribbon, something snaps inside me. Father holds his hands out, and it's unclear whether he wants to accept the gift or refuse it. Maybe it is just a signal that he is waiting.

"Oliva, my dear, this man has decided that we should have the cassata for dessert today. But I brought you to the pastry shop because I want you to choose for yourself what you want, without anyone else interfering." Father turns toward the glass door and opens it wide so that everyone who has gathered outside can hear. Then, with the tip of his finger, he lifts my chin. "So, don't be shy. Telling the truth is never going to hurt you. Do you want it or not?"

I look at Paternò's hands gripping the tongs as if he were pointing them at me. His mouth is twisted into a smile but his eyes betray his rage. Father clamps my left arm like he did on the evening of the patron saint festival. Nobody breathes, inside the store or out. The words rise in my throat, tumble into my mouth, slide around on my tongue, but catch behind my teeth and the only thing I manage to do is shake my head.

"You see?" Father says.

Paternò clenches his jaw and stares at me. I feel a cramp in my belly, like when the marquis is on its way. A dull ache deep down that could even be pleasure.

"Let's go, Pà," I whisper, and rush outside.

24

We walk away from the pastry shop with a small package hanging from Father's index finger. He had bought some almond cakes and left money on the counter, which the man didn't touch.

We go the same way home. This time, the comments reach us loud and clear. Everyone knows what tone of voice to use in order to be heard in the crowd.

"Paternò has dishonored him and he goes and buys cakes from him?"

"Bought? What are you saying? He must have been given them. For him, it's a bargain."

"It's not a gift. It's humiliating!"

"Salvo Denaro has the blood of a bedbug!"

"If that man had kissed my daughter in front of the whole town, I would be landing him with two big, fat jawbreakers!"

Father doesn't look down under the brim of his hat and continues to greet everyone as he goes past, calling out to each by name. Some answer, many do not. I decide not to look at my feet any longer. I lift my chin and slow my pace down. We chose the cakes we wanted at the pastry shop and we paid for them with our own money. We haven't accepted any gifts from strangers.

Mother and Cosimino are waiting for us at the door.

"We've been looking for them everywhere and where have they been? Off for a stroll like two young lovers on their first date," Mother complains. Father takes his hat off and goes to the bathroom to wash his hands. His silence is worse than a slap for Mother, so she takes it out on me. "And what on earth are you doing wearing my skirt?"

"You gave it to me!" I said, without thinking.

"I said you could wear it for special occasions. And anyway, it wasn't ready yet."

She lifts my skirt, baring my thighs. "Can't you see the basting is still there? What are people going to say? That the seamstress's daughter goes around wearing half-stitched clothes? God forbid!"

I cover my thighs with my hands and try to pull my skirt back down. "So now you don't care what people think!" she says, laughing bitterly as usual. "Father and daughter waltz around doing whatever they like. And why shouldn't they when I'm here to take care of things? When the whole Fortunata episode happened . . ."

"I told her to put something nice on," Father interrupts. She's so shocked to hear him open his mouth that she shuts up. "Your husband has recovered his good health, Amalia, and we went to buy a Sunday treat. Would you have preferred to stay a widow?"

Mother reads the name on the wrapping paper and slumps into her chair, waving one hand in front of her face and bringing the other to her breast. "Widow? That's not going to happen. You'll be the one burying me, mark my words. I threw my life away for a pair of green eyes. My mother was right. Do you realize how long it took me, an outsider, to be respected in this town? When Amalia Annichiarico walks down the street, nobody says a word against her. I married off our first daughter after she was compromised. Well, at least she's always been a sensible girl and listened to her mother."

She glares at us, places her hands on the table, and makes as if to get up but swoons again. Cosimino rushes to her side and helps her. She sinks back into her chair, massaging her temples.

"I don't know and I don't want to know why this young man has gotten it into his head to have you, of all people," she says, observing me as if I were a thief. "He's not ugly, and he's not poor. But he hasn't come to ask us for your hand, as God commands, nor has he sent anyone in his place. He's lived in the city for too long, where they do things differently. He may well have serious intentions."

Words stick in my throat and Cosimino pales.

"Paternò is a loan shark," he dares to say. "Saro says his father is being strangled by the man's interest rates. He's not a good person."

"That's none of your business," Mother says. "Your father and I will decide who marries your sister."

Cosimino storms into his room, slamming the door behind him. She has never answered him back like that.

Father picks up the scissors and cuts the ribbon tying the blue package.

"Amalia," he says calmly. "Do you like marzipan?"

Mother rolls her eyes and then looks over at the package, which is still closed.

"What does marzipan have to do with anything right now, Salvo? Your head is always in the wrong place."

"I seem to remember that you don't like it. Correct me if I'm wrong."

She sits there, looking drained even of her anger. "Yes, Salvo. You're right. I don't like marzipan."

"Well, our daughter, Oliva, doesn't like cassata. She told the young man in the pastry shop loud and clear. Everyone in the street heard her."

Mother rests her elbows on the table and cradles her face in her hands. Father leans over her and with his index finger slowly lifts the fold of wrapping paper to reveal the contents of the package.

"That's why I thought about it and decided to buy the almond cakes so that we'd all be happy."

A tear runs down her splayed hands. It doesn't get as far as her cheek because he reaches over and rubs it dry with his thumb, like he does with his plants.

"Don't despair, Amalia. Things will work themselves out if everyone is sensible, you'll see."

25

A few days after the walk to the pastry shop, Mother pulls two stacks of pure white sheets and towels out of the chest and starts working more furiously than ever. She spends her days sewing for the townsfolk and her evenings until late embroidering my initials onto every item. In the morning, her pupils are shriveled with fatigue. Every now and again, she grabs a tape and measures my height and circumference. Is she preparing my trousseau so that she can give me away to that man?

When she was preparing Fortunata's dowry chest, I imagined she would never set so much as a floorcloth aside for me. She knew perfectly well that Fortunata was the marriageable daughter while I was the one who would stay at home and keep her company in her old age. Who would ever ask for my hand, scrawny and dark-skinned as I was? Instead, she has prepared everything for me, too, and now she's hurrying to get it all ready, to embroider the linen, adjust the nightdresses, thread satin ribbons, shorten petticoats. Whenever she comes up to me and wraps the soft tape around my hips or breasts, she looks stunned. In town, people are saying I have cast a spell on Paternò. She can't get over the fact that, of all the beauties available, he should have become obsessed with me. Maybe even Mother is scared the spell will break like in the fairy stories and I'll go back to being the pumpkin I was before. That's why she's working against the clock.

Father has started going back to the market with Cosimino, who managed to bring in a few extra customers while he was bedridden. Sometimes Saro goes with them and comes back to our house to eat. After lunch, we stretch out on the grass like we used to do when we were young, except that Cosimino comes straight out to join us because even though it's only Saro, he is still a man.

"Oliva, go in. Mamma wants you to clear the table," my brother says. I get up, the back of my skirt damp from the grass and my blouse stuck to my shoulder blades, and head toward the house. When I get to the door, I turn around. Saro is following me with his eyes. He touches the strawberry birthmark on his left cheek, looks down, and fishes in his pocket for a cigarette. The way he looks at me is not like Paternò, or like Gerò Musciacco's leer at every woman who is not Fortunata, but I can feel it weighing on me nonetheless: he's a man, I'm a woman. And the clouds up there in the sky will be without a shape from now on.

I cross my arms, shrug, and go back in to tidy up the kitchen. Intermittent peals of laughter reach me through the window.

26

Y ou don't take a prize horse to market," Mother said. "If someone wants your hand, they'll have to come to the house and ask for it."

After which, she forbade me from going out. When I'm bored, I retrieve my old schoolbooks from the shelf and repeat a lesson aloud. Liliana comes around every now and again with the excuse of a dress fitting. While Mother fixes her dress, we go into my room and leave the door open, since closing it would not be proper. We talk about sweet and savory dishes as long as Mother's eavesdropping outside but, as soon as a song she knows comes on the radio and she cranks up the volume and starts to sing, we can confess our real thoughts. I ask Liliana whether there is a suitor in her life, and she says there isn't. I tell her there must be someone she likes, and she laughs and covers her face with her hands. She likes the shirtmaker's son, she admits, as well as the brother of a classmate of ours from elementary school who now helps out at the bar. She even likes the Scibetta sisters' cousin.

"The guy covered in acne?" I ask. I'm not at all in favor of acne.

"He has nice shoulders," Liliana argues. I'm confused because I've never thought about a boy's shoulders.

"What's so great about shoulders? I can understand a smile, eyes, or hair, but shoulders?" Mother is right, Liliana has crickets in her head.

"Have you ever kissed?" I dare ask, as the song draws to a close.

"Almost," she taunted.

"Did he touch you . . . ?"

The song Mother likes comes to an end and she stops singing, too. I'm as curious as the skinny Scibetta sister but I don't ask her anything else. Liliana looks toward the door and then loosens two buttons on her blouse. I can see her belly button, pursed like a little mouth.

"I brought you the movie magazines," she says, pulling out a pile of them tied up with string. She hands me the bundle and hastily buttons herself up again.

Mother's steps come closer. I jump up and hide the magazines under the covers.

"Your hem is ready," she says, peering into the room and handing Liliana her skirt. "Try to be careful. It's the third time you've brought it back with the hem hanging down. When there are two salaries coming in, children get spoiled."

Liliana heads for the front door.

"Thank you, Donna Amalia. How much do I owe you?"

"I'll talk to your mother. Girls shouldn't handle money, it's not proper."

Liliana and I brush cheeks as she leaves. I watch her from the window as she walks on her own toward the big road. After all, there is nothing in store for me except waiting until everyone is asleep so that I can untie the bundle of magazines, copy the faces of the actors and actresses I like the best, each in their own secret album, and gaze at the photo Liliana took of me as if I were one of them. I mentally file it under the label "unfortunate brunettes" because love has not yet knocked at my door.

"Everyone speaks ill of that girl," Mother says, planting herself beside me on the bed where Liliana had been seated only moments ago. "But I've never cared what people say. They just like to hear their own voices. It's not her fault if her father is a Communist and sends his wife out to work, is it? The poor thing is innocent, if anything. It's true she gives herself airs but she's a good girl at heart. Do you really think I don't know that she unpicks her hem just to have an excuse to come and see you? It must mean she's very fond of you."

I've never heard her speak like this before. Usually, she either pities or fears people. She smooths out the bedspread and for a second I'm scared she'll notice the bump made by the magazines. But she's distracted, thinking about something else.

"Your friend is a good girl."

She lifts her arm and puts it around my shoulders. Her scent hits me suddenly. I'd forgotten how sweet it is. We sit like this for what seems like forever. She is as close to me now as she was when I was a child and every little joy or hurt was filtered through her body. I observe her other hand in her lap, which is the same shape as mine. I press my head in the hollow between her shoulder and her cheek and close my eyes. We're cut from the same cloth, I think, and I remember when we used to mix flour and water and our hands were glued together in the same sticky coating.

"You're a good daughter, too," she murmurs, and that's what I become, just like that.

"That's why I thought . . ." Her voice catches, just a tiny hitch, and her breath changes, the muscles on her neck contracting, as I'm forced to pull my head away from the safe place I'd found in her. "I thought that we should invite her to your wedding. What do you think, Olì?"

27

She has betrothed me to a perfect stranger.

"He's an outstanding young man, and good-looking, too," she says merrily, as if we'd won first prize at the festival raffle. She comes back from the bathroom with a hairbrush in her hand. She sits behind me, unties my hair, and lets it fall onto my shoulders.

"Where did he come from? How did you find him?" I ask, envisioning her at the market rummaging in the pile, seeking out a bargain.

"Of course. If I don't get involved, nothing ever happens . . . Luckily, Mrs. Scibetta is a special friend of mine. It seems he is quite a catch."

"Mrs. Scibetta, with two daughters to marry off, has found a husband for me?"

She doesn't answer but starts to prepare me. "His name is Franco. It's a nice name, isn't it? He lives in the city and was born into aristocracy."

The marquis has indeed arrived, I surprise myself by thinking, like when I was a girl and I imagined a nobleman coming to take me away.

"But I've never set eyes on him," I protest, as Tindara's face of disgust flashes through my mind.

"Let things take their course! Next week, he'll be coming here to introduce himself and speak to your father so that everything will be settled."

The bristles of the hairbrush plow through my hair gently until they meet a tangle, then I feel a painful tug before the stroking resumes. That is what Mother's like, too: first she tugs and then she gives you a caress.

"And if I don't like him?" I ask, squirming with embarrassment.

"Whether you like him or not," she says, tugging on my hair, "it'll pass. He's a nice-looking young man, Mrs. Scibetta told me . . ." For a second, she stops brushing as if she is momentarily seized by doubt. "But a good marriage doesn't depend on that. Take me, for example. As you see . . ." She doesn't finish the sentence. Instead, she puts the hairbrush down on my bedside table and starts running her fingers through my hair.

"You're exposed at the moment," she says, dividing my hair into three strands before starting to braid it. "You rejected a man who makes people pay dearly when they say no. Don Ignazio has confirmed it. He says Paternò is a man to be reckoned with: he takes what he wants. We need to act quickly, for your own good as well as for ours."

I wanted to tell her that I haven't done anything. I have never said either yes or no to the man. On one side of the counter, there were his eyes, which penetrated my flesh, on the other side, there was Father's face, which betrayed no feeling.

She pulls at the strands as if they were ropes, and, little by little, the braid reaches past my shoulder.

"Mrs. Scibetta says his father is a loan shark. Cosimino was right. The Randazzo widow told me the son is hot-blooded all right. He came back to Martorana to escape a jealous husband out for revenge. He's not someone you reject publicly and expect to be left in peace. With a good marriage proposal, you'll save yourself from his tricks."

My braid is finished. She holds the end with two fingers while with the other hand she delves into her apron pocket and removes a red velvet ribbon to tie it with. She rests the braid over my shoulder and comes around to look at the result.

"Now you look nice and neat," she says, holding my chin between her finger and thumb. "Make sure you keep yourself clean."

I tilt my face toward her so that I can feel her open palm against my skin, her fingertips as rough as her voice. Then she pulls away.

"Come, help me embroider the napkins."

"Yes, Mamma," I obey, without asking further questions.

28

You need to suffer for your beauty," Mother says as she goes into the kitchen and puts the baked pasta dish into the oven. I look down at my shoes, the same ones I had to wear at the patron saint festival: if the shoes are making me look pretty then without them I must be plain. Beauty is always in the eye of the beholder. Maybe that's why we love eyes.

"They're coming," she announces excitedly, looking out the window. She rushes up to me, straightens a hairpin, and smooths my blouse down over my hips with her hands. She's like a little girl with a doll.

"Go and call the men!"

Father is already in the vegetable patch, like every morning, crouching down near the tomato plants. Looking at him like that, in his work overalls with a handkerchief tied around his neck, I kid myself that the whole thing has been invented by Mother, that this Franco will not come, that I won't be given away, that I'll be able to stay here at home sketching the faces of movie stars in secret at night.

"Aren't you going to wear your good suit?" I ask him.

"No, I wouldn't prefer that," he replies matter-of-factly. I hold out my hand to help him up and I give his hand two little squeezes as I do so. The heels of my shoes sink into the loam and every step I take plants me into the earth like his vegetables. I'd like to stay here and flourish, nourished by water and wind, allow my leaves to fall one by one as they turn yellow, cling to a knotty bamboo stick so that I can grow straight.

"Let's go and meet this man," he says, without emphasis, as if he were saying, "Let's go and have a glass of water with mint syrup."

"I'm scared, Pà," I venture.

"Don't be scared. If he's fine for you, he's fine for us."

I don't know what's fine for me. As long as I was running in my short skirts with Saro and Cosimino, and praying to the Virgin Mary for the miracle that I would never become a woman, I thought I knew everything. But now I don't understand a thing.

The table is set for six people. The rules of sitting at table are: don't speak with your mouth full, don't wipe your plate with your bread, don't ask for more if there are guests. Cosimino's hair is greased back and he is wearing long pants and a white shirt. I look at my parents' wedding photo on the sideboard and see that he's as handsome as Father was when he was the same age. I check whether I look anything like Mother and conclude that I don't: I'm still scrawny and dark-skinned. My beauty was short-lived: one dance at the patron saint festival.

"Is Saro coming?" I ask, indicating the extra chair.

"God forbid!" Mother answers in a whisper. "It's for the person accompanying him."

The car stops in the lane. I peer out the window, too, to catch a glimpse of the visitors. At the wheel is a middle-aged man with salt-and-pepper hair. He gets out and stands outside the door, checking the number to make sure he is in the right place. His steps are nervous, he is short in stature, and his cheeks are hollow. Mother opens the door and makes as if to greet him, but he looks down without smiling, turns around, and returns to the car. He is leaving, I hope. Instead, he opens the passenger door.

A tall young man steps out wearing a well-cut suit, starched shirt, and sunglasses like a movie star. He looks like Handsome Antonio. The older man whispers something in his ear, he rests his hand on his forearm, and they walk the short distance to our door together. I feel the blood thumping in my veins, as if I were one of the characters in Liliana's photographic novels forced to marry an ugly old widower who has a handsome son my own age. That's why Mrs. Scibetta has introduced us. My heart is beating in my throat. I wipe my clammy hands on my yellow skirt.

The old man stops at the threshold and Handsome Antonio stands behind him. He is fair-skinned and has a dimple on his chin. I try to imagine whether behind his dark lenses he is looking at me. I suck my belly in but then I remember when Fortunata used to preen herself and immediately release the air.

"It's a pleasure to meet you," Mother says. "Please come in." She waves her hand as if she were sweeping the air and invites them inside.

The old man stands in front of Father, who is attempting to loosen the handkerchief around his neck with his index and middle fingers. Handsome Antonio follows him, without letting go of the other man's arm. He doesn't take his sunglasses off, even in the house. The old man looks even older from close up, his skin is slick with sweat and as gray as his suit, which smells of stale smoke.

"Baron Altavilla," the old man says, without moving so much as a finger. I feel sick: he is introducing himself as if he were a king despite claiming the hand of a wife the same age as his son. I try to catch Cosimino's eye to see how he is reacting but he is standing behind Mother, who is smiling politely.

The old man touches Handsome Antonio's back, making him swivel around and face Father as if he were a marionette and the old man a puppet master. Father holds out his hand and says, "Franco, how do you do?" When Antonio smiles, his teeth flash white.

29

H e caught the disease when he was a child," the old man tells Mother, who is the only one conversing with him. Father, at the head of the table, is behaving as if this were an ordinary Sunday. Cosimino listens to the story as rapt as when he listened to the story of Giufà as a child. Franco is sitting opposite me. I observe him on the sly: he eats without looking down into his plate; every now and again the old man pours him some water and brings his hand to the glass. He doesn't speak much but he has a nice voice.

"His parents consulted the best doctors," the old man went on, "even up north."

All of a sudden, Mother is suspicious. "Is it hereditary?"

"No, no one else in the family has it," he reassures her. "They will have healthy children."

My blood quickens: my girlfriends have told me that you need to lie in the same bed as your husband. I look at his hands moving as he lifts his fork opposite me. They are smooth and white, very different from Father's. Before having a child, those hands will have to sign the church register, brush against mine at the wedding banquet, slip under the nightdress Mother has sewn for me, and touch my flesh.

"We should raise our glasses to the couple on their engagement, Salvo," Mother proposes with her cough-like laugh to prod Father out of his silence. He takes a long time to finish his mouthful and then he wipes his mouth with his napkin. "I wouldn't prefer that," I imagine him saying but, instead, he lifts his glass, half filled with red wine, looks at me, and says, "Congratulations."

The old man arches his eyebrow, forming three horizontal furrows across his forehead.

"My nephew Franco is a good-natured and well-meaning young man," he explains, enunciating clearly as if Franco were deaf rather than blind. "His parents were unable to come from the city because, as I told you, the baroness has an inflammation of the kidneys, but they send their regards and will be happy to return your hospitality. God gave them this one child, who is their only joy despite his unfortunate condition. Girls in the city are too modern. They no longer cherish the wholesome values of old. They want to go out to work, they want to go out with their friends, they want to go to the cinema, to dance. They don't realize that they soon spoil, that they lose their purity."

"Many of them are broken jugs," Mother says, nodding. "My daughter is intact."

"So is Franco: he has never touched a woman," the older man assures her, turning to inspect me as if he were checking to see whether Mother was telling the truth.

"We've cultivated Oliva like a flower," Mother confirms, covering my hand with hers.

"We believe so," the old man answers, carrying on with his inspection. "It has come to our attention, however, that the girl has been in contact with a man. It seems she had a certain 'sympathy' for him, as the young would say today."

"No sympathy whatsoever," Mother rushes to clarify. She tucks a loose wisp back into her bun with the tips of her fingers even though every hair is already in place. "A hotheaded young man had set his sights on my daughter but she never gave him encouragement of any kind."

She looks at Father imploringly. "My husband made it very clear to him that we weren't interested in his proposal, and so"—she lowers her eyes and stares at the embroidery on the tablecloth—"the young man in question has made peace with that. Since that day, the girl has never left the house."

Franco's uncle scratches the furrowed lines on his forehead. Mother grabs my hand with her icy cold one. Everything is painful for her, even giving her daughter away in marriage.

The old man examines me again as if wanting to worm a secret out of me. Finally, he sighs and looks out the window.

"The girl has completed middle school, is that correct?" he asks, never using my name.

"She did two years of high school, too, but then we took her out," Mother says apologetically.

"Franco likes someone to read to him in the evening before going to bed," the uncle says in a conciliatory tone.

He rubs his cheek with the back of his hand as if he were checking how long his beard has grown since morning, then he rests his chin on two fingers for a while, and finally nods. Franco and I sit in our places, opposite each other, frozen. The old man empties his glass in one gulp and gets up from the table. The exam is over.

30

After lunch, Franco and I are told to go for a walk in the land around the house so that we can get to know each other while the others discuss the nitty-gritty of the nuptials. The blind man approaches me and rests his hand on my arm, his grip much lighter than Paternò's. My brother is unsure whether he's supposed to accompany us and turns to Mother for instructions. "Let them go, Cosimino," she says with a mischievous smile. "Your sister is engaged and young people nowadays have the right to a little privacy."

My brother pulls back, amazed, and we go out. I'm surprised, too. Maybe she is letting us go out on our own because Franco can't see and therefore can't do me any harm. We walk in a silence that doesn't feel awkward, as if there were no need for us to say anything. Then I realize that he's blind, not dumb. So I start worrying that it is rude not to speak but I can't think of anything to say. I'm scared of offending him, I'm scared of everything: of walking un-chaperoned beside him, of leaving home and moving to the city as a bride, of ending up sad and lonely like Fortunata, of being placed in the hands of a complete stranger, the same hands that will have to touch me in order to make a baby. Scared of having to take care of a blind man every day of my life. Scared of not existing because his eyes can't see me. Where does love enter if not through the eyes? *Amore è uno desi oche ven da' core per abbondanza di gran piacimento*—I can hear my teacher Mrs. Terlizzi's voice reciting—*e gli occhi in prima generano l'amore e lo core li dà nutricamento*, as the ancient Sicilian poet put it.

The blind man grips my arm but it is actually him leading me, and without realizing it, my steps synchronize with his. I keep searching for something to say but the only words echoing in my mind are the lines of that poem. I turn to look at him, stare at his face, and then cast my eyes down again immediately out of habit. Then I think about it: if he can't see me, I don't need to keep my eyes to the ground.

Franco comes to a sudden halt behind Pietro Pinna's toolshed, in a spot where my house is out of sight. "Can you see anything?" I ask him suspiciously. His mouth twists in a grimace and I'm ashamed: I have kept quiet all this time only to come out with the one question that is not proper to ask.

He takes his dark glasses off. I pull my arm away from his in fear. I wave a hand in front of his face but the white irises are as unresponsive as burned-out light bulbs.

"You must do something for me," he says, feeling for my hands. I take a step back. Even though we are engaged, I don't want him to ruin me before my time has come.

"Are you scared?"

"No," I lie, my heart rattling in my chest.

"It's something that costs you nothing but that is very

important for me." He touches my hand, strokes the back and then, with the tip of his index finger, brushes against my palm. No one has ever touched me there. I feel a tingling sensation in the middle of my body. The blind man continues to touch every finger, one by one, moving up and around my nails, then he stops and takes a step toward me.

"Stay there, don't move," he says. I'm rooted to the spot, holding my breath. *Amore è un desi oche ben da' core*, I keep on reciting in my head.

"Close your eyes," he suggests. "That way, we're equal."

It's not proper, Mother's voice in my head warns me, but I close them anyway. Standing there with my eyes closed in front of him, I feel stripped naked but then I realize he can't see me and I catch my breath again. I'm expecting to feel his lips on mine like in the photographic novels Liliana brings me hidden under her blouse, and a warmth spreads through me, low down, under my belly button. But nothing happens. All I can hear is the wind that always rises at this time, rustling the plants in Father's garden and now lifting my yellow skirt from my ankles to my knees. I stretch a hand out to pull it back down but then I stop. Nobody can see me, after all.

"Don't move," the blind man says, and I obey. After a few seconds, I feel the pads of his fingers on my forehead, starting from the center where Father used to plant his good night kiss when I was little, and fanning out toward my temples, rubbing against the grain of my brows, touching my eyelids after navigating my eyelashes. His thumbs touch my nostrils, his palms flatten against my cheeks and then descend to my jaw and envelop my whole face. His pinkies delicately lift my earlobes and, finally, his index fingers touch my lips. Instinctively, I pull them into my mouth, between my teeth, and he freezes. With a sigh, I pull them back out. Franco takes his hands off my face, leaving only the index finger of his right hand to trace the outline of my mouth agonizingly slowly and then disappear.

We stay in this position, the blind man and I, while the sun starts to set. I'm in favor of sunsets.

"You're beautiful," he says. That's when I open my eyes and we head back home.

31

They're marrying you off to a blind man?" Liliana asks with the same disbelief I showed Tindara. The stacks of books on her desk are piling higher while my old schoolbooks are stuck on a shelf. The darkroom is unchanged. Liliana dips the white sheets in a tray with metal tongs.

"Will you be my maid of honor?" I ask her in the murky depths of the room as we wait for the images to reveal themselves.

"What does your mother think?"

"She wants you to do it."

On the satin paper, I can just make out a woman dressed in black with sunken eyes and fleshy lips peering out from behind half-closed window shutters. She looks as though the house has swallowed her whole.

"It's Fortunata!" I burst out. "When did you take it?"

"Doesn't she come to church with you?"

"She never leaves the house."

"And have you never wondered why?"

"Musciacco is jealous," I say. "Franco is different," I add, more to convince myself than her.

"You've only met him once." She picks up the sheet with

the tongs and floats it on another tray filled with reagent liquid.

"That's not true, he's been back. We went into town so that people would see us. Mother is giving me a bit more freedom now that I'm engaged. Today she let me come to see you."

"This freedom will come to an end and you'll be walking from one prison right into another."

"Franco has been good to me. If it weren't for him . . ."

Liliana lifts the photograph out of the tray and pegs it on the line as if it were a pair of underpants hanging out to dry.

"You sound like he's doing you a favor."

"He's getting me out of a difficult situation."

Liliana goes on tinkering with her tools.

"Do you remember Miss Rosaria?" she asks me after a while.

"Miss Rosaria was . . ."

I stop myself. She wasn't disgraceful, it wasn't true. ". . . she was unlucky." Then I realize that my sister, Fortunata, has also been unlucky. And so had Nardina, Saro's mother, and the Scibetta sisters, both the fat and the skinny, and Miluzza, who will end up a spinster, and Agatina, who was stabbed five times, and Tindara, forced by her parents to fall in love at first correspondence. Being born female is unlucky. Period.

"Miss Rosaria taught us to think for ourselves."

"I like Franco. He's gentle, unlike most men."

We both stare at the picture of Fortunata. She's blond and my hair is raven black, her eyes are big and green while mine are like little black olives, she's tall and shapely while I'm short and scrawny. I compare her features to mine and mentally divide them between similarities and differences, as if this exercise might disentangle our destinies.

"Come to the meeting this evening," Liliana says point-blank. It's not a request, it's an order.

"I can't, I'm busy," I answer straightaway, thinking of Mother.

"So, it's a lie that you're freer now that you're engaged."

"I don't want to run into that man," I say, the scent of jasmine so distinct in my mind I can smell it in the air right there.

"Paternò? He's gone," Liliana says.

"Where?" My heart tumbles into my stomach.

"To that uncle he has in the city."

I flop into the chair in front of Liliana's desk. I'll soon be married and I'll never see him again. I'm relieved but also suddenly bereft, already missing something that was mine and nobody else's. Liliana hands me the photo of Fortunata and I don't take it. I want to remember her when she still had a face. She looks like a ghost in this picture. When I walk out of her bedroom I see her father sitting in an armchair in the living room reading a newspaper called *L'Unità*.

He looks up and examines me.

"You're Salvo Denaro's daughter."

I nod.

"You came to our Thursday meetings, I believe, unless my advanced age has clouded my memory, that is."

"I came just once," I say with a wisp of a voice.

"If you were to have the good grace to visit us once again, we'd be greatly honored." He smiles kindly at me and then hides his face once more behind the densely printed broadsheet. Liliana joins me, holding a pile of magazines and a coral necklace.

"These are for you," she says.

"The necklace?"

"It's a wedding gift. Coral brings good luck. I have a pair of earrings in the same set. The bride and her maid of honor are supposed to match."

She presses the gift into my hands. I wonder whether Franco will like it. Then I realize he won't be able to see any of it: the necklace, the dress, the shoes, the flowers. Me.

32

A real man should have strong arms to work with, a good head to think with, open eyes to be vigilant with. And he shouldn't let his wife and daughters go here and there," Don Ciccio the haberdasher says, clutching his beret in his hand.

Liliana and I are sitting in the front, next to Calò. I don't need to hide behind the fishing nets this time. I'll be sixteen next month, I'm engaged, and soon I'll be married.

"What about women?" Calò asks in a soft, almost feminine voice. Liliana writes everything down in her notebook.

"A woman should know how to preserve herself," the same man picks up from before, "and depend on her husband just as a climbing vine depends on a trellis." Many of the men who have gathered in the hut nod their approval. He goes on, "If a woman were the one to wear the pants, it would be the end of the world," and bursts out laughing.

I look at Calò to see if he agrees but his face betrays nothing. He simply listens to everyone and every now and again poses a question.

"So, if I understand correctly, the wife should stay at home and obey her husband. Do you agree? Do the women here in this room hold the same view?"

"I think it's unfair," a middle-aged woman says. The

men turn and stare at her. "It's unfair but it's necessary," she explains. "Girls need to be chaperoned when they're out and about because if they keep coming and going on the street, people will start wondering what they're doing. Men are on the hunt, it's in their nature, and if you behave like a lamb, a wolf will eat you up."

Liliana stops writing and raises her hand, as she used to do at school with Mrs. Terlizzi.

"The Grasso widow is right," she says. "But, the problem lies with women, too. They instill the same rules in their daughters that they had to abide by in the past. If mothers taught their sons to respect women, to treat them equally, if they allowed girls to live freely without locking them up in the house, if they encouraged them to study and train to go out and work . . . Are men the only ones responsible for this mentality, or are women at fault, too? I think we need to lead the way!"

The few women present nod with as much conviction as they would to a little girl reciting a poem.

"The Lord only gave me one daughter," the Grasso widow said, "and until I managed to betrothe her, I couldn't let her go free. Then, after the wedding, it's the husband's responsibility."

"I think Liliana is right," a male voice at the back strikes up. "The new generation of youth should step away from old rules and men should encourage it. If we unite in the struggle, everyone is better off. Otherwise, the world keeps turning and we remain stuck in place."

I crane my neck to see who it is. It is Saro, who I didn't see come in. Liliana whispers in my ear, "He's been to every meeting for the past few months. Every now and again, he comes to the house to speak with Father."

"Has he become a Communist, too?" I ask.

"No, he says he supports the Bourbons, like his father, but he wants to learn more and he likes understanding things."

"Maybe he comes so he can meet you," I whisper back, checking for her reaction. She shakes her head. Saro glances at us from the back of the room and nods in acknowledgment. I haven't seen him since that afternoon my blouse got damp on the grass.

"There are cases, for example," Saro says to the widow, "where we are raised together, we drink the same milk, we share everything, and then we end up being segregated anyway, boys on one side, girls on the other, as if we belonged to separate worlds. We're not even allowed to speak to each other and then we end up learning of each other through the gossip mill."

It sounds like he is addressing everyone but he is looking at me.

"But this level of familiarity between men and women can be dangerous," Don Ciccio suggests, winking. "You start out talking and you end up doing . . ." Lots of them laugh.

"So," Calò summarizes calmly, "men and women cannot be friends?"

"Friends?" the man says. "If a man wants to be friends with a woman, he only has his own interest at heart. Am I right, Saro?"

Saro doesn't say another word the entire meeting. I look over at him now and again to see whether his eyes ever seek Liliana out. When we leave, he's gone. He left without saying goodbye. We cross the big road as the sun is setting.

"You didn't speak at all," Liliana points out.

"What was I supposed to say?"

"Do you think women should serve men, stay at home, and not go out to work?"

"My view counts for nothing. That is how the world is, was, and always will be."

"Yes, but what do you think you'll do once you're married? Do you think Franco will let you . . . ?"

"Franco is a generous man and he'll take care of my needs."

"Generous or not, that's beside the point. I want to be a teacher or a photographer when I finish school and maybe go on to live in the capital and become a deputy in the parliament, like Nilde Iotti . . ."

Our steps are the only sounds we can hear on the almost empty street. A car with its headlights off is trundling along slowly behind us, a few meters away.

"Good for you," I comment, linking my arm with hers. "And for Mr. Iotti if he agrees . . ."

"Mr. Iotti? Who's that?"

"The husband of this Nilde woman you're always talking about, right?"

"There isn't a Mr. Iotti. She's not married," Liliana explains.

"No husband, no name," I say, parroting Mother.

Liliana shakes her head and furrows her brow. She presently stops and looks at me with a perplexed expression, as if I were unable to see a donkey standing in the middle of the kitchen.

"You were top of the class at school. Do you want to end up a housewife like all the other women in Martorana?"

The rules for being a woman are: get married, have children, take care of the house, I repeat in my head. The rules for being a man are . . . I hear a noise behind us and just as I turn around to see what it is, the car that was trailing us pulls onto a side road.

"I don't have crickets in my head," I say to Liliana, putting an end to the conversation.

We stop at the crossroads. Our paths are separating: Liliana's house is on the other side of town, near the sea, where they're beginning to build new apartment blocks. In the distance, a car engine rumbles and I feel my blood run cold.

"I'm feeling a bit funny," I say. "Can you walk with me for a bit?"

We quicken our pace and walk together toward the dirt track. By the time we get to Father's land we are almost running. The lights are on in the house. He's there, kneeling down outside the chicken coop, his head in his hands, saying nothing. Next to him, Violetta, Rosina, and two other chickens lie dead.

"What happened?" I ask, the soft grass prickling my knees. He shakes his head.

"Let's go inside, Pà," I say, lifting him by the arm.

"I wouldn't prefer that," he says, staring first at the empty coop and then at the stiff chickens on the ground. This time Mother won't yell at us in Calabrian: we didn't paint the inside of the coop yellow.

We stand in a circle as if we were at a funeral.

"It's my fault," I whisper in my friend's ear. Father hears us.

"Chicken fever," he declares, and goes back into the house. Cosimino comes out and grabs Liliana by the arm.

"I'll walk you home," he says. Liliana doesn't complain and sets off meekly under his protection. Men and women are not equal and she knows it.

ne, two, three, four, five," Mrs. Scibetta counts. Mother puts the sugarcoated almonds in a crocheted doily and places a little card inside with two ornately written names on them: Oliva Denaro and Franco Colonna. She passes the bundle on to Miluzza, who ties it up with a little white ribbon and snips off the end with a pair of scissors. I like my name next to his, as if I could lean on the column evoked by his surname.

The Scibetta sisters and I carry on with our embroidering. Instead of the wooden bench, today they have given me the place between them on the sofa.

"You must send my regards to your daughter's future mother-in-law, Amalia," Mrs. Scibetta says from the armchair while she counts out the almonds for the wedding favors. "Next time you see her, that is."

Mother presses her lips together, given that we haven't met Franco's parents yet.

"Luckily, they live in the city so certain little details won't have reached their ears," the gossip continues, intentionally needling her.

"As they say," the fat sister joins in, "what the eye doesn't see, the heart doesn't grieve over."

The skinny sister interrupts her sewing to cup her hands over her mouth but her laugh is still audible.

"One of the advantages of marrying a blind man," the fat sister goes on, "is that he won't be able to see what's going on."

"He's blind, not deaf," Mena protests.

Miluzza gives me a sad look. "They say he's as handsome as a movie star. Is it true, Oliva?" she asks, changing the subject.

"What was the name of that film?" Nora asks.

"*Handsome Antonio*," Mena suggests.

"My daughters don't go to the movies. It's not proper," Mrs. Scibetta takes pains to point out. "They've only seen the billboards in the piazza."

"Of course," the fat sister says defensively, "I only know the gist of the film because people talk about it."

"I hope your fiancé isn't as feckless as the movie's protagonist," the skinny sister remarks without even attempting to hide her laughter.

"Even if he is, Oliva, who cares? He's marrying you when you have no dowry worth mentioning and he's making you a baroness," their mother adds. "With the trouble you've gotten yourself into, you should be thanking Saint Rita."

"Saint Rita is the patroness of heartbroken women," I answer without looking up from my work. "Franco and I are marrying for love."

The sisters don't say a word. Mother clears her throat, which sounds like a laugh coming from her.

"Love!" Mrs. Scibetta says disdainfully. "Young people today are too romantic, aren't they, Amalia? They should obey their parents, without question. Even Paternò, when his father banished him from town, didn't complain. Of course, these nouveau riche types are so full of airs. I wonder what he wanted for his son? A princess, maybe? When he found out he had fallen for a girl with nothing to her name, he threatened to disinherit him. Then again, the young man has been nothing but trouble. He's hot-blooded and there's nothing much to be done about that. That's why we need to keep our daughters home."

"You lose value if you circulate too much," the fat sister confirms.

"On display today, on display tomorrow," the skinny sister adds, "a man's mouth is bound to water. But if you whet his appetite and then deny him, he'll react badly. You need to carry yourself carefully."

"My daughter has never sinned," Mother says, emerging from her silence. "Her only sin is to have many qualities"—she turns to Mena and Nora with a mischievous grin—"and many suitors."

She goes quiet again and not another word is exchanged. All you can hear in the Scibetta living room is the rattle of the sugarcoated almonds as Mrs. Scibetta counts them out. When we leave, they don't invite us to the Rosary recital and they don't give us any sewing to do. Mother has endured years on the wooden bench without saying a word, and now, with one remark, she has lost her best customers. This was her wedding gift to me.

As we walk home arm in arm, we see Cosimino running toward us on the dirt track, his eyes red and his arms in the air.

"They've killed all our plants with salt! We came back from market, me and Pà, and the field was flooded."

"Good God!" Mother shrieks, letting go of my arm. "What happened?"

"Someone put salt in the well and then flooded the land!" He rubs his hands on his work overalls looking downcast. "Nobody will admit to seeing a thing: we're on our own!"

34

What do you mean we need to postpone?" Mother yells.

"Amalia, calm down," Nellina says, lowering her voice.

"And I come to hear about it in the middle of the marketplace, just two weeks before the wedding?"

"The news has just come in," she explains. "I myself only heard this morning. The Colonna family sent a message to say that the baroness's condition has worsened. You wouldn't want to celebrate a wedding on the same day as her last rites. I was on my way to tell you but then I saw you on the street . . ."

Mother rubs her eyes, she can't even complain in Calabrian because it would be improper. "He should have communicated this in person," she says. "Just as he came to the house for the engagement, he could have come to bring us the news."

"He's an only child, Amalia. He can't leave his mother alone on her deathbed."

Nellina leads us into a quiet street, away from the crowds. I tug at her arm like a capricious child. "Has he changed his mind?" I ask her. "Is it because he doesn't want me anymore? Nella, tell me the truth . . ."

"My dear girl, of course not. It's a tragedy, we should feel sorry for him."

"Did anybody tell them about my husband's land?" Mother asks.

Nellina turns away. "What land? I don't know . . ."

"By mistake, a few weeks ago, Salvo put salt instead of pesticide on the plants. You know his head is always in the clouds. Anyway, some of the vegetables died. You know how these things go, though. People will embellish a story, embroider it, until a little incident becomes a novel."

I think back to Father's face last week as he inspected the sick plants. "This is all we have," Mother says as we go inside, "dead plants and dead chickens." The pittance Mrs. Scibetta paid Mother had been thrown away for one defiant comeback after years of downing poison. Maybe she thought Franco would be taking care of us from now on, but now even that pillar had begun to crumble.

"Amalia, a family as important as the Colonnas are not going to make a fuss about a few tomatoes rotting on your little plot of land. They're a respectable family, don't worry. Franco is not the kind of person who would fail to live up to his commitments just because of a couple of threats."

Mother covers her face with her hands. "Who has threatened him? What are you telling me, Nellina?"

"I haven't said anything!" she screeches, her eyes wide with fear. "Don't put words in my mouth!"

From the end of the road, we see the priest arriving, his hands behind his back. "Sorry, Amalia, I need to go and get Don Ignazio's lunch ready," Nellina says, wringing her hands. "You'll see, everything will be all right. You, too, Oliva. Don't worry about anything. You'll be married soon. You need to be patient a little longer. You're so young! How old are you?"

"I'll be sixteen in July."

"Good girl, in a month, then. Don Ignazio, Don Ignazio!" Nellina waves at the priest, who is walking toward us from the other end of the street, and signals for him to stop. He sees me and Mother and lowers his eyes. Nellina catches up with him before he gets any closer and leads him away at a brisk pace.

Mother and I are left alone on the street. "She didn't come to tell us at home because she was scared," Mother whispers as if she were talking to herself. "Poor girl," she says, shaking her head as we turn back. "Poor girl!"

35

From my bed, I can hear the rain beating on the windowpanes and the thunder rumbling in the distance but the air is clammy and I'm suffocating under the sheets. First, everyone wanted me, and now nobody does. And if nobody is ever going to love me, how can I love myself? I sit in bed with my head in my hands. If I had been born a boy like Cosimino, I could live on my own and I wouldn't need to belong to a man. Instead, I was born a girl and the feminine singular doesn't exist, in spite of whatever Miss Rosaria claimed.

At dawn, I hear Father's footsteps outside my door.

"What's going on?" I ask him. It's still dark and he's already shaved and dressed. My eyes sting with drowsiness.

"Are you going out for snails in your good clothes?"

"Hurry up and get dressed. This morning we're going to ferret them out in their own home," he says, going back into the kitchen.

Mother and Cosimino are still asleep when we set out. The ground is wet and the mud clings to my shoes. As we walk toward the bus stop, the sun peeks out from behind the clouds. We cross the empty square, where the shutters of the café are still drawn. A few old ladies hear our steps echoing in the silence and come to the window to spy on us from behind the almost-closed shutters. I give Father's hand two little squeezes as we get on the bus and we head for the back row on the right: me in the window seat and him on the aisle. There's no one else. When the driver sets off, I feel weak at the knees. I've never been on a bus before. Our progress is slow to begin with and I watch the town waking up: women in black veils on their way to the first Mass of the day, men heading either for the fields or for the sea according to their occupations. The market stalls are being set up. The pastry shop is closed. Then the bus starts accelerating, we get to the other end of the big street, and we turn onto the main road that leads to the city. After the last houses, there's a signpost with the name of our town crossed out, as if it were dead. It's the first time I've ever left Martorana, and I feel as if I'm dying a little bit, too.

"It takes about an hour, and then we're there," Father says, as if we were on an Easter Monday jaunt.

After last night's rain, the early morning air is crisp. He looks out the window at the landscape, his eyes half-closed against the dazzling reflection of the sun on the sea. He doesn't like the sea. He prefers land. Nobody can be master of the sea, he sometimes says regretfully.

After a while, the bus slows down and comes to a halt.

"Are we there already?" I ask, my heart flying out of my rib cage.

But the driver calls out the name of another town.

"Still a while to go," Father says.

The bus sets off again, following the winding coastline. My stomach is churning.

"This morning, I wanted to go and harvest snails," he starts telling me. "Because after this dry spell there would have been hundreds of them. I put my work clothes on, my rubber boots, and my jacket, but I couldn't find my hat."

He stops as if he's come to the end of his story but I don't get his drift. At the end of the fables with talking animals, there was always a lesson. "In fact," he goes on, "I looked everywhere, but it wasn't there. I don't like going out without a hat."

I look at him: his head is bare, blond with a few gray hairs I have only just noticed that weren't there before.

He pats his head. "Do you know why I couldn't find it?"

I shake my head.

"It rotted in the water," he answers, then pauses a little before going on. "Together with the tomatoes, the vegetables, and all the other products of my garden."

His expression is flat, as if he were telling me what he had for breakfast. "I went out to do some work without my hat," he says, stroking his head, "but then I started to get angry. The strange thing is that the closer I got to the field, the angrier I got, and I started to get annoyed by other things. A blister on my left foot, a kitchen chair with one leg loose, a board on my cart that had come undone, and your postponed wedding. So I decided I was going to fix everything. I medicated my foot, I tightened the chair leg, I nailed the board, and I got myself ready to go out."

The bus stops and the driver calls out the name of another town.

"If something isn't working," he starts again as soon as the bus sets off, "you need to try to fix it."

I have never heard him talk for so long. Maybe he has started getting angry at his own silence. The idea that Father's tongue comes to life only when he's on a journey occurs to me, as if it's movement that shakes words out of him. "I should thank whoever it was that ruined my land, because the anger I felt made me say to myself: Salvo, either this wedding takes place now, or it will not take place at all, and your daughter will be left in an awkward situation."

He takes his eyes off the landscape that slips away behind the window and looks at me.

"Do you want Franco?"

I look at my hands and search for an answer.

Then the bus stops and the driver announces our arrival in the city.

36

The lawns in front of the church are full of daisies. Mother calls me from a few feet away, I stop and pick a flower and pull its petals away one by one: he loves me, he loves me not, he loves me, he loves me not, he loves me, he doesn't love me anymore. I throw the last petal away. It lied: he still loves me.

———

Franco's building was close to the opera house, just as the gray-faced uncle had described it. Father and I walked arm in arm into the hall. This was going to be where I lived, I thought as I climbed the stairs. A girl my age came to open the door. She was soft, blond, and fine-boned, and could have been my father's daughter. A gob of envy rose up in my throat.

"The master and mistress of the house are not receiving today," she said hastily. "You must come back next week."

"No, thank you, I wouldn't prefer that," Father said and didn't budge.

———

"So?" Mother asks. "Which flowers do you want? Traditionally, it's orange blossom but you can choose."

I look at the display but can't decide. I'm not used to knowing what I want.

"We can put roses, peonies, lilies, and jasmine in the bouquet," the florist suggests.

"Not jasmine, Biagio," I say, remembering the cloying scent of the sprig behind that man's ear, his white suit stained red with blood orange, his whistling serenades in the street, his eyes following me, his hands holding me tight at the patron saint festival, his voice in the pastry shop that made my blood quiver.

"I'd like daisies."

"Daisies? They're wildflowers, they're not for a wedding!" Mother corrects me. "Don't you agree, Biagio?"

Father and I stood at the door for what felt like a long time.

"I'm ashamed, Pà," I complained.

"I was ashamed, too, in principle, because of the hat," he said, flattening his hair with his hands. "Then I said to myself, 'Salvo, it wasn't your desire to present yourself to these people bareheaded. So what is there to be ashamed of? The shame belongs to the person who ruined your hat, not to you. And to these people here, who seem to fear someone may ruin something of theirs.'"

He said these last words loud and clear so that they could be heard. At that very moment, the blond maid reappeared and announced, "You may come in."

We crossed the hall and were led into a big room where
an elegantly dressed lady, followed by a short, balding man,
came to meet us.

———

"The orange blossom is fine," Mother settles with the florist.
"We'll put daisies in your hair. Are you happy, Olì?"

Am I happy? I'm sixteen today, I'll be married next week.
Liliana will be getting her teacher's certificate next year, and
a city newspaper has bought some of her photographs. I
think I am. I think I'm happy. This is the only way I know
how to be happy.

"We need a flower for today, too," Mother tells the florist.
"It's her birthday." She lifts my head with her fingers under
my chin as if she were showing off something valuable. A
woman's worth, I think, depends on the man who wants her.

"If you allow me, I'd like to offer the signorina a flower
for her birthday." Biagio hands me a red rose with a long
stalk. "No strings attached," he says, his palms outstretched
before him.

———

"I'm happy to see the lady of the house has recovered her
health," Father said in his usual calm voice. There wasn't a
trace of anger or irony in his words. Franco's mother wore a
face that made the wrinkles around her eyes more evident.
"By the grace of God," she muttered, her palms pressed together in front of her breast.

"I am delighted to hear it," Father went on, "and I hope to see you in good spirits on the wedding day that has been settled."

The woman pursed her lips as if she didn't want any words to come out of her mouth. "My health," she managed to say in the end, "is subject to the preoccupations and grievances that afflict me, and recently the friendship between our children has caused me a great number of them. It appears evident that we come from different backgrounds and that an agreement between our two families is unlikely to take place. If you've already betrothed your daughter to someone else, it's not fair that our family should bear the brunt. It's not my habit to invite visitors to leave, but in this instance I really must ask you to go."

She tossed her eyes and then proceeded to inspect Father from head to toe as if she were highlighting all the deficiencies of his person. The bald husband didn't say a word, perhaps out of habit.

––––––

"Watch out for the thorns," Mother says. As we cross the piazza, all eyes are on us but nobody whispers maliciously as we pass by. Their gazes are filled with admiration and, for the first time ever, I feel that she is parading me with pride.

––––––

Franco came into the sitting room, looking pale and disheveled. He was wearing a light brown smoking jacket and leather slippers. He didn't look like Handsome Antonio any longer, he looked more like a movie star in the category "unlucky in love."

"I, on the other hand, am in the habit of keeping my word," Father said to the woman. "Franco was betrothed to my daughter. If he has changed his mind, he needs to tell us in person."

He led me to him. "Franco," I murmured. I closed my eyes as I had done that first day behind Pietro Pinna's shed and I waited for his hands to feel for my face. But he didn't move and he didn't speak. He dug his hands into the pockets of his jacket. Was this the column that was supposed to sustain me? Were these the arms that were supposed to hold me?

"Let's go, Pà," I said, turning toward the door.

"Oliva, wait!" I heard the scuffling of his slippers behind me and Franco's voice calling. "As you can see, Mother is feeling better," he whispered, his voice trembling. "There are no other impediments."

He didn't say another word. The lovers' ditties, the sighs, the gazes had come straight out of Liliana's photographic novels. Mother was right not to want them in the house. We traveled back in silence. It wasn't the movement of the bus that made the words tumble out of Father's mouth, after all. He looked out the window as the countryside went by and nodded off every now and again. He was no longer annoyed. The betrothal was back on track. All that was missing was his hat.

———

Halfway down the big road, Mother stops in her tracks. "Olì, I've just remembered that I have to go to see Mrs. Scibetta. She's called for me again with some urgent work." She tucks a lock of hair that has come out of my braid back into place. "Let's go, we'll be quick," she says, heading off in the opposite direction. "No, Mà. You go to see Mrs. Scibetta. I'll make my way home."

"What? On your own, at this hour?"

"What's going to happen? Is someone going to kidnap me?"

"People talk, Olì, and you're a beautiful girl now." She takes two steps back as if to check me out and clears her throat. "Go straight home," she says, taking her lace shawl off. "And put this on. It's damp in the evening. And don't prick your finger," she adds, handing me the rose.

I wrap her shawl around my shoulders and it feels like she's hugging me. I start walking, holding the rose between two fingers.

"Oliva, Olì," she calls out suddenly from the other end of the street. "Be careful."

37

When we were little, Cosimino and I celebrated our birthdays together. Every July 2, we would both get a year older: five, six, seven, eight. Mother would measure us against the kitchen doorjamb and draw a line with our names and the date on it. Then we stopped growing together and our lines no longer coincided: every year, he would grow a bit taller and I a bit older. Now that we're both turning sixteen, he's gained ten inches on me and I've gained ten years on him. I'm destined to be a bride, a homemaker, and later a mother. He's still a boy, hanging out with his friends at the café. Time has flown more quickly for me and will be consumed in a greater hurry.

The big road is deserted. I tighten my grip on the stem of the rose, avoiding the thorns, and pull the shawl closer. Daisies are easier than roses, they answer lovers' questions and don't hurt people. The farther I get from the piazza, the more deserted was the road. I stick close to the walls so that the voices that rain down from the open windows keep me company.

Somebody turns onto the big road from a side street and starts walking behind me. I dare not look back but I can hear the soles of their shoes pounding the asphalt. I walk more briskly and turn to see whether it's a face I know. *Rosa, rosae, rosae,* I start chanting in my head. The steps come closer. *Rosae, rosarum* . . . I see a car pulling out at the junction of the big road with the dirt track that leads to my house. It slows down and then stops. I slow down, too, and catch my breath. Inside the car, there's a young man and a blond woman, maybe husband and wife. They look around, then consult a map. The man behind me catches up, gives me a nod of recognition, and vanishes around the corner. It's Don Santino, Tindara's father, the father-in-law by correspondence. The car door opens, the woman gets out and beckons me over.

"Can you tell me the way to the city, young lady?" she asks. "Are we going the right way?"

Close up, she looks older. Her hair is fine and you can see the dark roots growing back. There are deep ridges on both sides of her mouth, as if she'd had to make an effort all her life to smile.

"The city?" I ask. "I don't know. You need to get out of this town first." I stretch my arm out and point in the other direction and turn my body as if to confirm it.

The woman pulls at my wrist while the man suddenly appears behind me and grabs me by the waist so hard that I can't breathe. I have no breath to scream. I desperately look for someone to help me but the big road is empty.

"Let me go!" is all I can say, my voice barely a whisper. I try to struggle out of his grip, using both my arms and legs. He lifts me up and I find myself kicking the air. The woman opens the back door of the car and the man drags me inside.

"It's my birthday today. They're waiting for me at home," I say, and the older woman laughs meanly.

"Happy birthday, my beauty," she answers. "You'll be getting your present tonight," she adds, and sticks a rag in my mouth to stop me talking. The car sets off and the dirt track disappears into the distance. The rough cloth stinks and makes me gag. I feel like I'm suffocating. I can't recognize the landscape around me, my house must be very far away. My fists are clenched and I'm still clutching the rose between my fingers. Some of the petals fell onto the road, taking my place. And I'm left with the thorns. I'm not at all in favor of thorns. When I open up my right hand, the palm is stained red. Bloodstains are hard to get out, that's what Mother says.

38

The blond woman lights another cigarette. She's been chain-smoking the whole journey and the smoke makes me feel sick. I don't know how long we've been traveling. When the car stops, they yank me out. I can smell the sea but I can't see it. The woman grabs my wrist again and drags me toward an isolated hut. When she sees my bloody hand, she says, "I haven't touched a hair on your head. When he comes, you need to tell him you did this to yourself." She sounds worried.

"Take her through here," the young man orders. The older woman opens the door with a key, pulls me in, and closes it after her. Inside, it's dark and there's a sweet musty smell, like rotten perfume. She jerks me toward a room at the end of the corridor and makes me go inside. She inspects me closely, maybe to try to understand how a man could possibly be interested in me, then she shrugs and leaves without saying a word, slamming the door and drawing the bolt as she leaves.

I wait for my eyes to get used to the shadow. The windows are closed but a tiny ray of light comes through a gap under the roof. There's a wardrobe on one wall, a dressing table on another, and on the third, above the bed, a picture of a woman with long hair hanging loose over naked breasts.

When we were little, All Hallows' Eve was the only day we were given presents. "Go to bed," Mother would say, closing the shutters to make the house dark. "If the dead see you are sleeping, they'll bring you new shoes and toys, but if they find you awake, they'll pull your feet and won't leave you as much as a pin."

In one corner of the room, there is some linen: two towels and a folded white nightgown on an embroidered bedspread. It looks like a room for newlyweds, the linen like my dowry. I lie on the bed and wait.

It's the dead who bring gifts to the living, everyone in the family who has died, Mother used to say. They come at night, through the keyholes and other cracks, and drop off their presents. I used to lie under the covers and breathe as quietly as possible so that I would hear the dead when they came in. If Cosimino spoke, I'd snap, "Don't say a word and be good, or the dead will pull at our feet." He would clam up in fear and I would bury my head in my pillow and go through my multiplication tables as Miss Rosaria had taught us. Starting with sevens, which were the most difficult.

I pick out the embroidery with my fingers and suddenly pull away. This room isn't for me: it's not my dowry, I'm not the bride. I run to the door and tug furiously at the handle as if I could break the lock. I go back to the middle of the room, grab the bedcover from one corner and pull it off the bed, stripping the sheets and tossing the pillows, towels, and nightdress into a big pile on the floor. I shove the whole lot under the bed.

When you are little, you know that when someone dies, they will come back occasionally bearing gifts. I'm not scared of the dead. I lie on the cold stone floor wrapped in mother's shawl and hold my breath.

Don't say a word and be good, if the dead find us awake, they'll pull at our feet. But I'm more scared of the living than the dead.

39

From the next room I can hear a radio, which must mean the blond woman is back. After a while, I hear the bolt being drawn back and the door opening. She appears wearing the same clothes as when they grabbed me.

"*Non arrossire quando ti guardo. Ma ferma il tuo cuore che trema per me.*" *Don't blush when I look at you*, the song on the radio goes, *Stop your heart from trembling for me.* She sighs and looks around the room with dismay. "You young folk make trouble and leave us to pick up the pieces," she mutters, pointing at the stripped bed and the room in disarray. She stoops over me on the floor and grabs my shoulders, her hands as strong as a man's. I curl up into a fetal position to make it harder for her.

"Get up, my beauty," she says, adding benevolently, "You don't want him to see you like this, do you?"

I fold my arms across my face. "Who are you talking about? I don't know you. What do you want from me?"

She lets me go, gets up, and sits on the edge of the stripped bed. *Don't be scared to give me a kiss.* For a moment she closes her eyes and sways her head to the music. "You're not the first person I've helped get married," she says, smiling. "Two young things fall in love and the family is against the match or can't afford it. So . . . they come here for a *futina* and . . .

the deed is done. I don't do it for the money. I do it to help people. Because I'm still a romantic girl at heart," she says, and then starts singing along to the song coming from the radio next door in a high, out-of-tune voice.

No, don't be afraid, don't linger any longer . . . She looks around her as if the walls could tell their story. "This used to be a whorehouse," she says, pointing at the naked woman in the picture. "Now it's for couples to get married in. I've always labored for love." She laughs.

She slides down onto the floor and sits next to me. I pull the shawl up over my head. She comes closer and uncovers my face. "Don't you get it, my beauty? He told me to treat you like a queen. No, like a rose. That's what he said. You're lucky."

Lucky, I think. Like my sister, Fortunata.

"If someone is fond of you, they don't maul you, scare you, or force you," I say, bursting into tears like a child who wakes up and sees there are no presents, not even a slice of candied fruit.

She comes closer again. Her breath stinks of smoke and her irises are dark blue. Maybe she was pretty once. "Don't blush when I look at you," the radio repeats. "Listen to me. Crying will only make your eyes hurt," she says, passing me her handkerchief. "Whatever you do, tell him," she says urgently. "Tell him that I treated you well."

I take the shawl off my head and start banging on the floor with my fists. "I want to go home," I yell, my voice broken with sobs. "My mother and my father are waiting for me. I'm getting married next week. Someone will come to get me," I wail, the white dress sewn by Mother, Liliana's coral necklace, the orange blossom and daisies from the florist flashing through my mind.

"What wedding? What fiancé?" the woman mutters softly, on her knees as she pulls the sheets and bedcover out from under the bed. "By the time you get out of here, there'll only be one man for you. Who's going to take you once you've been broken?"

A girl is a jug, Mother always said.

"You've been lucky," she said, billowing the sheet over the bed and bending down to tuck in the corners. "He's a good-looking young man, he has good standing, and he could have had any girl he wanted." She smooths the sheet down on one side, and then walks around the bed and does the same on the other side. "You're improving your lot, my beauty," she says without looking at me, as if she were talking to herself.

"Whose daughter are you, anyway? What property does your father own?"

"My father doesn't own anything anymore," I sob. "This man has taken everything from him."

"It's the power of love. He wants you all to himself. Some people would die to be in your position."

I leap up and run for the door, grab the handle, and push with all my might. "Let me go, I beg you," I say, on my knees in front of her. "You're a woman just like me, you must understand."

She picks up the pillows and fluffs them up on the bed just like Mother does every day. "Me? I understand perfectly, it's you who has a problem understanding," she says, setting the nightdress out on the bed. "I was just like you." She strokes the material and starts folding it. "Do you think I was born blond?" She combs her hair with her fingers. "I had a fiancé. I loved him and he loved me." She laughs bitterly, picks up the towels, and folds them in four. "But he didn't believe me, he wanted proof of my love. I was naïve, I thought that if I didn't give him proof, he would leave me for someone who was more passionate than me."

There's no pain if love is pure, the song continues. Try as I might, I couldn't imagine her young, her hair a different color, it was too long ago. "So I gave in, just once. The next day, he left me," she tells me. "It was a trick to test me out. He told me I was easy to get, that I couldn't resist flattery. I only did it to make him happy, I didn't even like it. Actually, it hurt. So I was dishonored and on my own. I had no father and no money. Women only have one thing of any value and when that's gone, they're worth nothing."

She pulls a packet of cigarettes out of her skirt pocket and lights one. "Later on, though, I found out that everyone wanted me, but just for one night," she says, taking a deep puff and laughing sadly. Her eyes are so deep they look black.

"Your case is different," she says, suddenly gentle. "You can relax, my beauty."

I stand up, leaning on the door, as if I by pushing hard enough I could get through.

"Once he has forced himself on you, he has to marry you or he goes to jail."

"But I don't want him!" I scream, thumping on the wooden door.

"What do you mean, you don't want him? A woman without a husband is like half a pair of scissors, she's useless." It's like listening to Mother. She takes my hand and leads me to the standing mirror. I follow feebly like a docile little girl. On the dressing table, there is what is left of the rose I was holding. In the reflection, I can see tears running down my dark, hollow cheeks. I can see my high cheekbones and full mouth. "Don't cry, girl. It won't change anything." Framed by the mirror, her face appears behind mine and, for a moment, I can see what she must have looked like. "It won't change anything," she repeats, as she stubs her cigarette out in the ashtray. *Stop your heart from trembling for me*. The song comes to an end and the room goes quiet.

"This man here, or another there, or a thousand others again, it's all the same," she concludes. "It hurts at first, then you don't feel a thing."

40

I kept sleep at bay all night, terrified that I would be defenseless when he came in. Just like when I was little and I used to wait for the dead. "Don't say a word and be good," Mother would say, and I would keep my eyes peeled, exploring the darkness.

At dawn, I hear a car engine, doors slamming, and a voice, ". . . a woman belongs to the man who plucks her like a rose."

He comes to the door and pauses on the threshold. I curl up in the middle of the bed with my knees over my breasts, trying to create a protective shell. He strolls toward the dressing table and picks up the rose with the torn petals by the stem.

"You're as beautiful as this flower. *Rosa fresca e aulentissima*, remember? Actually, more beautiful, because this one will droop by the end of the day while you will continue to bud. You're the most beautiful girl in the whole town," he adds, and I think back to what Mother said before our paths diverged.

I don't know whether I'm beautiful, and that is one more reason why I wish I had been born a boy, like Cosimino. Nobody tells him what he is like, he simply knows it. A woman's body is a burden.

"I had the bed made up with my mother's linen," he murmurs, stroking the sheet and moving closer.

I stay balled up, my head inside my shoulders. I don't move, I don't speak, I don't breathe. Like a snail.

"This is for you, open it." He sits on the bed and places a small box on the pillow.

"Open it!" he repeats, impatiently. I don't move a muscle. He lifts the lid. They're coming. Gifts from the dead, I think to myself.

"Pure silk. In the city, all the fashionable women wear them. Such finery. You have to wear it later when we go out, instead of that worn-out shawl."

Later. Between me and that door there's a before and an after. A line I don't want to cross, because that line is me, it is inside me.

He stretches out and takes my foot in his hand. His fingers stroke the instep, slip themselves between my toes, one by one, like when I was little and Mother would dust the sand off. I can feel the heat of his lips on my skin, as soft as dough.

"I'm kissing your feet, you're my queen. Rose, freshly picked rose . . ." His mouth works its way up to my ankle slowly. He pulls me toward him and I grip the headboard but I suddenly feel drained, lacking any energy.

"There's no way the most beautiful girl in town is going to marry a man who can't even see her. As soon as I found out they'd betrothed you to that blind man, I made sure to save you right away."

His hands have traveled up to the hem of my skirt, grazing against my knees.

"A princess before swineherds," he says, kissing my ankles and then my shins. He grabs my hips and pulls with the full strength of his arms until I lose my grip and slide down next to him. He brings his face closer to mine; the sickly smell of jasmine slaps me.

"If you let me go, I won't tell anyone. I'll go home quietly and that will be that," I whisper.

"By the time you leave this room, you'll be my wife. It's your lucky day, and mine."

I'm lying on the bed, still wrapped in Mother's shawl. I don't move. A blade of cold dawn light slices through the chink in the roof. His face sweaty, his chest showing through his gaping shirt, his curls combed back, his eyes closed. He clamps my hands down on the bed and brings his face even closer. The smell of his skin suffocates me and I turn my face away.

If the dead find you awake, they'll pull at your feet, Mother used to say, but I would stay under the covers, my eyes wide open and my ears pricked, ready to pick up any sound. I'm not scared of the dead, I used to say. I want to see them for real. They won't hurt me.

He frees my wrists and pulls my face back toward him. I close my eyes and wait, frozen, as if he were still pinning me down. He bends down over me and plants his lips on my forehead. Like Father used to do when he was putting me to bed. Then he presses them onto one eye,

then the other, he brushes against my ear, and then my
cheeks. The doughy warmth reaches the right-hand corner of my mouth and stops there. He rests his chin on my
collarbone and his hair tickles my cheek. For a moment,
our breathing is synchronized. He murmurs something
so softly I can't hear what he's saying.

"I want to go home," I say in his ear.

I feel a jolt, as if he'd been stung by a wasp. He detaches
himself from me and sits up in a fury. "Hasn't it sunk into
your little head yet?" he says, grabbing my head with both
hands. He stops himself and goes back to the gentler tones
he used before, except that his voice is trembling with rage.
"You're made to be with me, don't you get it? I've known it
since you were a little girl and you used to lick the sugared
ricotta off the tip of my knife. Can't you see what you're
like? You're provoking me. Your poor little Virgin Mary face
drives me crazy." He stands up and starts pacing the floor,
back and forth. "You came to that Communist meeting,
you stopped and talked to me in the piazza, you accepted
an orange out of my hand, you danced with me at the patron saint festival, you were walking out on your own in
the evening. Don't you see? You wanted me to take you."

He picks up the rose from the dressing table and twirls
it in his hand. "I'm not taking you home. Forget it. For your
own good. How would you end up? Like Angiolina. That
old bag with dyed hair who's had more men than there are
days in the year. Who do you think you are? You should be

thanking me," he says, even louder. "You should be saying thank you. To me!" He throws the rose at me.

I close my eyes and hear his steps fade. "I have all the patience in the world," he adds, before leaving. "You'll be the one to call me. In a few days, you'll be begging me. Apples fall when they're ripe."

The door slams, the bolt is drawn again, and after a while there is only silence.

41

The last time Angiolina came, she left a carafe with some water in it and a few slices of stale bread. She hasn't been back since. I feel cramps of hunger. Maybe no one will ever come. Like when we used to play hide-and-seek when we were little. Saro counted and I would run off and hide in his father's workshop. I froze, holding my breath and my heart banging noisily. I don't know whether I was more scared of being found or of nobody finding me.

Virgin Mary, I try and pray. Mother most pure, Mother most chaste, Virgin Mother. You have never known a man, you don't know how strong their arms are, how warm their mouths are, how harsh their voices are. I knew how to recite the Rosary in Mrs. Scibetta's living room, under Mother's supervision, protected by women's voices as they joined together in prayer and in tittle-tattling, warning me against the dangers of the world. Now I'm alone. Feminine, singular. Is this what happens to a woman when she is on her own?

I get up from the bed. How long has it been? A day, two days, a week? The silk scarf is lying in a corner of the room. I bend down and pick it up, feel how smooth it is, and then I tie it around my neck and look in the mirror. Is this how I will look when I get out of here, wearing Paternò's scarf instead of Mother's? I angrily try to rip it with my hands but I have run out of strength and fall facedown on the bed.

"Come," I whisper, and jump at my own voice after so long. I walk over to the door and start banging on it with what little energy I have left. "Come back, let me out! I can't take it any longer. It's all my fault. I'm to blame. I'll do what you want, open up! I'm hungry, I'm thirsty, I'm scared. I don't want to be on my own anymore."

The banging echoes feebly around the room. Maybe there's nobody there. They've all gone. He doesn't want me now. Like when we used to play hide-and-seek when we were little. In the end, they'd forgotten me here.

I slide down onto my knees in front of the door, my ear pressed against the wooden surface. Not a sound. Then I hear a noise, in the distance to begin with, and then coming closer and closer, a hoarse voice and then silence again. An hour goes by, or maybe two. Time no longer exists.

I feel as though I may have dozed off at a certain point and, in my dream, I am clutching a little bouquet of orange blossom. The church aisle is long and cold. From the entrance I can just see a black dot in front of the altar, waiting for me. Father holds his arm out for me to take, and we start walking.

"What are you doing wearing a hat, Pà, you should take it off in church," I warn him.

"I wouldn't prefer that," he says, and we keep walking up the aisle as the guests turn and look at us. Every step

I take, the groom seems to get farther and farther away. I can't make out his features.

"Who is he?" I ask Father. "Who are you giving me away to?"

"Only you can know that," he answers flatly.

I don't understand. "You're walking me up the aisle," I say in tears. "Tell me, who do you want me to marry?"

Suddenly, the nave of the church, which looked so long, shrinks and I find myself face-to-face with a man in a dark suit. It's Franco. He's handsome and as elegant as the first day I met him. I look at his long, tapered fingers, the ones that held my face behind the toolshed. He brings his right hand up to his temple and takes his dark glasses off: the bright blue irises are no longer lost in shadow. The pupils dilate and look straight at me.

"Franco, can you see me?" I ask him, filled with emotion.

"You thought I was blind," he answers, as if he were telling me off. "But I know what you've done. I know you were calling another man and you were begging him to come into the room."

His words echo throughout the church. I don't know what to say. The guests talk among themselves and Mother shakes her head in the front row.

"Everybody saw you, Olì," Franco says. "I wasn't the only one."

The priest slams the missal shut and a roar like a clap of thunder rumbles through the church.

42

When he opens the door, he finds me crumpled up in a corner, the palms of my hands scratched from banging on the door, my nails torn. He doesn't look at me, he doesn't speak, he doesn't smile, he picks me up and carries me across the room to the bed as if we were newlyweds. My eyes are throbbing, weariness radiates from my belly outward, to my legs, my arms, my feet, my hands, my head, and every atom in my body subsides into the soft surrender of the mattress. I lie there frozen and wait, like when Mother and Fortunata took me to have my ears pierced the day before my confirmation. I don't want to, I had said, and they forced me to go anyway.

His body presses down on mine, digs into it as if he were burrowing into me. I close my eyes tight, hold my breath, and repeat in my head Mother's words as she held my forehead still that day: you won't feel anything. But just as it wasn't true then, it isn't true now. The pain back then blends with the pain now. The heat of his body weighing down on mine and the numbing ice on my right earlobe, the pungent scent of alcohol and of his sweat, the little block of cork placed behind my ear and the pillow he shoves under my hips to arch my back, his hands pushing me down hard, just like Mother's, Nellina's needle piercing my flesh. This time, though, I can't scream, turn my head away, and run. I'm not my own mistress, and realize I never have been. The rules of the body are: don't gesticulate, don't laugh with your mouth open, don't stand near the window. I learned these when I was little, and I've always obeyed them. Yet I do not know my body. It's alien to me. But he knows what to do with it. He sifts through it bit by bit to glean his pleasure, while I lose mine forever. Don't say a word and be good, I say to myself, don't say a word and be good. Just a prick and it's over. The needle this time is forcing itself into me, pushing, penetrating, tearing. A stab of pain tears through me. I don't know what to hold on to in order not to shatter into pieces so I hold on to him with all my might because he's alive and I'm dying. I feel blood gushing, trickling down my leg and dripping on the white sheet. Then all my senses shut off one by one and I don't feel a thing.

Good girl, Fortunata said that day in front of Nellina's house, you're going to grow up. But I didn't want to. I've been made a woman through force.

———

When I open my eyes, it's all over. Paternò is panting, his face is slick with sweat, his curly hair plastered on his head. He raises himself on his elbows without looking at me then he turns onto his side. His body, lying by my side, is that of a sated spouse, and after a few minutes he sinks into a deep sleep. The same body that until a few minutes ago represented fear, heaviness, the violence of muscle forcing my muscle, flesh penetrating my flesh, is now lying there indifferently, in silence. There has been no change in him, no open wound. He can go to sleep in peace, he is not scared of me, he doesn't need to worry that I might hurt him while he's fast asleep. His legs splayed, his chest thinly coated in dark hair rising and falling calmly, his small, almost feminine feet with the second toe longer than the big toe, his muscular arms, his stubby fingers with bitten fingernails, a mole the size of a lentil on his left collarbone.

He lies next to me indifferently, but he now has rights over me. I belong to him and he, too, will belong to me for the rest of my life, whether I want it or not.

With a sudden jolt, his steady breathing is broken and he wakes up. Without looking at me, he gets out of bed and walks around the room gathering his clothes, which he pulls on hastily.

"This was how it had to go," he mutters, as if he were talking to himself. Finally, he unlocks the door and walks out, this time leaving it open behind him.

———

I stare up at the ceiling and lose myself in the arabesques formed by the cracks. I'm inert, as if my lifeblood had been extracted from my bone marrow. I brush against my belly with my fingertips but they don't feel like mine, the hands touching me are someone else's. I explore every inch of my body to find out what has changed and try to mend it, like with my torn earlobe, but there's no tangible difference between before and after, the break is inside. I'm a broken jug.

Imperceptible to begin with, and then stronger and stronger, a spasm rises from my stomach to my mouth and transforms itself into a wave of nausea. I sit up and spew a jet of warm, frothy liquid. The vomit has freed my body, but the brick sitting on my stomach is still there.

When I was little, Mother would come to my sickbed and her presence was enough to make me feel better. She's not here now and I can't make myself feel better on my own. Sleep, she would say, sleep, she would repeat, sleep and it will pass. But sleep is for the innocent and it doesn't come to make me feel better. I get up and walk over to the dressing table, pour some water into the bowl, and rub myself with soap, once, twice, three times, ten times. The stench of vomit goes away; the stench of him will never go away. It's fused with my skin.

The girls at school used to say that you were stained after. What stain? I asked, and they laughed their heads off, holding their cheeks in their hands. I pull up the counterpane to hide the stain of my betrayed body.

I go out into the corridor and the light pricks my eyes even though it's gray outside. A clap of thunder rumbles nearby and makes me jump. I run back into the room, like Father's chickens when they found the coop open and sat there waiting for someone to come and lock them up again. I go to the dressing table and pick up the rose. The last petals fall off the crushed sepal, like red droplets, onto the floor.

43

I don't know what time he comes back. I am lying on the bed in a state of numbness with no will to do anything, like Father after his heart attack. I can't move. He slips in between the sheets and wants to have his way with me again but at that very moment we hear noises outside. He opens the shutters and looks out. "Move," he says. He pulls the sheets off me and yells, "We need to go."

I was brought to the house with force and now I'm being forced out. I throw Mother's shawl over my shoulders as we hurry out a back door and run into the darkness. He yanks me by the wrist into the bushes, my wooden clogs make me trip, so he stops and turns. He looks like a thief. He picks me up and carries me.

We can hear the voices of the carabinieri behind us. "Stop or we'll shoot." I can make out their outlines in the light of their torches: one is tall and the other short.

"Wait, don't run," I yell. The branches are scratching my arms. "Shut up!" he intimates angrily. The tall carabiniere raises his gun, shouts another warning, "Stop!" and fires a shot in the air.

I squeeze my hands to my ears. The whole world goes silent. The dark silhouettes of the carabinieri are coming toward us. I press harder and it's as if I'm going deaf. I feel as if I will never hear anything again, but then I hear another shot even closer. He stops in his tracks so I raise my arms, free my ears, and shout, "That's enough! There's nothing for it now."

The carabiniere lowers his weapon and walks toward us. He's blond. He must be from another town, maybe he doesn't know our laws. You break her, you take her. That's what Mother taught me.

My hand slips out of his but he won't stop. He keeps running and, after a while, vanishes into the trees. I am alone. I drop to my knees, pull the shawl around me, close my eyes, and wait for the carabinieri to come to me. When I open my eyes again, I see another figure behind the others: a man without a hat is walking very slowly toward me. Father approaches me, squats down on the damp ground, takes his jacket off, and drapes it over my shoulders. Then he lifts me up, takes my hand, and gives it a little squeeze.

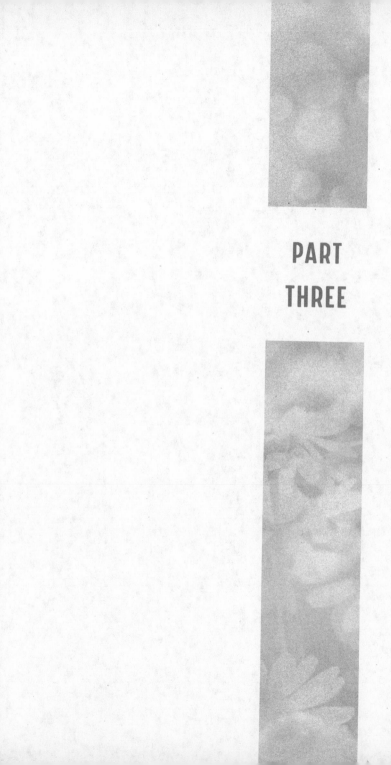

PART
THREE

44

When I was nine, I had scarlet fever and I was quarantined in my room for three weeks. Mother said Cosimino was fragile and she would bring my food and medicine in with a handkerchief tied over her nose and mouth. Time felt like big solid walls that could suddenly melt into tiny little waterfalls. From inside my room, I could only guess what was going on outside. Daylight came and went, at night the moon shone over Father's land. Miss Rosaria sent me books to read and on the floor next to my bed the ones I had finished piled up in an increasingly precarious tower. After three weeks, I was better: the pile of books was taller than my bedside table. I caught my reflection in the windowpane and saw a stranger: the flesh on my body had melted away, the bones protruded, two dark rings circled my sunken eyes, making them look even deeper. The first time I went out, my muscles felt weak but my head was full of stories, just as my nights had been filled by moonlight.

My room today is dark, even the moon has turned away from me. I can't see Father's field. I'm quarantined here as if I were contagious again. I can hear steps and voices gurgling like water being sucked down a drain. Every now and again I get out of bed and grope for objects, imagining I am

Franco. I open the shutters but no light filters in. At new moon, Miss Rosaria once taught us, the moon doesn't show its face because it joins the sun and only shows its shadow. The sun is a jealous man who wants her all to himself, and I'm just like the moon now: dark and distant.

I stop in front of the bookcase and run my fingers along the spines one by one but none of these stories talks about me anymore. All my teachers have lied to me: the multiplication tables are a trick, the pluperfect tense a ruse, active, passive, and reflexive forms, acute and grave accents, subject and object complements, the Ides of March, "thirty days hath September," *spero, promitto, iuro* take the future infinitive, "in fourteen hundred and ninety-two Columbus sailed the ocean blue," they're all an elaborate hoax and I'm here, woefully alone, falling, falling. The darkness feels unbearable, like a blindfold over my eyes, so I fumble around for the light switch. I pick a book out of the case but I can't take in a word of what I'm reading, the parallel lines are long black creatures slithering across the page, the sentences are not linked, and meaning drains out of the words as if they were sieves. Culture doesn't save us, Miss Rosaria. I have always studied and it has been no use to me. I stretch my arm out and, in one fell swoop, knock everything down in my path: the objects from the shelves, the pens and notebooks from the desk, the books from the bookcase. In the dark, I tread on everything I once treasured.

The books lie at my feet, their spines cracked unnaturally, like bodies with broken limbs. The jackets have slipped off their spines and the pages, having lost their protection, expose their lies for what they are: the Little Women will never grow up, Dorothy never reaches Oz, Pollyanna loses the glad game, Alice can't find the shrinking potion, and Lucia Mondella, in *The Betrothed*, was unable to save herself from the thugs by praying to the Virgin Mary. Just like me.

I drop to my knees and lie on that bed of books, neither tired nor hungry. My body is no use to anyone anymore. I'm no longer marriageable, and I'm not welcome in the circle of women reciting the Rosary or embroidering. Who wants their dowry linen to be stained by shame?

I can't lie still, so I squat down by the bedstead, pull it away from the springs, and fish out my secrets: the old notebooks with my charcoal and sanguine pencil sketches, the hand mirror, the stub of lipstick, and Liliana's photograph. I throw everything except the photo portrait on the pile of things to discard. I inspect it at length, tracing my lineaments with my finger. I reflect myself in those eyes that had not yet experienced shame. I tear it in half, then in half again, and again, until it is reduced to satin-finished scraps. I gather them together into a little pile, pick them up in my cupped hands, walk over to the window, and scatter the pieces over Father's field.

45

Mother moves in and out of my room, her eyes circled with grief. Every time she comes in, she opens her mouth to speak but doesn't produce any words, as if she were wearing a mask to avoid being contaminated. Look at me, Mamma, I would like to say to her, I'm still the same jug: same hands, same hips, same lips. Nothing I did smashed me to pieces. I followed all your rules: I didn't look at the man, I didn't suck in my breath to make my breasts stick out, I didn't put any lipstick on, I didn't slow down in front of the church so that I could be followed, I didn't sneak into the movie house. I would have married the man you chose for me. I've never disobeyed you. I've always said yes. I'm your daughter: a stranger who looks like you but who you may not like.

At the first rustling of a leaf, she runs to the window to see if anyone is coming. She counts the days and waits but no one comes on the first day, and the situation doesn't change on the second, third, or fourth. The blond woman Angiolina had said he would have to marry me and so I, too, am sitting here waiting to hear the steps of my jailer to come and set me free. I don't know whether it would be better if he came or if he never did.

I spend my days emptying my room of all its objects. With a vinegar-soaked rag I wash the floor, wipe all the surfaces, door handle, and the windows. When everything is clean, I look at the pile of books. "I told you to give them away, they just gather dust and dirt," I yell at Mother through the closed door but it's late, everyone is in bed, I'm the only one who has made an enemy of sleep. So I lie on my bed and start reading the first pages of *Anne of Green Gables*: "You don't know what's going to happen through the day, and there's not much scope for imagination." I no longer have any scope for imagination. I close the book, stick it under my pillow, and finally fatigue spreads irresistibly through my limbs and puts my thoughts to sleep.

Angiolina walks into the room where I am being held prisoner and throws the shutters open. Moonlight floods the floor. She stubs out her cigarette, drapes Mother's shawl over my shoulders, and gives a raucous little laugh like Mother's. "What are you doing in here?" she asks. "Run along home!" "I can't," I answer, pointing at the door. "It's open," she says. "It's always been open. You're the one who wanted to stay, nobody forced you. All you needed to do was turn the handle." I leap to my feet and push her away. Angiolina falls down but goes on laughing in that awful way. I run out into the street, barefoot, my hair flying, sweat dripping from my temples down my neck, my skirt catches on my legs, my arms windmill at my hips. I run as fast as I can until I find the road that leads to my town and stop only when I get to the piazza and find myself standing in front of the pastry shop. I look at my reflection in the window: I see a scrawny, disheveled, dark-eyed child staring longingly at the cream cakes.

wake with a jolt, starving for the first time since I was kidnapped. Frozen on the bed, I feel my hip bones with my hands: they are jutting out through the skin, as sharp as gimlets. Acid erupts from my stomach into my mouth, making me dizzy. My body is still alive and is telling me I am hungry. I run into the kitchen, envious of everyone else's capacity for sleep. It's still dark outside, the moon is still hiding in the shadows. Stifling every sound, I open the larder, fling the sideboard and other cabinet doors open, and grab everything I can find. I cram my mouth with the leftover pasta from lunch that I hadn't touched, I bite into the hardboiled eggs set aside for supper, the stale bread scratches the roof of my mouth. I jam my tongue with a piece of cheese and sink my teeth into a wrinkled apple. The food slithers down my throat and engorges my gullet. I twist the top of the jar of capers off and stick my finger in, the rough grains of rock salt scrape against my skin. I take the lid off the olive jar and roll the olives in my hands: they are like me, small and hard. I need to fill my body to feel it again. The pot with the orange marmalade for Sunday breakfast is up on the highest shelf. I clamber up onto a chair and upset it, allowing the treacly substance to trickle down my arm. I lift my nightgown and spread it over my legs all the way up to my groin. I lick my finger and start gorging on the rest of the jam until I feel sick. The chair wobbles and rocks until I crash to the floor.

I soon hear her steps. Mother appears in the kitchen and looks at me, bursting with pity. "Oliva," she says. She flops onto the floor, getting her nightdress dirty with all the discarded food. "Olì," she says again, as if she were talking to herself. She moves closer and lifts her arm. I close my eyes, waiting for the slap. Instead, she takes my face in her hands, then my neck, my shoulders, and finally she wraps her arms around my back and squeezes me tight. We sit there on the floor hugging, our cheeks glued together with the sticky orange marmalade.

The house is still quiet when we get up. She leads me to the bathroom and fills the washtub, like when Cosimino and I were little and she would leave us there to soak and play. She tests the temperature with the tip of her elbow and pulls the stained nightgown off my head. I stand there before her, naked, and don't feel shame. She settles me in the tub, rubs the soapstone to lather her hands, and then passes them over my whole body before rinsing me. She removes the plug and we both sit there under the spell of the opal whirlpool being sucked down the drain. She holds out her arm to help me get up, takes clean towels out of the chest, rubs my hair, and dries the drops of water from every inch of my body. When she reaches my toes, she dabs the porous linen between each of them. "There you are," she murmurs as she does my buttons up. "You're all clean now."

47

Just before lunch, there's a knock at the door. Mother and Father exchange glances then she gets up to see who it is. Nellina says hello and the three adults lock themselves in the kitchen to talk. Their voices are muffled and every now and again there is the sound of chairs scraping on the floor. From the corridor behind me appears Cosimino. He hasn't shaved since our birthday and he's beginning to look like a hoodlum. We both flatten our ears to the door to eavesdrop on the conversation, and as we do so, our faces are suddenly as close as they were when we were in our mother's belly. I can feel his breath on my hair, the familiar smell. It has been the same since we were both little and I was the one looking after him when we were left alone at home. Now that we are older, he is a head taller than me. I rest my shoulders on his chest and he doesn't pull away. Slowly I lean my whole weight on him.

"Tomorrow?" Mother says.

"Before lunchtime," Nellina confirms. "At the pastry shop."

"I wouldn't prefer it." Father's voice is the deepest.

"Whether you prefer to or not, there are no other saints in paradise," Mother snaps.

"Do we really have to give her away to that rotten piece of flesh?"

"Where are your feet? On the ground or in the clouds?" she yells, banging her palms on the table. "That is how the world is, was, and always will be."

"A compromise must be made, Salvo," Nellina says. "Don Ignazio says we must."

"Nellina, remind me. How many daughters does the priest have?"

Nellina doesn't answer but Mother yells at Father, "The day you were born was the day I was cursed!"

"Calm down, Amalia," he answers coolly. "All I'm saying is that sometimes it's best to only give advice on things you know."

"There's no point arguing with you: you're a waste of space and marrying you was a fate worse than having a daughter! Nellina is the only person who has helped us through the years and this is your way of thanking her?"

"Salvo," we hear Nellina say. "If there were another solution for the girl . . . but we've tried everything possible. Franco's mother, after what happened, has withdrawn her consent and who can blame her? Now, for the good of your family, for your own good . . . You don't want to take justice into your own hands, do you, after what happened to you last year? Do you want another heart attack?"

Cosimino winces. He must be remembering that night.

"Justice?" Father says, his voice deeper than ever. "Justice is another matter."

After these words, nobody shouts and we can only make out the words *marriage, dress, home* . . . Cosimino and I pull away from the door. He grabs my wrists and looks me dead in the eye.

"I'll go and teach that man what's what," he says in his new man's voice, which has been breaking over the past few months.

I shake my head. "No, Cosimino. Neither you nor Papà. It's up to me to deal with the situation. This is a woman's job."

We go to bed without saying a word. When I wake up in the middle of the night, I think I can see Mother's silhouette in the doorway leaning on the frame and looking at me. But my eyes soon droop and the image fades away.

t's still dark outside, but Father is already in the kitchen, his rubber boots on, and a hat on his head. "Where did you find it?"

"I bought myself a new one."

"What you need to buy is a new daughter."

He perches on the corner of the bench, takes his hat off, and twirls it in his hands, inspecting it from every angle. "The meeting is today," he says slowly, as if he were saying something inconsequential. "They want to make a proposal."

Angiolina was right, then. He took me and now he has to marry me. Otherwise, I will end up either a spinster or a fake blond like her.

I turn to look at Father. There's no anger in his face.

"What proposal can there possibly be?" I ask, pulling my dressing gown tight.

"You must decide."

"Do you want to give me away to that man?"

His hands shake and he drops his new hat. I go to pick it up and rest it on his knees. Father drops his head and tenses his shoulders as if I had loaded a weight onto them.

"I don't know how to use a rifle, Olì. It stains your hands

and I like to keep mine clean. Bloodshed is a cycle that can never be broken."

The few times he opens his mouth, Father speaks in riddles. He doesn't dictate rules like Mother.

"You know I was orphaned at sixteen: your grandfather set out in his boat and never came back and your grandmother died less than a year later of a broken heart," he says. "We grew up on our own, me and my little brother. Nitto got married young to the most beautiful girl in town, but a few months into their marriage, someone put a bug in his ear. Rumor had it that his bride was unfaithful. Blather today and blather tomorrow, his blood began to boil. They had a fight and she suffered an injury to her face. She returned to her family and the next day sent her brother. An eye for an eye, Nitto ended up dead. We no longer had a father so defending the family honor was up to me. I went to pay a visit to the man who slaughtered my brother."

For a moment, Father was once again the Greek god bathed in sunlight that I used to see him as when I was little.

"On my way, Pippo Vitale, a childhood friend who had gone into the carabinieri, detained me. He took my rifle and locked me in a cell for two nights to cool me down. When he let me out, he handed me my weapon and said, 'This is yours. Are you still thinking of using it?' 'I wouldn't prefer that,' I answered. I was on my way to kill the brother, but the father would have retaliated, and on and on the feud would have gone, without end. I have Pippo Vitale to thank today if I can don a new hat because doing so six feet under would be quite a feat," he concludes, curling his lips in a grimace of a smile.

I turn to look out the window. The road is still deserted. There will be a proposal, I will be married off to that man, people will greet me in the street. But then? What will I do? Will I go back to drawing pictures of movie stars? Will the clouds still look like marfoyles? Will I still enjoy picking the petals off a daisy?

"What happened to your carabiniere friend?"

"He's still at the station."

Angiolina had said that man had to marry me or he would go straight to jail.

"Shall we go and harvest some snails before it gets light?" he suggests.

"Mamma doesn't want me to, I'm not little anymore."

"You'll always be little to me."

I get dressed in a hurry, he dons his hat, and we set out with the first light of dawn.

49

We come back with brimming buckets. Cosimino has shaved, leaving just a mustache, which is fashionable today for young men. Mamma sees us coming and lights the gas under a little pan. She has twisted strands of her hair around swatches of cloth to curl it.

"Breakfast?" she asks. We sit down and Father starts tearing the crusts off the bread, dropping them into his bowl of milk, and then pouring coffee and sugar on top. I do the same, bring the spoon up to my mouth, and feel the crunch of the sugar granules on my teeth. We eat in silence then part and go into our rooms to get changed into our good clothes. Our movements are perfectly harmonized, following a silent score. Everything has been written and the rhythm erupts of its own accord.

I find the yellow skirt and flowery blouse laid out for me on my bed, a top and a bottom forming an invisible girl, an apparition of me. I hold the skirt up to my hips and scrutinize myself in the mirror. Then I open the wardrobe and put it away: it's for special occasions, that's what Mother said. On an iron hanger, there's my old black pinafore. I stroke the rough material and Mr. Scialò comes to mind when he used to dictate in that flat voice of his, "Be sweet and obedient / so people will consider you / more highly." I close the wardrobe door and stay in my work clothes. I don't want to look attractive. I don't want to follow any advice. I don't want to obey anyone ever again. Where did it get me? Instead of multiplication tables and irregular verbs, they should have taught us to say no. After all, we've been learning to say yes since the day we were born.

When I go back into the kitchen, Mother looks at me and shakes her head. "Your shoes," she says. I take my clogs off and put the shoes with a low heel on. Father and Cosimino are wearing their Sunday suits. Apart from the mustache, they look almost identical. Overnight, they have become the same person. We move around the house stepping lightly, exchanging a few polite words as if we were strangers. And yet we have never been so close.

"Let's go," Father says. We leave the house and set off down the dirt track. The night clouds have dispersed and the sun is an ax looming over our necks. On the rise of the road toward the piazza, we walk arm in arm: me and Cosimino in the middle, our mother and father on either side. Cosimino's curls are greased down in a dark crown of tar, Father's sweat drips onto his starched shirt collar like a distillery. When we reach the junction where the car was waiting for me that day, I lean on Cosimino and we turn onto the big road. We move like puppets pulled by an invisible string under the curious stares of the crowd. Some people come out onto their balconies. Others exchange comments. As we walk past the church, Don Ignazio steps out and nods at us.

On the first floor of an elegant residence, first the shutters open, then a hand appears, followed by an arm, a face, and finally a torso. Two sunken eyes peer out of the square gap and follow my progress all the way. Fortunata gives a feeble wave, then disappears again behind the shutters. I will end up like her, swallowed and spat out, held captive between four walls. The rules of obedience are: follow the road, look docile, and nod.

I am still looking up when I feel the ground give beneath me, my knees buckle, and I fall on the asphalt. It isn't frailty, it's my shoe: the heel has come off. I hold on to Father to pull myself up again, while Mother brushes the dust off my clothes with her hand. I pick up the broken heel and hobble on, one leg shorter than the other. I am limping like Saro. I look up at the clouds but there are no funny shapes today. We walk past the carabinieri station and leave it behind us on the left. The shoe with no heel is beginning to annoy me, and the other one is hurting. The pastry shop is at the other side of the piazza. Not far now, and I will be handed over. Both shoes are getting harder and harder to walk in. He is standing there outside the store window in his white suit, a sprig of jasmine behind his ear. I remember the cloying smell, the locked room, the crumpled sheets, Angiolina's dark roots growing out, the stench of cigarettes. Either he marries you or they take him straight to the carabinieri, she mocked. He takes a step toward us, lifts an arm, and brushes his hair back with his fingers: he has had his way. I turn to Father but I can't read an answer in his expression. Exhausted, I stop.

"I can't go any farther," I say, and pull my shoes off. A wave of relief radiates from the soles of my feet upward through my whole body. I look Paternò straight in the eye, then make an about-face, starting, barefoot, in the opposite direction.

50

"Maresciallo Vitale is on a call, we need to wait awhile," the young carabiniere with a mustache just like my brother's tells us.

The station waiting room is dark and smells of mold. Cosimino has stayed behind in the piazza, keeping an eye on the pastry shop while the three of us sit on a wooden bench inside. Mother looks first at Father then at me, trying to work out what has just taken place, but nobody says a word. In her best dress and with her curled hair, she looks like the bride-to-be while I look a century older. One minute we were walking toward him and the next we walked into the station with everyone looking on. Whether it was the midday sun, heatstroke, or the broken heel, I don't know. I was so uncomfortable I couldn't take another step. That's why I stopped.

Father gets up, says something to the junior officer, and walks into the corridor.

"Can we go now, Olì? Have you rested enough?" Mother whispers, staring at my bare feet. Her voice is half-scolding, half-kind, as if I were a little girl throwing a tantrum.

When we were little, she would drag me and Fortunata to the first Mass. Cosimino was allowed to sleep in because he was fragile. "Santa Rita cured you of your scarlet fever," she would say as she dragged us girls out of bed and pulled warm clothes over our heads. It was still dark when we left. Fortunata and I would cling to each other, sheltering from the wind. "I'm hungry," I would whine, to delay our departure a little. "I'll give you a piece of pie on the way," she would cajole us. As we continued, I would dig my heels in. She would feed me a tiny morsel and I would take another few steps. "Good girl," she'd say. "You're a good little child." She went on like this all the way to the church door.

Sitting on the wooden bench, Mother touches my hand and I close my fist.

"What will you do afterward, Olì? Have you thought about that?"

Crumb by crumb, like a good girl, I carried on walking until we got to the church door. The nave was icy, the old ladies of the parish smelled of mothballs, and I would drift off to sleep. But I had been obedient, that's what Mother said, and the prize was her love.

"I'll stay broken, Mà," I whisper in her ear. "There's no other solution."

I open my hand and show her the scars left by the thorns the day they snatched me. She runs her finger along them and closes her eyes not to see them.

"You can come in." The young officer with the mustache smiles at us. Father is standing next to him and beckons us forward. We follow the junior officer down a corridor and up a flight of stairs to the first floor.

"Come in," a voice calls out from behind the door when he knocks on it.

Maresciallo Vitale is sitting behind his desk. He gets up and nods slightly in greeting. Mother and I sit down and Father stands behind us.

"A hot-blooded young man has been disrespectful to you, I hear." He looks down at a folder full of sheets of paper. The message is: my case is not as important as the files in front of him.

Father places a hand on my shoulder. "Pippo," he starts, but then corrects himself, "Maresciallo Vitale, she was raped . . ."

"Rape with the intention of marriage. They say the man is willing to . . . make reparations?"

I pick at the deep gouges in my palm and shake my head. Father's hand increases the pressure on my shoulder. Neither of us says a word.

"Is the *signorina* legally an adult?" Vitale asks, continuing to inspect the folder before him.

"She turned sixteen a few days ago . . ." Mother answers, the words lost in her mouth as she thinks about the evening of my birthday.

"Right then, I'll speak to you as her parents," he says, closing the folder brusquely. "She doesn't want to marry him anymore?" he asks, as if they were talking about a lovers' tiff.

"Maresciallo," Father says, clearing his throat. "My daughter Oliva never intended to give her hand to that man. There was no agreement between the families and no regular marriage proposal was ever made. He made overtures, and faced with our indifference, he reacted with force, damaging first my property, then my daughter."

Vitale took his glasses off and mopped his face. "What do you want to do, Salvo?" he says. I can see him as a young man, as I imagined him in Father's story, taking the rifle from Father's hand and locking him up for two nights.

Father toys with the hat in his hands. "I want . . ." He pauses mid-phrase.

Vitale gets up and slowly circles the room. He walks back to his desk and picks up his pack of cigarettes.

"My daughter came here for justice," Father continues, still standing behind me.

The maresciallo digs a lighter out of his pocket and weighs it in his hand. "Justice is slippery," he says. The lighter flame trembles as the fan blows air on it. "There's the justice of the law and the justice of men, but they're not exactly the same thing." He takes a drag of his cigarette. "This is your town, Salvo. This is your family. This is your daughter: you need to do what's right for her. When you walk out of the station, she'll be the one hearing things behind her back . . ."

"I'm not a disgrace," I say, leaning forward in my chair, still clutching my broken heel. Father's hand slips from my shoulder. The maresciallo frowns and sucks in another mouthful of smoke. I thought I had shouted these words but he behaves as if he hasn't even heard them.

"The girl is very young, maybe she's confused," he continues, without looking at me. "At this age they want one thing then latch on to something else . . . a father's role is to guide her to make sensible decisions. Salvo, you have a beautiful daughter. Do you want to condemn her to an unhappy life?"

"I've already condemned one," he answers.

The cigarette has become a pillar of ash precariously balanced on its stub. Vitale rests it on the edge of the desk and stares at it as if it were a wager that he had won against himself.

"The Paternò family are big fish around here. They know a lot of influential people. The damage has been done but there's always a way to make peace. What are we talking about here?"

"What about the law . . . ?" I say, leaning on his desk and tipping the ash pillar over the edge.

"The law is for people with money," the maresciallo interrupts me as he cups his hands, sweeping up the ash and dropping it in the ashtray. "Do you want to make a formal accusation? Fine! I'll call the agent and we'll write: 'Salvo and Amalia Denaro join criminal proceedings as a civil party seeking damages against Giuseppe Paternò for rape with the intention of forcing a marriage . . .'"

Mother arches her back as if she had been beaten. "There'll be a trial," Vitale goes on. "You'll need a lawyer, you'll need to prove the man's guilt, not just with words but with objective evidence."

He's sitting right in front of us and he looks at me for the first time. "The *signorina* will have to prove that she is no longer intact, that she was before, and that she was not complicit with the *fuitina* as is often the case with elopements in these parts. Has she ever been seen speaking to Paternò? Has she ever been seen dancing in the square with him, in full view? Has she ever accepted any gifts? Serenades? When she was taken, was she walking alone or was she being chaperoned? Was it morning or was it at dusk?"

I close my eyes. Anger is caving my stomach. I realize I will be the one on trial, not him.

Vitale wrinkles his nose and screws up his eyes, as if he were irritated by a fly landing on his nose.

"If it were my daughter, Salvo, you know what I'd do?" he concludes. "Nothing."

The broken heel slips out of my hand. It drops to the floor.

"Hard feelings pass, things have a way of fixing themselves," he says, enunciating clearly. Then he picks up a big blue leather-bound book from the corner of his desk and starts skimming through it in front of Father.

"Article 544 of the Criminal Code," he says, leaning over the desk to read. "For the offenses provided for in Chapter 1 and Article 530, the marriage that the perpetrator of the offense contracts with the offended person voids the crime even with regard to those who have participated in the crime itself; and, if there has been a conviction, the marriage ceases its execution and criminal effects."

"Meaning? Speak clearly, Pippo," Father asks.

"It means that once they are married, the crime is legally

annulled and the girl's honor is reestablished," he answers, slamming the book shut with much more energy than required.

"And you call that justice?" Father asks, as if he really was curious to hear the answer. Mother puts a hand on Father's arm. She has always been the one to talk and she is not happy sitting here in silence.

"It's the law," Vitale snaps sharply.

"The law was made to save that piece of shit and to condemn an honest girl? If that is the case, the law should be changed."

"Would you like to modify it yourself, Salvo? Is that why you got up early this morning?" He smiles, but soon turns serious again. "If you want to convict Paternò you first need to put the Criminal Code on trial," he says, thumping the book with his knuckles.

Father looks down at the blue book and scratches his head as if he were contemplating something incomprehensible.

"And anyway, if you think about it," the maresciallo goes on, "the rule was designed to defend honest girls, to guarantee they would be married and make sure they weren't abandoned and left empty-handed by those who wanted to take advantage of them. After all, you know better than me how these things work: young people who don't want a marriage arranged by their parents end up using the *fuitina* as a way to marry whoever they want."

Mother swivels her eyes toward the window and holds a

hand up to her throat. She is probably thinking of her journey across the Strait, her stomach heaving with seasickness.

"It might happen when families don't have the money for the service or for the wedding banquet. Sometimes they organize a fake kidnapping. What if the groom changes his mind? What happens to the honest girl, as you put it? She ends up alone and dishonored, nobody is held responsible, and she'll never be able to get married. So, the law obliges a man to take responsibility and honor the agreement he entered into."

"But Pippo, I explained this to you before: there was no agreement in this case."

Vitale sits there in silence for a few minutes. The only sound is Mother panting as if she were out of breath after running.

"Salvo, I believe you. I'm absolutely sure of it. I have a daughter, too, a few years younger, and I'm saying the same thing I would say to her. I'm speaking to you as a father and as a friend, not as an agent of the law. That has always been the way between us, and you know it." Father rubs his chin and sighs. "This is why I'm really trying to put myself in your shoes. Do you mind?" He inhales the smoke deeply. "Let's imagine that you manage to pay a lawyer, considering they also ruined your field and killed your animals. That you'll ignore the town gossip, because we all know the real court as far as honor is concerned is that of public opinion. That you'll keep your daughter sheltered at home until the day of the trial, which could be up to a year.

Then there'll be a court case. The girl will have to tell everyone what took place, every little detail of it. The lawyer for the defense will plant a bug in the judge's ear that your daughter was complicit, that she'd already met with him and been intimate with him, do you see? That it wasn't rape but love. You know how it will end? The boat belongs to the person who sails it," he concludes, stubbing yet another cigarette in the ashtray. The ash pillar wager collapses this time as he gesticulates wildly in exclamation.

"Go home and wait." Vitale gets up and walks toward the door. Then he turns to me. "Your father was just a little older than you when he was about to make the biggest mistake of his life. I said the same thing: let time pass, don't rush into things. I'd like to give you the same advice: go home and let your thoughts rest. You have all these crickets in your head, you young things: love, heartthrobs, romance. But do you know what marriage is? It's a contract. A partnership based on reciprocal interest. He maintains you and you are faithful to him and guide him and your children. After the wedding favors, each party takes on their own life. You won't even necessarily meet for meals. A wife is a woman who has found her place in society, and therefore has more freedom. Eventually, if the good Lord makes you a widow, you can do what you like with your life. Anyway, what is a life of solitude for a woman, without a man's embrace? Flesh needs warmth. It's not me saying it, it's nature. Laws come and go, but nature is always true to itself."

When we walk out of the station, the sun scorches our heads more brutally than before. Cosimino has left and the three of us no longer walk arm in arm. Each of us has their own step and their own thoughts. Why was I born a girl? I ask myself. Twenty years ago, Maresciallo Vitale advised Father to break with tradition and denounce his brother's killer rather than continue the blood feud with a bullet, but today he told me to go home and accept the man who hurt me.

Father has lapsed back into silence. Mother walks with her head bowed. I hear her muttering the same phrase over and over: "That is how the world is, was, and always will be." She's right.

51

My head is on fire and the shadowy interior of the house feels like a sanctuary as we step inside. I go to bed. Mother sits in a chair at my bedside and soaks rags in cold water to place on my forehead, which allows me finally to give in to the rising fever and sink into a welcome state of oblivion.

There's a knock at the door. "Don't let anyone in, Salvo. They're only coming to watch the show," Mother roars.

I can feel her on tenterhooks beside me, like a she-lion guarding a den with her cubs in it. "The priest, the carabiniere, the matchmaker . . . they all want to say their piece. I can see now that you're wise never to open your mouth," she says to Father.

She closes the shutters to keep the heat out. I may be hallucinating because of the fever but I have never heard her speak like this.

"After all my efforts to bring my girls up properly, what have I ended up with? One daughter walled up in her house by a bastard and another one ruined by a brute."

She takes the compress off my forehead, dips it in a basin at her feet, wrings it in her hands, and puts it back, nice and cold again.

"We've lost everything: our land, our animals, our dignity. What's left for us?"

I feel the strength draining out of my body, her voice reaching me as if in a dream.

"When I first came here, many years ago, I was an outsider. I did everything I could to be accepted but it's no use. It's like trying to straighten a dog's legs. We must get away from this place. We need to leave and never return."

Father comes closer and sits next to my bed. My eyelids are heavy. I manage to open a narrow slit.

"Amalia," he says, holding her face in his hands. "The sinner flees, not the sinned."

"You heard the maresciallo, didn't you?"

"Pippo Vitale told us what we already knew. But Oliva is still young, we sent her to school, and now we need to listen to her."

I have no thoughts and no voice. My eyes are throbbing and I can hardly make out what they're saying. I hear steps moving around the room and then nothing, like when Cosimino and I slept in our twin beds and, before falling asleep, I would imagine being onstage at the patron saint festival with my angel wings tied to my shoulders. "Sing, Olì, sing!" Mother shouts from the crowd. I take a big breath through my nostrils, fill my chest, and push the air up to my throat but my mouth is stubbornly mute. Everybody is looking at me. The girls in the choir smile with satisfaction: I don't deserve the solo. The music starts up again. I count the beats until I have to come in, and prepare to project my voice, but nothing comes out. They're all in front of me: Father, Cosimino, and even Fortunata, beautiful and proud, her blond hair piled up on her head like the singer Mina, sending kisses with her fingers and singing *Le mille bolle blu*. "Oliva," Mother pleads. "Sing!"

I can't produce a sound. Mrs. Scibetta and her daughters clap offbeat. Saro looks disappointed. I thought you were the best but you've gone and ruined yourself, he says, and walks off. Then a woman in a low-cut dress and hair flowing below her shoulders steps up onto the stage. To begin with, I think it's Miss Rosaria, but when she turns around, I see it is Liliana. She smiles at me and walks up to the microphone. The crowd in the piazza quiets down to a hush. All I can hear is a voice calling me.

"Oliva, Oliva, Olì!"

52

ow are you feeling, Oliva?" Liliana brushes my forehead with her lips and sits on the chair Mother was sitting in before. "Lucky your fever has gone down. It must have been heatstroke," she says, crossing her legs with her dress over her knees.

"How's school?" I ask, staring at her perfectly formed white kneecap. She smiles and with one hand pulls back the loose hair covering her face. I put all my weight on my elbows and push myself up into a sitting position. Liliana hands me the glass of water from my bedside table. As she lifts the glass, I catch a glimpse of the pale roundness of her breast through the armhole of her dress.

"You need to be careful how you dress," I scold her.

"Careful? What of?" she says, smiling again.

"I was buttoned up to my neck with my mother's shawl covering my head and look what happened to me. You're asking for trouble like that."

Liliana looks down at her dress and starts picking at one of the pink flowers as if she'd dropped food on it and was rubbing it off.

"If someone says something offensive to me on the street, is that my fault?"

She sounds just like her father, with those little questions that mean something without actually saying what it is, so I decide to answer her even though I'm still feeling weak and I don't really feel like talking.

"If you go out dressed like that, and the only thing that happens is that somebody says something offensive to you, you're already lucky. I had every single thing I had ripped from me by force, without having done anything wrong..."

Liliana stops scratching at the flower on her dress and starts looking at a fingernail as if it had just vanished under her skin.

"So you're saying it should have happened to me instead of you? What have I done wrong?"

"You and your father are good at putting words into people's mouths."

I don't want to give her the satisfaction of seeing me cry so I stifle my tears before they come. My face is so congested that I feel the fever rising again. "I didn't deserve it" is the only thing I manage to say.

"No, Oliva, you're wrong..."

An uncontrollable sob rises from my chest and I let out a long wail.

"You're wrong," she says again, wiping my face with the handkerchief Mother left on the bedside table. "Nobody deserves it. Whether you're buttoned up or dressed provocatively, whether you're God-fearing or an atheist, the fault lies with the man."

"You don't get it," I answer, still heaving with sobs. "Men don't have feelings. Miss Rosaria was wrong. They're not like us: for men, love is a sick quivering of the flesh that needs release. Women either defend themselves or become accomplices."

Liliana shakes her head. "What did you just tell me? That my dress is short and low-cut?" She looks at her dress as if she were checking. "Do you see? We're just as bad: too short, too long, too provocative. We parrot men's words rather than try to change them. What happened to you has nothing to do with love. Love is not imposed, it's exchanged . . ."

I interrupt her before she can go on. "You go to school," I say. "Next year you'll graduate as an elementary school teacher: you know lots of things but, luckily for you, you know nothing about this!"

I can't look her in the face. I am ashamed of how I judged her based on her dress and her hairstyle and I turn to face the wall.

Liliana strokes my hand. "You did the right thing to go to the carabinieri," she says after a while. "You're using your terrible situation to help others. Just think of all the unhappy marriages, all the abuse, all the tragedies there are out there!" Her voice sounds like Miss Rosaria when she used to praise me for being the first to complete my grammar exercises.

"You're wrong. I only went there because my foot was aching," I declare, pointing to the broken shoe on the pile of things to throw away in a corner of the room. "Anyway, Maresciallo Vitale didn't exactly give me a round of applause. He was about to throw us out. He told us that you need money to get a lawyer, that we would have to go through a trial, that I would have to submit to a physical examination and mortifying questions. That I am the one that needs to prove my innocence, that in this case the man is in the right, that the law is on his side, and that if I don't marry him, it is my loss."

"It's his loss if he goes to jail," she says impetuously, raising the hand that she has been squeezing as if I had won a prize.

"Jail? People with money are always innocent. His father is well-connected." I free my hand from hers and cover my eyes with it. "The maresciallo is right: I was flattered, he made me feel like the fairest of them all. Vanity is the daughter of . . ."

"He looked at you and you felt you were beautiful? So what?"

"It's not proper."

"Why not?"

"That's enough!" I cover my ears. "Stop it. I didn't want him to do what he did."

"That's precisely the point, Oliva. You didn't want it! It's one thing to look at someone and another to take them by force. You're a girl, not a chicken in a coop. Do you remember the evening I brought you your photo? 'Shoo! Shoo!' you said to the poor creatures, hoping they would run free, but what did they do? Without so much as a cluck, they strutted back into their cage. Is that what you want to do?"

I turn my head and look at the bedstead.

"That photo no longer exists, that girl no longer exists. You don't get it, do you?" I yell at her. "I may be a chicken, but you're more stubborn than a mule."

"What, me? Me?" Liliana crosses her arms and uncrosses her legs. If she walks out of this room, I will be alone in the world. She puts her weight on the arms of the chair and starts lifting herself up.

"Me?" I imitate her, pulling a face. She stops halfway up. *"Me-aw, ee-aw,"* I bray, pulling myself up in the bed. She sits down again, looking at me quizzically. *"Ee-aw, ee-aw, ee-aw!"* I whinny, shaking my head like a mule. She stares at me, flinches, as if I might butt her or even bite her. *"Ee-aw, ee-aw, ee-aw."* I leap out of bed, pulling the sheet over my head, and start bucking.

Liliana smiles and jumps up herself, grabbing a corner of the sheet, pulling it off the bed, and draping it over her shoulders. "If I'm a mule, then you're a dumb sheep: *baa, baa, baa.*"

"Well, you croak like a frog: *ribbit, ribbit, ribbit.*"

"Moo." Liliana follows me, laughing.

"Gobble, gobble," I answer, throwing a pillow at her head.

We chase each other around the room imitating all the animals in the universe. Then Liliana raises a closed fist in the air and yells, "Freedom, freedom for all creatures in the kingdom!"

We chant these words marching around the room and

then we jump on the bed, windmilling our arms, until we collapse together on the mattress.

Mother rushes in, throwing the door wide open, and sees us wrapped up in a tangle of sheets on the bed.

"What's going on here? Have you opened a harem?" She looks to me anxiously. "You're better," she says softly. "Pull yourself together. There's someone out there who wants a word with you."

53

Liliana's father, Calò, looks smaller than when he used to hold his meetings in the fishing hut, as if his bones had shrunk. He removes his glasses with a certain aplomb and wipes them with a square of cloth that he pulls out of his pocket. My parents are observing him from the other end of the table. Cosimino is out.

"I'm pleased to see you are recovered," he says in that reedy voice of his. "Liliana has been coming every day to check on your progress."

"I'm sorry to have troubled you," I answer, looking at my friend out of the corner of my eye as she holds the collar of her dress closed with her hands.

"You must know, Oliva, that you are not alone. We are a small community but when one of us is in need, we lend one another a hand."

I think of the stares we received as we walked through the piazza under the blazing sun and bite my lower lip.

"I was telling your parents that last time I was in Naples for a Party meeting, I had the opportunity to meet a comrade who deals with women's matters . . ."

"Oliva has a mother," Mother interrupts brusquely.

"Of course she does. That's not the issue here," he answers gently. "I'm asking you simply to be so kind as to listen for a few minutes, after which you can arrive at your own conclusions, as is just and right."

Mother twists her hands and looks out the window at the arid lot stripped of all its plants.

"As I was saying, before coming to see you I took the liberty of contacting this comrade. Her name is Maddalena Criscuolo, and I presented your case to her. She assured me that she would be able to find a lawyer who is an expert in this field."

"Antonino," Father answers. "I thank you for your interest but right now we don't have any money to spend."

"You don't need to worry about this, Salvo," Calò replies. He inspects his glasses to make sure they are clean and calmly puts them back on. "You wouldn't have to pay."

"He'll want something from us, won't he?" Mother asks suspiciously. "Why would this person go to all this trouble without compensation?"

"He does it because it is the right thing," he answers plainly.

"The right and the just end up in the ditch," Mother rebuts, sighing.

Calò's expression is flat, like when he used to listen to everyone's point of view during his meetings in silence. He scratches at the little beard that covers his chin.

"There are very few girls who are brave enough to accuse someone of rape, and do you know why? Because of fear, shame, or ignorance. Most people think it is best to avoid the scandal and, rather than charging the rapist, they condemn their daughter to spend her whole life married to him. Or they hunt down the rapist and put a hole in his head with a rifle. After a few years in jail, they walk free because the vendetta was to restore their daughter's honor. These laws are the result of an antiquated mentality. They were acceptable to our grandparents, perhaps, but not to our daughters. One walnut in a sack doesn't make any noise, it's true, but if there are several . . . This is the only way to change things."

"Signor Calò," Mother interrupts him impatiently. "Let's be frank: I don't want to start any trouble, nor do I want to send my daughter to fight other people's battles. And anyway, Maresciallo Vitale made it quite clear that the law . . ."

"How are families doing nowadays, Amalia? Children pop out like loaves: all you need is water, yeast, and flour. They come when they come and if a woman can't afford another child, what can she do? Have an abortion. But the church says it's a sin and the state says it's a crime, so she ends up going to a back-alley butcher in secret and sometimes she doesn't make it back home because she dies of an infection or bleeds out on the table. When husband and wife don't get along, what happens? They carry on living unhappily under the same roof, weaving a web of deception and subterfuge. I know lots of decent family men who juggle two or three families at the same time. Honor killings and rape-marriage laws may be in the Criminal Code but does that make these laws right?"

"Are we supposed to straighten out these wrong laws, Calò?" Mother asks. "Politicians should be doing that but, as they say, the heads agree and the tails fight. No one from up there has ever come down here to help us. But I'm an ignorant woman and I don't know much about anything!"

"But you know your daughter," Liliana says, coming to sit down next to me on the wooden bench. "Things are not what they used to be and we young people are different from the way you were. We're not resigned to accepting things just because they've always been that way. One no, on its own, can change a life. Many noes put together can change the world."

Mother doesn't answer but stares at her as if she were still a little girl reading from a book without understanding the words. For a moment, nobody knows how to continue the conversation. Then Father's voice breaks the silence.

"What you're saying is very noble, Antonino. You are involved in politics and your daughter is studying to be a teacher, while I consider myself lucky to know how to write my own name. One thing I can say for sure, though, is that if my daughter needs help, I'm in." He places his hands palms up on the table and looks at Mother. She sighs, closing her eyes, and nestles her hands in his, followed by Calò, then by Liliana. They look like the Knights of the Round Table that my teacher Mrs. Terlizzi used to tell us about.

"It's your decision, Oliva," Father says. "Speak without any fear: Do you want to take Pino Paternò to be your lawfully wedded husband in reparation for the damage he has done to you?"

I bring my hands out from under the table, open them, and slowly place them alongside the others. The words rise up from my stomach like the nausea that has remained lodged inside me since that terrible day and they come out of my mouth loud and clear.

"No," I say. "I do not."

And as I utter these words, I realize that they are the only thing I am certain of.

54

It's late by the time Cosimino gets home, and we have already eaten. He looks distraught, with dark bags under his eyes. Since we split up in the piazza, he hasn't come home once, not even to sleep. As soon as Mother sees him, her hand flies to her throat and she rushes to the stove. She doesn't say a thing. All she wants is for him to have some food, sit down at the table, and eat what she has cooked for him and what she will always cook for him until a woman whom he will call his wife comes along to take her place.

"I'm not hungry, Mà," he says, fobbing her off and vanishing into his room. Cosimino's lack of appetite, his gaunt expression, nights spent away who knows where. These, too, are the price to pay for going against the current. I toss and turn in my bed, unable to sleep. "Can you tell me a story to go to sleep?" he used to ask me when we were little. "A story, now? Go to sleep, it's late," I'd answer, giving myself airs. "The story of Giufà," he'd beg. "I can't remember it," I would lie. "Giufà and the refried tripe!" "I told you that one last night." "Giufà and the stolen cooking pot, then!" "I told you that one the night before last." I would lie there in silence but as soon as I thought he was about ready to give up, I would say, "I've just remembered one I read this morning in Miss Rosaria's book," and then begin, "Once upon a time . . ." until I heard his breathing grow deeper.

I hear steps in the corridor. "Are you asleep?" he asks me from behind the door. "When am I ever asleep? Come in." I drape my dressing gown over my shoulders.

Cosimino is wearing the same clothes as when he came home. Come here and lie down next to me, I would like to say to him, and I will tell you the story of Giufà and the brigands. But I don't say anything and he stands awkwardly at the head of the bed. "I've been at Saro's house these past few days," he tells me without my asking. "Nardina sends her love. She says come and see her."

"Send her mine, when you next see her," I answer.

How many years have passed by since he was scared of the dark and used to ask me to tell him stories to go to sleep? "Nardina says you're doing the right thing." The words come out of him like oil from the grindstone, drop by drop. He needs the force of an olive press to extract each word. "She says you mustn't pay any attention to what people say, that you should go your own way. That it's not your fault, that you're the victim."

The mustache, the cream-colored suit, the hair combed back with pomade: all to prove that he is a man, but the effort these words require make him a child again in my eyes. Being male, I realize, has its own difficulties. "Okay, Cosimino. I get the message. Have a good night."

He doesn't move. Maybe he is still scared of going to sleep like when he was nine years old. He stands under the arch of the door. "Saro says you're right not to accept that man."

Saro says, Nardina says. What about you? I would like to ask him. What do you think? But I don't ask him, maybe because I don't want to know and I really don't care what anybody thinks anymore. "Saro says marriage shouldn't be won by force." He takes a step toward me as if he is about to sit on the edge of my bed, stops, then inches backward again. "And girls are like clouds, that's what he said. That you need to watch what shape they make and should never try to force them into a mold."

Recalling the twin-horned marfoyle, my mouth curls up at the corners into a smile. "And how did you respond to that?"

"Me?" His cheeks burn red.

"I asked him . . . if he would marry a woman in that condition." He looks down at the ground. "A woman who has been dishonored, I mean," he says, correcting himself.

Girls are jugs, Mother says.

Finally, he looks up and our eyes meet. "And do you know what he said?"

I shake my head. I don't know.

"'I would throw myself at her feet, on the spot.' That's what he said."

55

I go to Sunday Mass in my everyday clothes rather than my Sunday best. There's nothing left for me to celebrate. When it's time to line up to take communion Don Ignazio looks at a loss. I make things easy for him and stay in my place. "You go," I encourage Mother. She turns and looks at the other women, about to get up to go to the altar, then changes her mind and stays with me in the wooden pew.

At the exit, my old friends gather. Some turn to look back at me. Tindara leaves the huddle of girls, comes up to me, and kisses me on both cheeks.

"Wednesday's my birthday, remember?"

"I wish you many happy returns," I say.

"We're having orangeade and almond cakes, I'm only inviting my closest friends, will you come?"

"I'm sorry but I have a previous engagement," I answer tersely. I have no desire to be the laughingstock of the party.

Tindara looks disappointed. "Wedding preparations do take it out of you, don't they?" she says sympathetically. "There's still a month to go before mine and I'm already done in. I don't know what shape my husband will find me in," she titters, covering her mouth with her hands.

I feel numb. What wedding? What husband?

"You mustn't take any notice of them," she says, glancing at the clutch of girls behind us. "They're just jealous because we're getting married and they're not. They'll always find something to say, right? First of all, they went on about my marriage being arranged, then they got bored of that and started searching for something else to pick at, like cats with tripe. Luckily for them, you threw them a bone. But you and I can tell it as it is: they're so provincial! I told them you were doing the right thing by playing hard to get. He was going far too fast and you made him slow down to a snail's pace. I'd add an extra clause in the contract while you're at it: his pockets are well-lined, his family owns the pastry shop here, and he even has some business in the city!"

I twist my arm out from under hers. They all believe I'm holding out to raise the stakes. They would rather I sold myself than be left on the shelf. Being money-hungry is acceptable, but being disgraced and unmarried is not.

"What's wrong?" Tindara asks, a little shocked. "I'm on your side. If we girlfriends don't stick together, who is ever going to be a friend?"

"I wish you all the best, Tindara, for your birthday and everything else," I say, waving at her and catching up with Mother, who has started walking up the big road. Tindara rejoins the huddle of friends and they start chattering. I walk away without saying goodbye. I no longer belong to the group. I no longer belong to anyone.

56

iliana comes to open the door. "Come in. They're here!" she announces happily, as if she were inviting us to a reception. Father takes off his hat and steps inside. I follow. Calò is seated at the table in the dining room next to a woman with short dark chestnut hair. As soon as I walk into the room, she gets up and comes toward me. I see she is wearing trousers, like a man.

"Here you are, finally," she says, as if she hasn't seen me for ages and missed me. She opens her arms, rests them on my shoulders, and pulls me into an embrace. I feel my blood run cold and hold my breath: since what happened, I haven't liked being touched. She feels my chest contract to hold my breath in and lets go. She takes a step back and holds my face in her hands.

"Antonino has told me so much about you that I feel like I know you," she says, as if she were justifying herself. "But you probably don't know anything about me." Her teeth are big and white. "My name is Maddalena Criscuolo and I'm a member of the Union of Italian Women."

I told Miss Rosaria that the feminine singular didn't exist. One way or another, women have to act together.

"Are you a lawyer?" I ask, in awe.

"I'm not, no." She smiles again and looks at Calò. Maybe she thought I would be brighter. "I'm a militant campaigner."

"What does that mean? Are you in the military?" I'm embarrassed to ask.

"Being militant means campaigning actively to improve people's lives," she explains, as if I were a little girl. "We are fighting on many different fronts," she says, looking at Father, who is engaged in tracing the grains of Calò's wooden table with his finger. "For divorce, for abortion rights, and defending women who are victims of violence."

At the words *divorce* and *abortion*, Father furrows his brow and crosses his arms over his chest.

"I thought we were supposed to talk to a lawyer," I say, looking at Father and attempting to justify our confusion. He looks up and knocks the table twice with his knuckles.

"Sabella is on his way," Maddalena reassures us. "First, I wanted a few minutes to get to know you, Oliva, and talk a little, woman to woman."

What does she want to know? What do we have to say to each other? A wave of fatigue washes over me, more overpowering than ever. My legs, my back, my shoulders, my thoughts are all tired, it feels as though the weight of all the words that I have heard since what happened are pressing down on my body, as if my whole skeleton is folding in on itself. Everyone seems to know more than me, they all have a ready answer, and yet nobody has once asked me how I feel. I press my hands into the back of the chair where Father has gone back to contemplating the table.

"Come into my room," Liliana proposes. "You'll be more comfortable there."

Maddalena and I follow her into her room: there are even more books on her desk than before, and more photographs, too. There's an open folder on a shelf with pictures in it that Liliana has taken.

"Calò told me his daughter was a good photographer," Maddalena begins, looking around the room. I don't make any comment. "What do you do? Are you still at school?"

"I finished the second year of teacher training but then I left."

I flip through the pictures in the folder and pick out the faces of the people in the town, one by one.

"Didn't you like school?" she asks.

Nardina in front of Don Ciccio's haberdasher's store, the fat Scibetta sister coming out of church with an ivory veil embroidered by Mother covering her head, Nellina outside the sacristy . . . What can possibly give her pleasure in these faces printed on glossy paper when she will bump into them every time she sets foot outside the house? I would pay anything not to meet them ever again.

"I did like it," I answer. "But it is not proper for a girl to know too much, Mother says. And anyway, after what happened . . ."

"Would you like to go back?" she asks.

"It is too late," I murmur. "What's done is done." I think

of Latin lessons with Mrs. Terlizzi, and of when I still believed that chanting *rosa, rosae, rosae* would work as a magic spell to keep evil at bay.

"You could get your diploma as a private candidate and then get a job as an elementary school teacher. Have you ever thought of doing that?"

"My father had a heart attack, what little land we had and the animals we bred were taken away from us. I get along by helping with the embroidery. Mother says I am quite good at it."

Maddalena doesn't answer. She flips through an album with red binding. She looks so focused that I don't know whether she has heard a word I've said. I start looking at the pictures with her: they're all portraits of women.

"I wanted to talk to you in private, Oliva," she says eventually, "because the lawyer will ask you things you won't want to talk about. He will ask you these things because it will help him help you. The more details you can give him, the better chance you have."

"What will they do to him?" I ask, my eyes fixed on Liliana's photos.

"He'll be accused of abduction and rape."

"The maresciallo said no one would believe me and the judge will let him off."

"It can happen," she answers. "Sabella is good but I can't guarantee the outcome. If you want to go ahead with this, it's for yourself so that the truth will come out."

I feel a stab in my stomach: I don't know whether I'm in

favor of truth now. The truth is that I often felt my heart race when I saw him at the bottom of the road waiting for me to walk by. The truth is that I was disappointed if he wasn't there, if he didn't follow me with his gaze as far as the junction with the dirt track that would lead me home.

Maddalena turns the leaves of the album and I suddenly see Mother: she's wearing the shawl she gave me the day I was abducted.

"I liked going to school because I knew all the answers. Now I don't know any. People expect to see me at the altar and maybe she would be happy to see me there," I say, pointing at the photo. "My brother would like me to marry Saro, a childhood friend, but he would be taking me in out of pity and I don't want to make his life a misery. Not to mention the fact that I would be putting him and his family in danger. They would end up having to pay for a mistake I made. And then there is Father. If I pull out now, he will be disappointed. There are too many humiliations, there is too much ill will, in this story. It might even have contributed to his weak heart."

My legs are shaking and I'm so ashamed I can't look her in the face.

"I have put so many people out for a mistake that was mine as much as it was his. This is the truth: I'm not brave and I'm not an example to anyone."

Maddalena takes my hand and places it on the photograph of Mother.

"Bravery is like a plant," she says. "You need to cultivate

it, find soil for it to grow in with sufficient sunlight, you need to water it. Two people witness a crime and recognize the killer: he's from a powerful family. What do they do? Do they go and denounce him or do they hold their tongues? If they are certain they'll be victims of a vendetta, they'll go home and play dumb. Nobody is a hero on their own. That's why the lawyer and I came here. Not to urge you to take action but to assure you that, if you want, you can."

For a while, neither of us says anything. From the window we can hear Mina on the radio singing "Renato." The chorus repeats, fades, and then the song comes to an end.

"What about you? How are you doing?" Maddalena asks me out of the blue. The only question I have never been asked has finally arrived. I stare at the picture in front of me.

"I don't know," I say, as if I were confessing this to the photo. "I can't even remember what I was like before."

Maddalena listens in silence as I caress Mother's face, wrinkle by wrinkle, heartache by heartache. That is how Liliana finds us when she sticks her head around the door.

"The lawyer's here," she announces.

57

He's sitting at the head of the table. He has a black leather briefcase from which he pulls out a few sheets and lays them out on the table.

"To begin with, I'd like to go through what happened," he says when I have sat down next to Father. "Let's reenact the events that took place on the evening of the second of July," he says, without further ado.

"There's not much to say," Father starts. "Oliva was abducted by a young man of ill repute. Everyone in town knows he's dirty . . ."

"That's not important," the lawyer interrupts, looking down at his handwritten notes, the penmanship tight but legible.

"What do you mean, it's not important?" Father asks, deflated. He glares at Calò as if he has been conned.

"Let me explain, Mr. Denaro." The lawyer takes his glasses off and runs his hand through his hair. "The judge is not interested in who the defendant is. They want to know what they did and if they did it."

Father brings a hand up to his temples. "So this is the law, is it? Someone in the right has to defend themselves against someone who has sinned?"

"There's no such thing as a sinner under the law: you

are either innocent or guilty, until you are proved otherwise," Sabella explains. Father hangs his head in silence. Calò and Liliana look embarrassed and, for a moment, I pity him because he finds it hard to express himself. I feel like fleeing from this place, running like mad like I used to after reciting the Rosary at the Scibettas'. Instead, I turn toward Maddalena and remember what we just said to each other in Liliana's bedroom.

"May I say something?" I say timidly. Everyone turns to look at me except the lawyer, who places a blank sheet in front of him and holds his fountain pen poised.

"Please do," he answers without looking at me but preparing to take notes. My heart beats so hard in my chest that I'm scared the thuds will echo around the room. Words have always been my friends but now I can't find them. They have run off. When I jumped to defend Saro or Miss Rosaria it was one thing but now I'm speaking up for myself. I begin but the words dissolve in my mouth because uttering them means reliving what happened, except that this time it is in front of everyone and I have nowhere to hide. I bring a hand to my chest and start torturing a button on my blouse, just like I used to with the buttonhole of my black pinafore when I had an oral test at school. I close my eyes and, all of a sudden, I'm in front of the teacher's desk. She is right there and all my classmates are watching. I have studied everything in depth, I know every single detail, and as usual I will get full marks. I take a deep breath and the words trip out one after another as if I were talking about someone else. As if I were no longer me.

"This is how it went: it was the day of my sixteenth birthday and I was walking home at dusk. I was alone."

Rosa, rosae, rosae, the magic spell is working again. The lawyer looks at me gravely and jots something down on the sheet in front of him. Every now and again, he arches one of his eyebrows but I have no idea what this expression on his face means, or whether he does it out of compassion or as a reproach. Liliana is pale. She has never heard my story, either.

"After a few days, I wasn't able to keep count, I dragged myself to the door and banged on it with what little strength I had left. I begged him to come back, just as he had said I would."

I can't face looking at Father so I keep my eyes firmly on the lawyer, who carries on writing, the nib of his fountain pen scratching the paper. Maddalena concentrates on a spot on the table: she must be disappointed, of course. She would never have given in to her abductor. She would have preferred to die of hunger, thirst, and fear rather than call out his name and beg him to come back. My voice breaks but I manage to get to the end of my account, to the carabinieri's voices, him running away, Father's shadow coming toward me through the trees.

When I finally stop talking, there is complete silence in the room. Even the fountain pen has lost its voice. Then the crashing of pots and pans in the kitchen breaks the spell:

it is Fina come to get lunch ready. Life carries on as usual for everyone else as if nothing has happened. Everything was easy before, even for me! The familiar clattering of crockery, thoughts flitting here and there, days going by comfortably in the slow motion of boredom. All this has been replaced with fear, which grips my throat as soon as I wake up in the morning and which often keeps me company even at night.

"Did anyone see you on the evening of the abduction?" Sabella asks, lifting his pen in readiness. The road was deserted, it was almost dinnertime, the storekeepers were closing up. Suddenly I remember the steps behind me, my heart missing a beat, and then Tindara's father nodding in recognition, overtaking me, and vanishing.

"Santino Crisafulli walked past at that very moment," I answer. "Maybe he heard something."

Maddalena nods and clasps her hands in front of her.

"I'm sorry," I add, since no one else was saying anything, "for all this trouble. I didn't believe that looking at someone or talking to someone would lead to anything so terrible."

The lawyer takes his glasses off. "Signorina," he says, looking at me sternly. "You don't need to apologize, and you shouldn't feel sorry, because you've done nothing wrong. Even if you had been betrothed to this . . . young man . . ." I shake my head vigorously in denial and he carries on. "Even if you had, as they say, encouraged him, even if you had been interested in him, I'll go as far as saying even if you had been engaged . . ." I twist my fingers until I feel sufficient pain to assuage the emotions raging inside me. "The only question is the following: Did you or did you not consent to relations with Paternò? Were you in a position to choose freely whether to accept his advances, or were you coerced out of exhaustion, hunger, intimidation, physical force, or humiliation?"

"I didn't want to, but . . ."

"There are different kinds of violence," Maddalena intervenes, finally. "There's physical violence and psychological violence: you suffered both. You didn't choose to go with him of your own free will, you were forced to do so against your wishes. That is not love, it's coercion."

Fina comes in with coffee. As she passes, she puts her arm around my shoulders. Sabella blows on the dark, frothy brew, knocks it back in one swig, and sets the cup back down on the table. He gathers his papers meticulously, places them all into a gray folder, slides them back into his leather briefcase, and gets up.

"As far as I'm concerned, Oliva, it's cut-and-dried. But the ultimate decision is up to you, in agreement with your parents, of course, since you are a minor. If you decide to go ahead as plaintiffs in the suit against Paternò, I'm willing to represent you as your attorney, pro bono of course, no charge."

I turn to Maddalena but she's busy talking to Liliana. So I go up to the lawyer and follow him into the hall. I lean on the wall, hanging my head. "It's not your fault, Oliva," Sabella says as he leaves. "You're just a girl."

58

Maresciallo Vitale filled in the required form, hardly saying a word. As we were leaving, he put a hand on Father's shoulder. We walked home by way of the side streets, and then I locked myself in the house and didn't step out again. Worse than Fortunata.

I wanted to send him to jail and I have ended up there myself. My days are always the same. My parents are scared of leaving me alone and go out as little as possible themselves. Pietro Pinna goes to market to sell our frogs and snails in our place: once people found out that we had pressed charges, they didn't trust Father anymore. Cosimino does a few odd jobs here and there but often ends up waiting for the days to go by with us.

One day the sun shines, another it's raining, when it's windy I stand at the window and watch the leaves as they float and draw shapes in the air. I take courage and venture out only at night: a corner of Father's land has survived the destruction and he has replanted a few vegetables.

Whenever there is a knock at the door, Mother's hands fly to her cheeks in terror and she instinctively pulls back. There are no more visits these days and we fear that, after the field and the chickens, we are next on their list. She peers through the spyhole.

"There's a woman in trousers and a boy's haircut," she says.

Maddalena comes in and hugs both of us. "I really wanted to meet you, dear Amalia." Mother shies away at first but then she remembers her manners and invites Maddalena to sit in the kitchen. She is carrying a heavy bag.

"Here you are," she says, opening it in front of us.

"More books: just what we need," Mother comments in Calabrian, adding behind our backs as we go into my bedroom, "We'll eat them for lunch between slices of bread."

Maddalena sits at my desk. My room feels more spacious, as if her presence has made it bigger. She looks through the books still in a pile in the corner and nods.

"You like reading, huh?"

"My teacher at elementary school gave them to me. I must have read some of them four or five times."

"These aren't novels, though," she says, pulling books out of her bag and arranging them on my shelf. I read the labels on the homemade colored-paper jackets: Italian, math, history, geography, Latin.

"I'm done with school," I object.

"You can continue on your own, doing exercises at home. Liliana, who's a little ahead of you now, can tutor you. She got hold of the books for you. You could take your teaching diploma as a private candidate and then you'll be able to work without having to depend on your parents or . . ." She pauses for a moment. "Or anyone else."

I run my fingers over the spines: I used to love putting

my black pinafore on, walking to school with Liliana, going to lessons, coming back home, sitting at my desk studying quietly. Maybe, if I started again, the days would be divided into hours, time would be divided into days, and my imprisonment would come to an end sooner.

"I don't know whether I'm up to it," I confess.

"I wasn't up to many of the things that I then went on to do," she answers, her straight white teeth gleaming as she smiles. "When I was twenty, a group of comrades and I got it into our heads to organize trains to transport poor children to wealthier families in the north. Do you know what people said? That Communists eat babies. But we went ahead anyway. Lots of women trusted us and sent us their children."

"Would you like a glass of almond milk with mint, Dr. Maddalena?" Mother asks, popping her head around the door.

"Thank you, Amalia. I'd love some." Maddalena gets up and we go back into the kitchen together. "I never went to university, though, so don't call me Dr."

"I saw you had lots of books," Mother says defensively.

"I earned a diploma as an elementary school teacher and I teach children," Maddalena explains.

"I thought you were involved in politics," Mother remarks.

"We are all involved in politics, one way or another," she answers. "Everything is politics: our choices, what we are willing or unwilling to do for ourselves and for others . . ."

Mother lines up three glasses, pouring the milky syrup in, and adds water. "It must be easier to do things for others living in a big city with a job for life and no worries about where your next meal is coming from . . ." she comments, stirring the drinks noisily. "I was born and brought up in a city, too." Mother closes her eyes as if she were trying to conjure an image from years ago. "Then I met Salvo. He wasn't much older than Oliva is now. I left on a whim and traveled in secret with him to this town." She opens her eyes and looks around. "We ran away because my parents didn't approve of the match. Twenty years ago, young people had no choice. *Fuitina* was the only way. Nowadays, on the other hand . . ." She darts a look at me and places a saucer under each glass. "Laws that were acceptable back then are worthless now. Things move on, and now saints have to pay, not assassins."

She picks a few leaves off the plant in the pot on the windowsill and rinses them under the faucet. The smell of fresh mint fills the kitchen. "I married for love, with no dowry and no wedding chest, and the children came straightaway. Fortunata came first, and then, four years later, Oliva and Cosimino. What can you do for others when you have three children to feed? You can hardly keep up with their needs. You were right not to get married. At least you are free." She tinkles the spoon inside the glass and watches the mint leaves sink into the almond milk.

Maddalena lifts the glass up to her lips and takes a sip.

"Actually, I have a daughter who is just a little older than Oliva," she says, placing the glass back onto its saucer.

Mother checks Maddalena's hand for a wedding ring. She notices and closes her fist.

"I got pregnant when I was eighteen, the father said he knew nothing about it and that it wasn't his."

Mother picks up the bottle of syrup, puts it on the sideboard, and comes and sits next to her.

"It's for the best, I thought. I'll bring her up on my own. During the pregnancy, I went to stay with an aunt in the countryside because my father wanted to keep it a secret. But I could feel her growing inside me and I imagined what her life would be like."

"Then what happened?" Mother asks, gripping her glass.

"They took her away without telling me as soon as she was born. They gave her to a couple who wanted kids but couldn't have them."

The silence that falls in the room is broken by the crack of broken glass. Mother's hand flies to her breast as she watches the white almond juice spill over the tablecloth. "Look at that. I've made such a mess," she exclaims, her eyes bright, leaping up to get a dishcloth. Maddalena and I get up, too, and pick up the shards of glass. "I'm so sorry, I'm so sorry," she keeps saying, wringing her hands. She gestures at us to sit down, meaning she wants to clean up her own mess.

Maddalena goes on picking the pieces of glass out of the

sticky liquid. "We women need to help one another," she says. "We have all messed up something in our lives."

We dance around the kitchen table and, in no time at all, the splinters of glass are all gone.

"When Antonino Calò told me what had happened to you," Maddalena starts, having sat down at the table again, "I wanted to come and meet you to tell you that you shouldn't be afraid: one woman's story is every woman's. When they took my daughter away, I stayed with my aunt in the countryside for more than a year. I didn't want to see anyone. I thought it was my fault that my life had come to an end."

"Did you ever manage to get her back?" Mother asks, her face still burning.

"I did some research and found the family that had adopted her. They were good people. They gave her the chance to study. She's at university now, doing mathematics. One day I waited outside her school to see her: she was surrounded by friends, boys and girls. For a second, our eyes met. She left her friends and walked my way. It was as if twenty years had dissolved into nothing and she still stirred in my belly. We were face-to-face but then she walked straight past me and threw herself into the arms of her boyfriend. He had been standing right behind me, having come to pick her up."

"Didn't you say anything to her?" I ask, pulling at my icy fingers.

"She told me everything I needed to know: she was

beautiful, healthy, happy, surrounded by friends, and had a strong pair of arms to support her. That's what I wanted for her. It didn't really matter that I wasn't the one to provide it. What else can we ask of our children, if not that one day they walk straight past us without even seeing us, that they go further than we did, and chart their own course?" Maddalena asks, looking at Mother.

Mother shakes her head, rolls her eyes, and puts her hand in front of her mouth as if she wanted to push all the words back inside.

59

A few days later, Maddalena left town, but she has started to write to us every week. I answer her immediately and ask Cosimino to take my letters to the post office. A letter every seven days is another way to help pass the time.

I keep her letters in the drawer of my desk, tied up with a pink satin snatch left over from a dress Mother had made for the skinny Scibetta sister. One letter, on the other hand, I tore to pieces and threw away. It wasn't from Maddalena but from Franco. When it was delivered and I saw the name on the envelope, I didn't want to read it. I remembered his profile, so similar to Handsome Antonio's, and thought back to the time when I believed that the languorous feeling in my stomach when we kissed behind the toolshed was love. I slit the envelope and took the sheet of paper out. In his letter, he said that he had asked his uncle to write the letter for him and his uncle had agreed. That he regretted every single day not having had the strength to contradict his mother. That he hoped I would be happy with the man who possessed the courage he lacked. All he wanted was for me to be happy and he wished me well. He would never forget me.

I crumpled the sheet into a ball and threw it away. Not out of anger but out of grief.

Liliana comes by every day after school and we do our homework together. Whatever she does in class, I catch up later. I have to catch up on last year's material while keeping up with this year's. At first, Mother didn't like the idea of me sitting the exam alongside the other candidates but then she came around to it and started sewing my dress for the day.

Father and I have started going out to harvest frogs and snails together again, enjoying the silence.

"Pà?" I ask him one overcast morning as we let ourselves back into the house. "Am I on the right path?"

He opens the door, takes his hat off, plops the buckets down near the chest in the hall, and, as usual, doesn't say a word.

"You're my father. Don't you have anything to say?" I push him, impatiently. "What do you do to help?" I shrug my wet jacket off and drop it on the floor. He picks it up slowly and hangs it on the clothes hook.

"What do I do?" He smiles as he squats down near the bucket and starts dividing the big snails from the small.

"You always loved coming into the fields with me and you've never been scared of work, unlike your brother and sister, who always shirked it since they were little."

His hands sift through the shells, which clack against one another gently. What does that have to do with anything? I wonder. He never gives a straight answer. Mother is right.

"Once, I wonder whether you even remember, you must

have been five or six, after two days' rain you came on a walk we'd never done before. On our way home you tripped and fell into an abandoned artesian well. I saw you vanishing down the hole before you had time to open your mouth and yell."

The episode came back to mind instantly as if it were happening right there and then. The cold in my bones, my feet kicking without managing to touch the bottom, the earthy taste of the water in my mouth and nostrils.

"I thought I would drown." I remember everything clearly and rub my arms with my open palms to send the goose bumps away. Then I close my eyes and I feel his strong hands grabbing me, pulling me out of the soft squishy mud, my head finally bursting up for air.

"You saved me," I whisper.

Father pours the big snails, which are worth more at market, into another basin and leaves them to purge. The little ones, the ones the family will eat, remain in the bucket.

"When you survey unexplored fields, it's always better if there are two of you." He sets the empty shells aside to use as fertilizer for the few plants we have left.

"You just asked me what I do. Well, this is what I do," he says as he finishes sorting the snails. "When you trip, I pick you up."

n Christmas Eve, at first light, Nellina comes to the door.

"I'm sorry," Father says, opening the door a chink, "we can't receive any visitors today."

"Why not?" she asks, sounding indignant.

"Because we're worried about our cat, who hasn't come back home."

Missing a beat, she eventually says, "But you've never had a cat."

"Maybe that's why it hasn't come home," he quips.

"Salvo, I know you're always in the mood for a joke but I've come for something important."

"At this hour?" Father continues, keeping her on the doorstep.

"It's about Oliva."

"She's fine, thank you. Do send my regards to Don Ignazio."

Mother intervenes and invites her into the kitchen.

"I've been told to tell you that if you drop your suit," Nellina starts, "the family . . . his family would give Oliva a gift. An important gift," she continues, rubbing her thumb and index finger together under my parents' nose. Cosimino and I listen in to the conversation from the next room.

"They want to bribe you with money," my brother says, smoothing down his mustache. "As if certain things can be settled by opening a wallet. A girl's honor has no price. Neither money nor the law comes anywhere near it. Courts, judges: the whole thing is a farce. If it had been for me, I would have done a lot more than sue them . . ."

I shush him with a finger. The voices are inaudible for a while and then I hear Father's rise above the others.

"Nellina, I think you must have been on your way to the cattle market this morning and lost your way. There is nothing for sale in this house."

Nellina feigns offense but soon regains her composure. "You are saying this now because everything is still fresh in your mind. But think about tomorrow and the next day and all the years to come. The money they're willing to give Oliva will come in useful in the future for her and for you, given that you're not swimming in gold."

The chair scrapes on the floor as Mother jumps to her feet.

"We are not willing even to hear the proposal out, Nellina. God forbid! You're only forgiven for coming here and putting it to us because you have never been blessed with children. Oliva is studying for her diploma to become an elementary school teacher," she says, raising her voice, maybe so that I can hear her. "We don't need charity from anyone," she adds in Calabrian. "I wish you a very good day!"

Cosimino and I look at each other in amazement. Our

mother has never said a word against Nellina or anyone else in the town. She has spent her whole life saying yes, sir, no, sir, out of habit, not to ruffle feathers, or just not to make any enemies. And yet here she is having learned to say no.

The priest's housekeeper, at this point, warns Mother that she should settle on a solution come hell or high water because the family in question is a force to be reckoned with and because there are occasions when we need to let go of our pride, which is one of the cardinal sins.

When she finally leaves, Mother and I start getting the Christmas Eve dinner ready without mentioning her visit. We do the same things we have always done: knead the bread, pour the oil, crush the garlic, peel the tomatoes, light the fires, wash the pans, polish the cutlery. We go on like this all evening without her ever having to tell me what to do. If I do something wrong, she doesn't correct me, she lets me do it my own way, as if she had given up on all her rules. Every now and again, she looks up and smiles at me, almost shyly.

Before we sit down at the table, we hear another knock at the door. Nellina's warnings come to mind and my blood runs cold. The knocking picks up again, louder than before. Mother peers through the spyhole but it is too dark to see anything. Father tells us in a whisper not to say a word and pretend we're not home. At the third round of knocking, a voice comes through the door. "Open up, it's me!" Dumbfounded, we look at one another. Each one of us thinks they are dreaming.

Fortunata comes in with a shawl wrapped around her wet hair, her teeth chattering uncontrollably. She doesn't say a word; her sunken eyes are darker than the night and she's shaking like a leaf, maybe not just from the cold. Like a beaten dog that doesn't know whether to trust an outstretched hand because it may be hiding a stick. Mother finds her some dry clothes and tells Cosimino to get a chair. We wait for her to finish eating and drinking without asking her anything and then she finally starts talking.

"I've been through four years of hell. Insults, injuries, indignities. I lost the baby because of his beatings. He said it wasn't his, that I had deceived him, that I was a whore and that I'd gotten pregnant with someone else to entrap him. If I wanted to force him to get married, he would soon show me what marriage was. Four years shut up in that house without seeing a soul, without exchanging a word with my family. And I bore it all without saying a word. I thought it was my fault that I had ended up in that situation. I thought: stick with it, keep going, a woman is strong if she can put up with things. I thought: silence, patience, sweetness are the things a man appreciates over time. Four years. He went around town doing whatever he liked and I was rotting to death inside. Rise above it, be meek, don't dig your heels in, I kept saying to myself. As you always used to say, Pà: 'a reed before the wind lives on' and I did just that, I bent, until the straw broke the camel's back."

I haven't heard my sister's voice since the day she got married, her dress tugging at her hips amid the Musciacco family's strained smiles. She has been there all this time, painfully getting through each and every day behind those walls as if it were perfectly normal to be buried alive once you are married.

"He came to the house with that man this evening and, all of a sudden, my patience ran out. 'We have a guest this evening, wife. Lay an extra place at the table: your brother-in-law has had a fight with his father so he's doing us the honor of eating with us tonight.' When I saw him there in front of me, a red mist came over me. 'Brother-in-law? My sister is taking this man to court, not to the altar,' I snapped. Musciacco slapped me and said, 'You're all the same, you girls in that family: you're up for anything as long as there's money in it. It's in your name, after all: *Denaro*, cash. At that point, I completely lost it. I walked around the table, stacking his grandmother's prize dinner service, and smashed every piece on the floor, spitting on the dishes. He was dumbstruck. He wasn't expecting it. He has never expected anything from me, ever. I ran into my room, threw a few things into a bag, flew out the door, and nearly broke my neck taking the stairs four at a time."

None of us says a word. Did we know what was going on or didn't we? If we didn't, could we have imagined it? And yet we did nothing. Our silence has made us all accomplices.

"I'm sorry, Pà. I really am," Fortunata says. "But if I can't stay here with you, I'd rather go to a convent than go back to that house."

Father is silent and then he goes up to his daughter and plants a kiss on her forehead. When he leans over, his fair hair mingles with hers.

"We've paid our dues this Christmas Eve," Mother sighs. "Let's go to bed now," she says, smiling with a new sweetness. "It's getting late. I'll make your bed up." She sets off down the corridor shaking her head, and Fortunata and I follow.

The men stay in the kitchen talking and we hear snatches of what they are saying.

"You must take her back there or we'll be in the wrong," Cosimino says. "Wives are supposed to live under the same roof as their husbands. It would be better if she goes back of her own accord, rather than Musciacco coming here and dragging her home. Do you want this to end in bloodshed? We are already up to our necks in trouble as it is."

For a while we don't hear anything else and Mother carries on tucking in the sheets. Fortunata shushes us but we can't hear what Cosimino is saying.

"I wouldn't prefer that," Father answers eventually, his voice less steady than usual. "I'll go and talk to them tomorrow and everything will be settled, you'll see. Go to bed. I'll stay here on guard."

We hear the scraping of chairs and stools as they are dragged across the floor and nothing else so we go to bed. The next morning, we find them both asleep in the kitchen, fully dressed, ready to defend the women of the house.

Mother tiptoes across the room and closes the shutters.

Then she looks back, her lips pressed together. Her efforts to marry us off have been in vain and we are both back home. It would have been better if we had been born boys like Cosimino, but we were born girls and life has complicated itself along the way.

61

Since Fortunata came home, time has started to pass more quickly, though my life hasn't changed at all. We clean the house, cook, and get on with the sewing. In the afternoon, I go into my room and get on with schoolwork. Fortunata offers to test me but after five minutes she starts yawning and often falls asleep with a book in her hand. Luckily, Liliana comes and we study together.

One morning, the skinny Scibetta sister comes to see us. Mother invites her in but makes her sit on the most uncomfortable chair and offers her a glass of water and mint without the almond milk. The latest gossip trips off her tongue as soon as she sits down, a blow-by-blow account of the goings-on in town. The whole of Martorana was at Tindara's wedding but there wasn't enough food and the wine was watered down, so people complained they had to stop off at the boiled meat stand and have a spleen sandwich on their way home. The priest hadn't been able to say Mass for two weeks because he'd had a problem with his vocal cords. Nellina, it seemed, had offered to replace him and it had taken the authority of a bishop to persuade her that the day a woman said Mass would be the day after the apocalypse. Saro had started working with his father; he travels to and from the city, where an important client has commissioned fitted cupboards for the whole house, and since he has often left in the evening and not come back until the next morning, people have started saying that he has probably found somewhere to roost at the end of a day's work.

I can't wait for Mena to leave. The one silver lining to being locked up at home is no longer knowing anything about anyone, being able to mute the static droning of voices just as you would switch off the radio. But she sits there and drones on.

"Isn't Cosimino here?" she asks, turning to peer into the other rooms.

"He's taken the bus into the city to look for work," Mother answers.

Mena sighs and starts cranking up the gossip machine again. Rosalina is upset at what she has heard about Saro because seemingly she has secretly set her eyes on him for a while and the heartbreak made her lose five kilos, and her mother took her to see Dr. Provenzano, who said no one has ever died of love and that if she were to lose five more kilos it would do her a world of good. Musciacco, on the other hand . . . My sister jolts at the name and almost drops the tray she is carrying, laid with fresh bread and a little pot of orange marmalade. Mena sees she is upset but plows on with her news bulletin regardless. Musciacco is telling everyone that he was the one to throw his wife out of the house and that she had forced him to marry her with her lies. Fortunata puts the tray down on the table and runs to her room.

Mena attempts to follow her but Mother and I make sure she doesn't. "I didn't mean to upset her," she moans, red-eyed. "I wanted to reassure her that she has nothing to fear, that Musciacco is not going to be looking for payback. After what she has been through, she is finally free. She should be happy."

I watch her without saying a word and I can't tell whether she means what she says.

"Free how?" I say eventually. "Free to be called a whore? Free to have people convinced she tricked her way into the family? Free to be repudiated by her husband? Is this what you call freedom, Mena?"

She looks up at me. Her clenched jaws and pinched cheeks make her look even more angular than usual. "What other opportunities do we have, Oliva? To stay on the shelf like me? Is that freedom? Am I happy with my lot? Don't people point at me as they do at you, Fortunata, Tindara, and Rosalina? Each one is branded with a different sin. At least your sister is no longer in the eye of the storm. She can go somewhere and start again. The marriage is no longer binding and luckily there aren't any children . . ."

She leaves the phrase unfinished and collapses on the uncomfortable chair. She must have remembered Fortunata's bulging belly, ill-hidden under the wedding dress, and now regrets what she has said. Poor Mena. I suddenly pity her. Unlike so many others in town, she doesn't feel she is in the right all the time. She is not a bad person. She is no different from me. We are all right and we are all wrong.

pring has arrived from one day to the next. Since I was little, this season has always given me cause for celebration because everything the plants on Father's land have received—seeds, fertilizer, pruning, antiparasite spray, light, warmth—slowly comes to fruition. Now the colors and smells of the garden have been switched off. Not only have the plants gone missing but so has the spring, both outside and inside me.

As we work on our embroidery, we turn on the portable radio, which is the only thing Fortunata brought with her from the Musciacco household. I sing at the top of my lungs and she gets up and shows me the steps of the dance the Kessler twins performed on television. She is as tall and fair as Alice and Ellen Kessler, while I am as scraggy and dark as a crow. We stand mirroring each other in the middle of the kitchen like mismatched twins, hold each other's arms, and dip, singing the nonsense lyrics, *dadaumpa, dadaumpa, dadaumpa*. We snap our fingers in unison to the beat and yell, *dadaumpa, dadaumpa, dadaumpa*. Mother complains that we still behave like little girls and have never grown up but every now and again she puts a hand on her hip and joins in the dance: *dadaumpa, um-pà*.

One morning, as we boil up the bitter oranges and sugar for the marmalade, singing the latest hit, "Quando, quando, quando," we hear a knock at the door. It is a bailiff serving us a subpoena for the first hearing. We turn the radio off and let him in. After that, the radio stays off.

The weather takes a turn for the worse as if it were winter again. I don't feel like doing any schoolwork and my books lie unopened on my desk. The only thing I manage to read aloud while we are knitting is Maddalena's most recent letter. She says Fortunata was brave to get away and that we should report the abuse she has suffered to the carabinieri. She also says that until there is a law allowing people to get divorced, it won't be easy for separated women to start a new life but that things could well improve in the future thanks to women like us from southern Italy who have suffered the most and are most eager for liberation. I'm in favor of liberation. At the end of the letter, she suggests that my sister could stay with a friend of hers in the city for a while, where it would be easier for her to find work.

Fortunata looks down at the ball of wool on her lap.

"I can't do anything on my own, not even cross the street. How can I leave this place? What would I do? At least you went to high school. I went from living under my father's roof straight to living under Musciacco's, and I know next to nothing about life."

Her hands flutter as the knitting needles clack and the wool is slowly coaxed from the ball.

"I'm sorry, Olì," she says, losing her grip on the needles. "I can't go to see Maresciallo Vitale. I'm not like you. You're stronger than me."

I take the knitting out of her hands and pick up some stiches she has dropped.

"I wasn't before, either. Here, I've picked up some stitches for you," I say, handing back her work. "That way, there won't be a hole."

A week later, wearing Mother's Sunday coat, and carrying the old canvas bag our mother carried onto the ferry for her honeymoon, Fortunata is off to catch a bus to the city, where she plans to stay with Maddalena's friend. With a hat and a touch of lipstick, she looks beautiful again, like she used to be in the old days when I had to accompany her every time she set foot outside the house. Only this time she is going out on her own: a few quick strides toward the big road and she had already vanished from view. Before leaving, she gives me a hug and says, "You see? We've been dancing *dadaumpa* together like the Kessler twins so much that I've turned into you."

63

I t's cold tonight. Fortunata's bed on the other side of the room is empty and mine is making my life a misery. The rules of sleep are: lie down, breathe deeply, and close your eyes. But as soon as my eyelids feel heavy, the thought of tomorrow wakes me up. Sleep comes in fits and starts, confused images wake me: a blood-orange stain spreading over a pair of white trousers, a whistle from the street, eyes watching me as I walk, hands holding me down, a spot at the very center of my body being lacerated, blood soaking into the sheets. Liliana's books on the threadbare counterpane, Fortunata's scraped knuckles banging at the door, rain in her hair, jasmine, roses, daisies, clouds in the shape of twin-horned marfoyles, Alice chasing a rabbit and getting lost, the rabbit leading her into a dark room and offering her a silk scarf. Alice running away at night as shots fired by the carabinieri get closer, the lawyer Sabella clicking the clasp on his black leather briefcase, the Queen of Hearts yelling "Off with her head!"

I open my eyes and dry the sweat on my brow. My back is drenched and my jaw is aching. In the bathroom, I run cold water over my wrists and trickle some down my neck. The house is completely quiet. I grab the lamp we use when we go out to harvest snails, unlock the door, and start walking over our land. I walk to where the olive tree used to stand before it died, where Franco first touched my face. I kneel down and start digging with my bare hands. I keep going in the dark, the damp air clinging to my shoulders, my fingernails breaking on the stony clods, until I can feel the rough leather. I scrabble a little longer and unearth the moldy old bag. I turn the lamp off and go back in, holding my things close.

I manage to undo the buckles, which have been half-eaten by rust, and open the stained bag. Inside, protected from the earth and rain, is the dress I wore to the patron saint festival. I lay it out on the bed. The embroidery and material are unspoiled. The time that has gone by since that day has consumed me but the dress is undamaged. I choose a needle and unspool a length of cotton from the embroidery drawer, sit on the edge of the bed, and, bringing my face closer to the weak bedside light, thread the needle and tie a knot at the other end of the cotton. I pull the lacerated edges of the material together and mend the tear with the tiny invisible stitches Mother has taught me. I make my way up the ripped material, which under my administrations now looks intact, even though I know it is not. Finally, with the scissors, I snip off the thread.

I take my nightdress off and imagine it is the eve of my wedding, the last night I would spend on my own, my body intact before it became the property of a man, on show for his pleasure. I run my fingers down my arms, my breasts, my belly, my hips, brush against my thighs, knees, ankles, and feet, toe by toe. I have grown a little taller since that night at the festival but my body is the same, maybe a little thinner. I undo the buttons one by one and slip the dress on. I pull the loose slat up and take out the coral necklace Liliana gave me. I hold my hair up and hook the clasp around my neck. I take a few slow steps across my room as if I were walking down the aisle, the wedding music playing in my mind.

"Do you, Oliva Denaro, decide never to take a husband, for better, for worse, for richer, for poorer, in sickness and in health until death do you part? Do you?"

Do I?

When I wake up, I'm still wearing the white dress I wore for my first dance.

64

They are waiting for me in the kitchen sitting around the table.

"I'm ready," I say. "Let's go and catch the bus."

Last night's fear has washed off my body like when you empty the bath and the dirty water is washed down the drain. My dress is now hanging in the wardrobe and the only thing left at the foot of the olive tree is my shame.

"There's no hurry," Father tells me. "Calò is taking us in the car. He'll be waiting for us at the end of the track with Liliana at ten o'clock sharp."

I sit with them, break the stale bread into pieces, drop them into the warm milky coffee, and sprinkle some sugar on top: it is a day like any other.

"I'm staying here with Mà to keep her company," Cosimino says, stroking his mustache. "We won't all fit in the car, anyway. When you get back," he adds, with one hand on my shoulder, "I want you to tell me everything, like when you used to tell me the story of Giufà." He's grown so tall: his long, thin body feels like an umbrella ready to shelter me from the rain or shade me from the sun.

I finish my last mouthful of breakfast and Mother is already clearing the table, gathering the bowls and spoons and taking them to the sink.

"I've got your good clothes ready," she says, as if she were sending me off to school.

"Don't worry, Mà. I'll keep myself clean."

She turns the faucet on and starts rinsing out the bowls. Then she stops and turns it off again.

"You don't need to. You are always clean." She dries her hands on her apron and puts one slightly damp hand on my cheek. "And remember: your tongue will get you far. You have to tell the judge everything, without being embarrassed. Like you did with the lawyer. In a few months, God willing, you'll get your teacher's certificate and you'll know more words in Latin than that wretch who abused you knows in his own language. You need to show them everything you know!"

———

Father and Calò sit in the front, Liliana and I in the back. The road to the city is long and winding. My friend squeezes my hand and chats about what we have to study for the exam we will be sitting early in the summer. I pretend to listen and give her a monosyllabic answer every now and again to keep her happy. The farther we get from home, the icier my blood runs, as if the nightmares I had last night might come true.

Calò stops the car in a piazza that is bigger than the whole of Martorana. A giant building rears up in front of us, built in three sections: two wings filled with windows and a central block with tall columns like an ancient Greek temple. Some of the divinities must actually live there, I catch myself thinking. We walk across the square until we reach the steps that rise up to the entrance. I look up and see JUSTICE carved in giant capital letters above the columns. I hope so, I say to myself, and start climbing the steps. Liliana seems to have read my thoughts.

"This isn't justice yet," she whispers in my ear as we walk through the main door. "One day, I'm going to change the law," she adds in a louder voice that echoes around the entrance hall.

"One day," I echo her. "It is all very well to say one day, but I'm here now."

I don't say anything else because Father pulls me toward him and tucks my arm under his as we walk to the huge room. Calò walks on one side and Liliana on the other.

"Oliva, don't be scared. It's like harvesting snails," Father says. "You need patience and intelligence because mollusks, like certain spineless individuals, have a special talent: they hide so as not to be spotted. But it's a talent for cowards."

Calò approaches a bailiff and says something to him. The man looks down at a big register and then lifts an arm and points to a corridor. The click-clack of Liliana's heels on the floor echoes up in the ceiling. I try to walk quietly in my soft white shoes and suddenly remember the moment when I stopped under the blazing sun, a broken heel in my hand. Even if I wanted to, I couldn't turn back now.

We get into the elevator and Calò pushes the white button with a number 3 on it. When it starts moving, my stomach heaves like that day on the bus.

"It's in Courtroom Twelve," Calò says, striding ahead of us. Near the entrance two women talk to each other intensely. One is wearing a man's jacket and slacks. As soon as she sees me, her full lips open in a dazzling, white-toothed smile. The other woman's hair is tied back in a ponytail, and her eyes are lightly made up.

"You look great with your hair tied up," I say to Fortunata. She smiles and lifts her hand to tuck in a stray strand.

"The lawyer is already inside," Maddalena says. "Let's go." Father and I are still arm-in-arm as we cross the courtroom. It looks like a church, with rows of wooden benches on each side and a crucifix on the wall. A man in a black gown comes in and takes his place behind the bench. We all stand.

The lawyer greets me with a handshake and extracts a file full of documents from his briefcase. He looks exhausted, as if he'd had a bout of insomnia last night, too. I, on the other hand, suddenly feel strong. My breathing is slow, my hands dry, my head high. Father, Calò, Liliana, and Maddalena are all here with me but I'm not here for their benefit. I'm doing this for myself. On the other side of the room is the defense: three men in dark suits and, in the middle, a man in a white suit, his hair combed back with pomade, but no sprig of jasmine behind his right ear. He's good-looking, there is no doubt. My girlfriends were right about that. Almost a year has gone by and nothing about him has changed. I have moved on and he has stayed still. That is another reason why we will never cross paths again.

As soon as he sees me, he stops smiling and throws me a cocky look. His gaze is hard to meet but it no longer has the power to render me either beautiful or invisible. Nothing will ever affect me the same way again, and the things I have lost I have lost forever: running like crazy in my wooden clogs, making up names for clouds, reciting Latin, drawing charcoal portraits of movie stars, pulling petals and asking whether he loves me or he loves me not.

PART FOUR

1981

65

It is easy to leave your hometown but your hometown never leaves you. Growing plants from cuttings is one thing, cultivating a garden is another. You can get up and go in no time at all, but coming back takes much longer.

The road hugs the coastline, curve after curve. I've always been scared of the sea, and your brother likes driving fast. He thinks if we get there early, he'll win a prize, do you see? His wife never says anything, not like your mother, who has never been at a loss for words. "Do you like the new car, Pà?" Cosimino asked me before we set off. I nodded to keep him happy. "Do you want to try it?" he said, opening the door for me. "I wouldn't prefer that," I answered, so he climbed into the driver's seat and has been stuck in the passing lane ever since. "An ass in a hurry will break its back," I say. He didn't even hear me. He looked over at his wife and lit a cigarette, the fiftieth since we left Rapisarda.

Amalia's fingers are wrapped around the handle above the passenger door, holding on for dear life as if she were on the bus, and she smiles down at Lia, who is sitting between us.

"You're growing so pretty," she says to her granddaughter, teasing her bangs away from her eyes. Lia shakes her head and her hair falls untidily over her face again. Amalia sighs and dries her forehead with her handkerchief. She finds it hard to go back, too. We planted ourselves somewhere else, like two broken trunks: I grew new vegetables with cuttings from the previous ones. New plants soon spring up but with people it's different: you can give them as much water and heat as you want, but the new roots never grow as deep as the old ones. Who knows why? If you work the land, you miss your own, even when it becomes foreign to you.

After your trial, the town split into two factions: she did the right thing, she did the wrong thing. Every time we went out, we were almost drowned in gossip. You never said a word. You got up in the morning to study, you went to bed after finishing your revision. Liliana came over and you would shut yourselves in your room. The house was so quiet you could hear a pin drop but there would have been trouble otherwise. You had gone a little feral, like after you had scarlet fever, remember? You were nine and on the first day you were covered in tiny red pinhead-size spots. We'd bring what little food you managed to get down, and occasionally some fresh ricotta from the Scibettas, into your room so that Cosimino wouldn't catch it, since he had a weaker constitution than you. Your fever was running high and your body was itching all over and your mother vowed to the Virgin that she'd go to early Mass every day if she would grant you the miracle of a full recovery. Three weeks later you were better. You were scrawnier than ever, with dark bags under your eyes, but you were standing straight and you didn't have any scars. All the kids in town stayed home because they didn't want to catch it and you were the only one out and about.

Outside the courthouse you wore the same expression on your face. You strode ahead without saying anything, you didn't let anyone approach or touch you, as if you were contagious. The spectators at the trial were amazed. They couldn't have known you were a lion in sheep's clothing. Your voice was firm as you answered every question, as steadfast as when you were tested at school. No, sir, there had been no agreement between us. No, sir, there had been no betrothal. No, sir, I did not appreciate his attentions. No, sir, I do not want to marry him. The judge couldn't believe that you were actually spurning the man's offer of marriage.

Any ass can say yes. Saying no, on the other hand, costs a great deal of effort and, once the noes start, they never stop. It's the only thing I ever managed to teach you, and from that moment on, the answer was no for everybody. No to your mother, who wanted to find you another marriage proposal. No to some of your old friends who came to visit. No to Mrs. Scibetta, who offered to take you in as a domestic. You were testy, stingy with your words. The day your exams started, you strode out bright and early onto the big road without saying goodbye to anyone, and after lunch, you closed yourself in your room. When Liliana came to pick you up on the day of your oral exam and asked you if you were nervous, you said, with a bitter smile, "After the courtroom, no examination is ever going to be as bad."

You passed with flying colors, your mother cooked pasta with fresh sardines, and we all dressed up in our new clothes for lunch. You came into the kitchen and looked at us darkly. "I'm not hungry," you said. "But today is a special day, we must celebrate," your mother insisted, filling your plate as she smoothed her shirt down. "Special days for me are over," you said, and you left us on our own.

Cosimino overtakes another car on a curve, which makes it the three hundred and twenty-seventh so far. Amalia is still gripping the handle with one hand, as persistent as a Virginia creeper, and pointing at the speedometer with the other. "Slow down," I say from the back seat. Cosimino's response is to honk at the car in front of us. What can a father do to save his children? I ask you.

Amalia taps her forehead with her open palm. "How embarrassing, Salvo! We haven't brought any gifts at all, not even pastries."

"She said on the telephone that she would get dessert," I reassure her. But I have remembered to pick some flowers from our garden, which you've always loved.

66

I need to get flowers.

I need to buy bread, air the rooms, open the table out and add the extra leaves, ask Miss Panebianco if I can borrow some of her chairs. Finally, I need to go and pick up the cake at the pastry shop.

I didn't want flowers in the house for years: your hands were the ones that grew things, Pà, with earth under your fingernails, superficial scratches and deeper cuts on your fingertips. You were a mine of information on how to draw life from the earth. How to plant a seed and wait for it to sprout. I did the same thing. I buried myself without knowing whether anything would ever germinate. I was a burned-out, sterilized clod of earth, as annihilated as your patch of land had been under the salt water, nothing would ever spring from my uprooted body. The day I got my teaching certificate, when I came into the house and found you all decked out for a party, I grieved for you all. You were happy and I was sad, because it was supposed to be the happiest day of my life. I would never have another one. I had not received justice, a white veil would never tickle the back of my neck, a ring would never be slipped onto my finger, I would never receive the caress of a man in love with me, I would never feel the calm fullness of a taut belly focusing on a pregnancy, nor would a soft little spongy hand ever hold mine.

Leaving Martorana was like trying to detach myself from my own shadow. The sense of injustice and shame never leaves you as you walk in the streets. It takes time, it takes other voices adding theirs to yours, it takes leaving and then returning. Because good or bad weather is never there to stay, as you always used to say.

That is why I got up early this morning. I will put on my new lipstick, a white cotton dress, and my turquoise sandals, I will lay the table carefully, I will cook pasta with fresh sardines, and we will celebrate, nearly twenty years later, my top marks back then. We will also celebrate my tenured teaching position, our silences, our snatched phone calls, everyone's birthdays, family anniversaries, a divorce and a few weddings, and, at the end of the day, my stubborn determination to be here in my town for all of these things and despite all of these things.

There is still a lot to do. I go downstairs, put my head around the door, and stay there for a moment: the pasty combination of heat and brackish air dries the breath in my throat.

67

There's no point in opening the window, the heat and salty sea air give no respite, and there's not a cloud in sight so there is no hope of rain. When you were little, you used to look forward to a storm so that we could go to harvest snails, and when it didn't come for days, you'd be disappointed. Watch the pan and the water will never boil, I would tell you. I said the same thing after the trial. You didn't get the justice you were seeking but you had sown a seed, and something will always grow on cultivated land.

As they read the verdict, that wretch was laughing his head off, as if it were stand-up comedy. A minimum sentence. How could that be? A woman with mousy hair, Angela Verro was her name, I'll never forget it, said in the witness box that she didn't hear you complaining or struggling in the room next door. Fear and revulsion can only be measured in yells and screams in this world. Can you believe it? For the first count, "violent conjugation" as the judge called it, the man was absolved with insufficient evidence. What evidence were they looking for? Is the word of an honest girl not enough? Is the courage to stand there and give everyone intimate details insufficient? Another witness told the judge they had seen you dancing with him and claimed you had encouraged him. Others again said that you had wanted the match but that I had gotten in your way and betrothed you to another man. And that this was why he had taken you by force: everything that virtuous young man had done was for love, if can you believe it, and according to the judge abducting someone on the street is the act of a lover rather than a brigand. I'd like to see whether he would be of the same view if his own little girl had received the same treatment. False witnesses were bribed to take the stand, a little grease helps turn the wheel, and he was certainly not lacking in that department. They said you had given your word more than once, that he had offered you an orange on the street and that you had accepted it! Even if it were true, tell me: Does accepting the fruit mean you want to take the whole tree?

"Salvo, how far off are we? I'm feeling sick," Amalia complains. She has taken her shoes off and has started massaging one of her feet. The time it takes to smoke another twenty cigarettes and pass a hundred and fifty-six cars with blaring horns, if all goes well, I'd like to answer, but instead, I put my hand on the back of her neck where I know her tension concentrates. Just as I did that day. The defense attorney, Criscione, asked a lot of humiliating questions and filed for a medical report from Dr. Provenzano but you had refused to submit yourself to the examination. It was as if you were the one on trial. Amalia and I looked at each other. The whole thing felt like a nightmare. I'll never forget Sabella's answer to the judge: I speak for the prosecution, not the defense. My client is not here to prove her innocence or her honorability. She is here to denounce a rape.

Luckily, Santino, Tindara's father, gave a witness statement and that was the only reason the wretch was found guilty on the second count. It wasn't true that the whole town was against us: even on the darkest night, there is always a star shining. When the judge finished reading the verdict, it felt like we were at the market. Some people clapped, others whistled, still others yelled. "The roaring mountain gave birth to a tiny mouse!" the wretch shouted as they led him away. "Where has this gotten you? It's all show and no go!" he taunted, pursing his fingers and shaking them in the air as if to say "What do you want from me?"

The nerves at the back of your mother's neck are a tangle of roots stretching out under my fingers. "Just a little longer," I tell her to keep her happy, even though there's still a long way to go and, to tell you the truth, I'm glad of it. Coming back after being so far away means getting reacquainted with every stone, every blade of grass, every clod of earth dried out by the hot air. Your mother takes her sewing out of her bag but stops right away. She looks at me as if she wants to say something but then she thinks again and turns to the window. Cosimino switches the radio on and turns the knob looking for the news. His wife stops his hand: "Leave this one on, I like it," and she starts singing.

She's a little out of tune but he smiles and waits for the song to end before changing the station. Their daughter takes a little tape recorder out of her bag and puts the headphones on. "Lia, you can't wear those things on your ears all the time," Mena yells. The girl doesn't answer. She's listening to a different tune.

go up to the window and tap on the glass with my knuckles. Carmelina turns the radio down and comes to answer.

"Today's the day," I say.

"It's all ready, dear. I've got the folding chairs here for you. Is Saro coming to get them?"

"Yes, thanks. He'll be over later." I stand there staring at the pink curtains at her window.

"Is there anything else you need, Olì? I made a delicious tart with fresh fruit in it, if you want . . ."

"Thank you, Carmelina, I'm getting the dessert."

"Are you sure?" There's a flicker of apprehension in her voice, the same hesitation I heard in your voice on the phone yesterday, Pà. Even from far away, you manage to worry without saying a word. "I'm going right now," I say. I wave goodbye as I walk toward the old part of town, which is on the other side from where I live.

My house is on the sea and you might not like it but you will say it's nice, leaving me as always free to do what I want but still wondering whether I have done something wrong. There is no land around it, you will see right away, but you have been surrounded by so much land that a little sea air will give you an appetite. I leave the coast road on my left and start the climb up into the old center. The climb has never felt so long and my feet soon start aching. *Rosa, rosae, rosae*, I used to recite when I was a girl walking home from the sea road. I thought it would make the climb easier but that was back when I still believed that words would win over injustice and suffering. If I were that age now, I would take my shoes off to feel the flagstones tickling my feet. Time passes, and it is not always in vain: I've distanced myself from that barefoot, unkempt young girl so successfully that I wouldn't know what to say to her if I met her now, just as I wouldn't know how to talk to a daughter. Instead of reciting Latin, then, I start humming a song that has been stuck in my mind. I stop at the lookout point and take a final glance at the white horses on the waves before I vanish into the old town, beating the heels of my turquoise sandals on the paving stones to the beat of the music in my head. I bought them in Sorrento with Maddalena seven years ago.

We got there from Naples on the local Circumvesuviana train and immediately got lost in the alleys smelling of lemons and jasmine. Maddalena stood in front of a cobbler's workshop, displaying different shaped and colored leather cutouts.

"These turquoise ones?" she suggested, pointing at a sample on a foot mannequin.

"They're too loud. They would be good for Liliana but not me," I said, turning away from the store.

"Great idea! Let's get them. We'll send them to her in Rome. Last time I spoke to her, she said she was worried about which way the referendum on divorce would go . . ."

"I'm sorry to hear that, but we all have our own worries. Maybe she doesn't need our sandals anyway? She already has everything she wanted. She even won a seat in parliament, alongside Nilde Iotti, just like she said she would when she was little."

"So what?" Maddalena stopped smiling for a moment. "You have everything you want, too. You're an elementary school teacher, you're independent. Okay, justice wasn't on your side but justice is another matter. It has nothing to do with you or me. Until there is justice in the world, we can't be free. Liliana is carrying forward the struggle for all women . . ."

"All women! Why do women have to be declined in the plural to get any consideration? One man on his own, with his name and surname, has value. But we have to stand together in a crowd to be considered, as if we were a different species. I don't want to be part of any army: associations, parties, activist groups, none of them interest me. I'm not like you and Liliana. I don't want to be engaged in politics. I mourn what happened to me on my own. What Paternò did to me when I was only sixteen . . ."

It was the first time I had ever said his name. Pulling those syllables out of my mouth was a way of substantiating the ghost, giving it an identity. The wind had suddenly died down and the sun seemed to be concentrating its rays on the back of my neck. I staggered, as if my flesh had been filleted from my backbone, and I had to lean on the outside wall of the store, where I slowly slid down to the ground. I pulled my knees up and sat there absorbing the coolness of the square pavers. "Why are things so hard for us, Maddalena?" I asked, closing my eyes so that tears couldn't come out. "Why do we need to fight battles, sign petitions, go on demonstrations, burn bras, flash our underpants, beg people to believe us, check how long our skirts are, what color lipstick we wear, how openly we smile, how strongly we want something? Why is it my fault that I was born female?"

Maddalena crouched down beside me and sat there with me for a few minutes.

"I went to my daughter's wedding, you know?" she said eventually. My eyes lifted of their own accord.

"Last week. She introduced me to her husband and all the family. She said, 'This is my mother.' And do you know what they said?" I shook my head. "They stared and said, 'Another one?'"

"You didn't tell me," I objected.

"One morning years ago, after your trial," she told me, "I found the courage to stop her outside her university and I talked to her."

"How did she react?"

"How do you think? Badly. She didn't want to have anything to do with me and for a long time I heard nothing more from her. I thought I'd made a terrible mistake and that's why I didn't tell anyone."

Even Maddalena, who is scared of nothing, has had to deal with her own shame, I thought to myself. Like everyone who has been a victim of injustice.

"A few weeks ago, she came to me," she went on. "Ten years had gone by since I last saw her but I recognized her immediately. She had a photo album with her: pictures of her as a baby, a young girl, a teenager. I took in the images avidly so that I could store them away: a whole life I had missed was stuck into the pages of that book. She came to see me because she had realized that in some of these photographs, she had the same smile as me. She told me that when she had the baby, she would tell it the whole story."

"So you're going to be a grandmother?"

"The third grandmother, to be precise."

I got up and offered her my arm to help her up. From the workshop we could hear the cobbler banging on the tiny nails. Maddalena peered into the store and then turned to me. "Shall we have three pairs of sandals made all the same?" she asked me.

Half an hour later, we were walking under the shade of the lemon trees. "I'm going back to Martorana. There is a permanent job in the school where I learned to read and write. That is where I want to teach."

"I know," Maddalena said, smiling. "And that is what I mean by being engaged in politics."

———

Here I am, at the top of the hill, at the junction with the big road that leads to the piazza. I'm sure that Maddalena has worn the turquoise sandals today to celebrate our victory.

You're right, Pà. Things happen if you know how to wait.

69

Things happen if you know how to wait," I tell your mother as she asks me for the umpteenth time how much longer, when will we be there, open the window, close the window. I stick two fingers into my shirt collar, which is wet with sweat, and loosen my tie. She purses her lips, as she does whenever she wants an answer from me that I don't have. Just because I am a man, a father, just because I wear the pants, as they used to say, doesn't mean I know the answer to everything, does it? I'm a peasant and what I know is how to put seeds in the ground and help plants grow even when there's a dry period, an unexpected downpour, or strong winds. I put a support in if they're weak and keep away the parasites that sap their strength. But if a plant finds its way, it grows on its own.

You decided to go to Naples to take up a job there. What were we supposed to do? We took you to the ferry port. Liliana stopped you at the bottom of the steps: remember the promise I made you, she said, and gave you a hug. You climbed the boarding ladder up to the door and vanished inside. Of course, I would have liked to keep you in my garden. Who wouldn't have? But the fact that you went away on your own meant that you had grown strong. Anyone who works the land knows this.

Cosimino honks the horn again and we pass the umpteenth car. Your mother is gripping the handle tight and reciting the Rosary to herself. "Salvo," she says between prayers. When she calls me by my name, it's either to tell me off or because she's scared. "Close the window, I feel the cold in my bones."

I wind up the window and the last tongue of torrid air licks my cheek.

"You shouldn't be scared, we're going home," I say, stroking her icy fingers.

"I don't have a home in Martorana anymore," she says.

"What do you mean, Amalia? Home is where our children are."

Home is where you hope one day to return, I think to myself, even if it has rejected you. Home is where you want to escape from, even though it taught you to walk and talk. When that wretch got out of jail after less than a year, people slapped him on the back as they passed by, as if he'd just returned from a nice vacation. Thank goodness you had already left! He strutted around repeating to whoever would listen what the defense attorney had said at the trial. I'll never forget it: girls want to be persuaded, you need to force a girl to break her natural reserve, a man in love has special rights. The attorney's words are indelibly branded in my memory: the only future for a young woman who is by no means pretty, and certainly not rich, is a marriage of convenience. Exploiting the natural flirtatiousness of her age, making eyes and smiling coquettishly, she had managed to gain the attention of one of the most eligible bachelors in town. Certain feminine arts are best learned in the family: her older sister, in fact, had ensnared the mayor's son by getting herself pregnant, and her mother had eloped in a *fuitina* when she was young, and only gotten married as an afterthought.

That is what he said, word-for-word. Call him an attorney. He's no better than a town gossip!

Your mother pulls at my sleeve. I look out the window and recognize the shapes and colors of the houses. Cosimino slows down, even though the road in front of us is free, as if the traffic were now inside his head. "We're back," he says. No one answers.

When the defense attorney finished his summation, you adopted that stony expression that you have maintained ever since. That was when you realized there would be no justice because you were on the wrong side of the law, which stated clearly that a man who rapes a woman has committed no crime if he offers her the compensation of marriage.

I was the one who led you down that dead-end street.

70

You were the one who led me up this street, Pà, one Sunday morning, under the midday sun. We stood in front of the counter and you asked me which cake I wanted. I didn't know. I was trying to guess what you wanted me to choose. This morning I'm retracing our steps, but this time I'm on my own: there's not even your silence to keep me company, which is easier to disappoint than a thousand recommendations. When I was little, I used to watch the brides go into church on their fathers' arms before being given away to their husbands. I wanted nothing more than for you to hold on to me forever.

"Good morning, Oliva," the old man standing next to the stand says.

"Biagio, good morning." I smile at him.

We always greet each other when I walk past his flower stand. He lowers his gaze, maybe because of the thorny red rose he gave me one afternoon many years ago. I stop and look at the stand. Biagio steps aside. "How can I help you?"

"I'm celebrating an anniversary today. I'd like a nice flower arrangement as a centerpiece for the table."

Biagio looks around: there are so many flowers. "Whatever you like, Olì, you tell me: gladiolas, dahlias, begonias, roses?"

"I like wildflowers. Do you have any daisies?" I ask. He nods and picks out a big bunch for me. I walk on. Every step I take, the yellow crepe paper swaddling the flowers makes a swishing sound against my pants. When I first came back, seven years ago, I felt like an outsider and I didn't speak to anyone. Fortunata had stayed in the city. You and Mà, together with Cosimino, had settled in Rapisarda after the rapist had gotten out of jail. There was nothing left for us down here, except the memory of that young girl in her wooden clogs and wild hair who used to secretly draw portraits of movie stars. I took out this rental by the sea in the new part of town so that I wouldn't have to bump into anyone and I kept myself to myself until the new school year started. I wondered what the point of coming back was, except maybe to play hide-and-seek with bad memories. Then, little by little, I started going out. Some people recognized me. They looked askance at me, unable to hide their bewilderment. When they found out I was to be the new elementary school teacher, they greeted me awkwardly. Good morning Signorina Denaro, they would say, worried I might be offended by the title *Signorina*, as it stressed the fact that I had never married. Good morning, I would answer, indifferently. I wasn't ashamed to be using your surname still.

One Sunday, a lunch invitation arrived from Mrs. Scibetta. "You should have told me you were coming home, my dear. You are family now, let's not let those tongues wag again!" The living room was unchanged. Rather than on the wooden bench, she invited me to sit in an armchair, but there was the same stale, dry bread that tasted like my childhood. Miluzza brought everything in on a tray, which reminded me of the old days when I used to try to imagine what my future would be like, whereas she already knew that hers would play out right there, working for the woman whose hospitality she had had to pay for with her freedom.

"Nora, Nora," Mrs. Scibetta shrieked. The fat daughter filled the doorway and smiled without any warmth. Of the two sisters, she was the one still on the shelf while Mena's framed wedding picture was displayed proudly on the dresser. I went to examine it more closely. You were all there, standing around the newlyweds. Maddalena had lent me a nice blouse to wear for the ceremony but at the last minute I decided not to go. That marriage was my fault, too. There was no work for you or Cosimino here. Antonino Calò had tried through his connections with the Party but the only opportunities were on the mainland, although you had a bad heart and Cosimino had a bad case of homesickness. Mrs. Scibetta struck while the iron was hot and offered one of her two daughters, whichever he wanted, as well as some family land in another part of the region. Cosimino spent two days and two nights playing odds and evens with himself and finally went to see Mrs. Scibetta. "I'll have Mena," he said. She wore the dress I had embroidered myself years before. He wore an old suit belonging to his newly acquired father-in-law that had been turned inside out for him, and

Don Ignazio had blessed their marriage until death do they part. The priest didn't know yet that the new divorce law would make it possible for a lawyer and a judge to separate a couple that God had united. A few years later, Lia was born.

Cosimino was the one who saved our honor. With two gold rings rather than a rifle. He sacrificed himself for the family and you let him, just as you had let Fortunata. I was the only one for whom you demanded freedom, with whom you walked around town arm-in-arm challenging the unwritten laws of what constitutes honor or dishonor. Why was your love for me so special? Why were your expectations of me so different? What feats did I have to perform for you?

Maybe it was our snail harvesting, our speaking without words, our hand squeezes, or maybe again it was the dripping yellow paint we both decided we would use to paint the chicken coop.

didn't consider for a minute that the yellow paint might harm the chickens. Sometimes things look good on the outside but there is hidden poison on the inside. Like when I took you to him at the pastry shop.

The car is crawling forward now. As soon as we come into town, Cosimino loses his bravado. He is looking around, for all the world like the reedy, feeble boy he used to be. The piazza is exactly the same: twenty years feel like a day. The church, the carabinieri station, the two bars with tables outside, the pastry shop window.

We stop right in front. That moment has stayed in the forefront of my mind. I wanted to take you there to shake off any remaining doubt. How could a man like that make you happy? That's what I was thinking, but what can I say? Maybe the truth is that there wasn't a single man in the world I could have imagined by your side. I wanted to give you the freedom to choose but I ended up doing it myself, taking you under my arm not to support you but to take you where I wanted you to go, and make you say the words I wanted to hear. Worse than a father brandishing a rifle, I've been, like one of those mob bosses demanding subservience with a hand kiss. I didn't want you to marry a bully as Fortunata had been forced to do but I lost you anyway, in a different way. Parents know that their children are destined to leave the nest. A father should leave his own interests to the side and let it happen.

After the trial, you went off to Naples and there was nothing left for me in my hometown. No land, no animals, no daughters. Fortunata had already moved to the city to get away from the gossipmongers and had almost immediately gotten a job in a factory thanks to Maddalena's friend. She was working in a tomato cannery. When we heard the news, your mother and I were astonished. Who would have thought it? Our dainty girl donning work overalls and punching the clock!

When Cosimino went to live on his wife's family land in Rapisarda, we went with him. What were we to do here on our own? Over the years, he has proved himself. The Scibetta land was abandoned and he got it back into production. Can you believe he exports oranges to the mainland?

Do you know what, Olì? Doing things your own way works out for the best. Fortunata's second husband is a union leader in the factory where she works and he uses his hands for work, unlike the first one, who raised his hand to her. Mena and Cosimino invite us to lunch every other Sunday. I think the marriage is a good one: two people living together without abusing each other either with their words or actions.

Do you know what children are? They are like those seeds carried by the wind that land in your garden. You need to let them grow before you know what fruit they will bear, and you can't decide beforehand what that is going to be. I thought I had three weak saplings in my field but I realized later they were three fruitful, resistant trees. Life can come forth even on land burned by salt.

72

Life can come forth even on land burned by salt: I learned this from you, Pà, from what you did with your hands. Digging, sowing, cutting, watering. I put the bouquet of daisies into my bag, being careful not to crush the petals, then set off at a brisk pace toward my destination.

I have put a shelf up in my classroom and filled it with books and flowerpots. At the end of the school day, the children take turns to read aloud while the others take care of the plants. Miss Rosaria would have liked this arrangement: maybe my reason for returning was to bring her back.

Over time, the children of some of my old classmates have arrived: Crocefissa's two girls, a year apart, both brunettes with charcoal eyes like their mother; Rosalina's eldest boy, with another one enrolled in nursery and a third on the way; and Tindara's daughter, fair and green-eyed, whom I recognized immediately because she was identical to the man in the picture Tindara had shown me in front of the church many years ago.

"You were right," Tindara says outside school one day when she comes to pick up her daughter. "I only agreed to marry him because he was good-looking, but as soon as he opens his mouth, I break out in a rash. He says 'white' and I say 'black,' he says 'dawn' and I say 'sunset.' And then—"

She breaks off, looking around her and lowering her voice. "How can I say this? He's a good-looker but he can't cut the mustard. Everyone's asking when we're giving her a baby brother or sister." She looks over at her daughter. "The saint only knocked once: if I'd become a nun the result would have been the same. Men are like watermelons: you need to try them out before taking them home. What do you say, Olì?"

When Marina enrolled, I didn't need to look at the register to know her surname. On the first day of school, she told me they had moved back from the city because her father had had to take care of the family business after her grandfather had died. She said that she missed her friends from before but that she was happy because in the afternoon she could go to the pastry shop and her father lets her lick the cream off the tip of a knife. She is a bright girl with dark eyes and a lanky body. Her mother picks her up every afternoon: she's small, quiet, and completely inconspicuous. When our eyes meet, we both nod imperceptibly in greeting. I could have been that woman.

Musciacco, on the other hand, never had children. After his marriage to Fortunata was annulled, a little balder and a little fatter, with a younger fiancée in tow, he used Don Ignazio's services again the following year. The much-awaited heir never arrived. The baby Fortunata miscarried after his repeated thrashings may well weigh heavier on his conscience than the conviction he never received.

73

There it is. The Musciacco family villa at the bottom of the main road hasn't changed but it looks smaller than it used to. Nowadays, they build something five times the size in a fifth of the time. There's no way around it: new money has overtaken the old.

I went there the day after Fortunata ran away. What I hoped to achieve I didn't know myself. I wanted to understand, maybe make peace with them. Back then, I still believed that if each side put forth their point of view, an agreement could be reached. As they say, mountains don't meet but people do. But I was wrong again.

I went up the stairs with my heart in my throat. Gerò kept me waiting half an hour and then let me in. He was smoking his cigar and drinking wine, lying back on the sofa. He didn't offer me anything and I wouldn't have accepted even if he had.

"You owe me an explanation," I said, standing in front of him, my voice trembling with rage. I was angrier with myself than I was with him for not realizing sooner what had been going on behind those walls. He answered that he had received Fortunata from my hands and that he had always treated her like a jewel. Can you believe he actually said that? She had been ungrateful, he said. Following her sister's example, she had been crazy enough to run away and once she'd spent more than one night outside the marital home, he would never take her back. "It's a matter of honor," he said, stubbing his cigar out in the ashtray.

"Fortunata has never left our house!"

"You were wrong to keep her there. You should have brought her back here that same evening. I'm a gentleman, not your daughter's puppet. You can keep her now but the whole town needs to know that I'm the one who has repudiated her on the grounds of desertion. And you should be thanking me for not making a formal complaint with the carabinieri. This marriage has been a farce from the very beginning and I'll be applying for an annulment at the ecclesiastical tribunal."

The cigar smoke was stinging my nostrils. Staying in that house any longer was like speaking to a mule: a waste of time and effort. I'd rather have her at home and disgraced than bring her back to this person, I thought. As I went down the stairs, a pain in the chest took my breath away. I stopped at the front door to rest and dry my brow. At that very moment, Paternò appeared, whistling.

"What are you doing here?" he asked. "I can't even pay a visit to a dear friend without having to get past you guarding the door." He headed for the stairs without deigning to glance at me.

My left arm was tingling. I opened my mouth but my voice was strained. "I'm not here for you or anything that regards you," I said hoarsely.

He stopped and stared back.

"Have you set the date for the wedding?" he asked, inspecting his nails distractedly.

"My daughter doesn't want you, get that in your head once and for all. But if you . . ."

"Well, then, we have nothing to say to each other," he interrupted, and went back to climbing the stairs, this time at a faster pace.

"Wait!" I tried to stop him. "If you apologize publicly and show some remorse for taking her honor by force, we'll withdraw the suit and there will be no trial," I murmured, my heart knocking against my ribs.

It was as if I'd told him a good joke. Paternò looked down at me from the top of the first flight of stairs, bent double, twisting his mouth into a laugh, and pulled his handkerchief out of his pocket so that he could pretend he was drying his eyes.

"What are you talking about? Are you kidding me or is this for real? What apology? I'm in the right, and the law is on my side. I wanted to marry her and that hussy of a girl had her chance. I even gave her a taste of our honeymoon so that she would know what she was missing if she carried on being difficult. But she chose to obey her father rather than follow her heart. Do you know what the truth is? You want to look progressive, but you're worse than the old frog-eaters in town: you order your daughter about and you'd rather she stayed on the shelf than marry someone you don't approve of, isn't that right? Your pride has been

Oliva's downfall, not my passion. You are the one that has ruined her."

He raced up the steps, two at a time. His steps echoed in the stairway and mingled with my heartbeats, which were galloping wildly. I heard him lean over the banister two floors up and yell, "Apologize? Never! You should be on your knees now apologizing to me for having dared drag my name to the carabinieri. You'll see how this goes: I'll knock your horns off. I know people, the verdict is already written: Your horns will be knocked off!"

Starting his whistling again, he knocked at the door and went in.

I sat on the first step and waited for the buzzing in my ears to die down. I didn't want to die right there and then and leave my daughters to their own devices. Sometimes in life the only choice is to keep going. I put my hat back on to hide the cold sweat on my forehead and slowly walked back home.

———

Amalia points out the roads of the town to Lia, who nods obligingly but goes on listening to some singer yelling. Instinctively, I bring my hand up to my left arm even though I haven't felt any pain since Cosimino paid for an operation on my coronary arteries with the best specialist in the region. There are some pains that get better with time and others that no surgeon will ever be able to excise.

I knew how your trial would go, Olì. That's the truth. But you had decided to go ahead with it and what was I supposed to do? I felt like a lion caught in a net: the harder I struggled, the tighter it got. There is no end to the mistakes you can make in your life.

74

There is no end to the mistakes you can make in your life. When I was little, it felt like I had a spotlight inside me: it lit up my path and showed me where to go to avoid the pitfalls, like when I was doing long division, even with a decimal point. Little by little, the light grew dimmer, and since I slipped up the first time, I've been afraid of falling ever since. I regretted coming back to Martorana almost immediately, and after that lunch with the Scibettas, I stopped going up to the old center and stayed down by the sea surrounded by the new developments.

One day, I took my courage in both hands and went to explore the dirt track that, come rain or shine, I had trekked so many times in my wooden clogs. My expedition was fruitless: our little house was gone and your land had been dug to lay the foundations of a modern apartment block in reinforced concrete. I came back empty-handed. I had been looking for something that no longer existed. I told myself that coming back was a big mistake and that I should have moved closer to you on the Scibetta family land. You never asked me, you never ask anything, but I knew you wanted me to: the house is big enough, nobody knows anything about our past, people look us in the face when we meet them on the street, you would say on the phone. I had decided to come and live with you.

One morning I heard steps outside my door. I knew who it was right away: that lopsided gait had accompanied my childhood games. "It's open," I shouted from the kitchen without moving.

"I've been waiting for you, Olì," he said as we sat on opposite sides of the table.

His hair had grown longer and he had a red beard that covered the birthmark on his left cheek.

"For me? What for?"

"For everything."

Saro wasn't smiling. His expression had the tenacity of someone who has spent more time struggling against the obstacle of his own body than against others.

"You know what I can offer you: my father's carpentry workshop, sawdust in our hair, an entire history of loving you that has been weighing on my chest since we used to play cloud games. And then, of course, there's my mother's secret recipe for anchovy pasta."

It was the best part of my childhood: Nardina and Vito Musumeci, summers in the shade of the giant tree outside the workshop, the smell of freshly sawed wood, cedar, walnut, cherry, each with its own scent, Nardina's voice calling us to lunch, the shutters pulled closed for the siesta.

Could all this be mine still? Would I still be able to look up at the sky and glimpse the outline of a marfoyle?

"No," I said. "No, Saro. The moment has passed."

Saro didn't say anything. He brushed my hand and left. A few days later I filled in the forms for a transfer, folded them into an envelope, and put it in my bag. Weeks went by and I still hadn't made it to the post office. One month later, though, I went to the workshop and asked Saro to come and take measurements for a built-in wardrobe. I watched him work quietly for a few days without asking me anything. Time passed effortlessly between us, words and silence mingled easily, and his careful, precise workmanship as he lined up the wooden planks made me feel I could entrust my bones, my cartilage, the pores of my skin to him. That he would take the same care with them.

When he had finished the wardrobe, he asked me what color I wanted it. I shrugged and didn't say anything, like that time you, Pà, took me to the pastry shop to buy a cake. I wasn't used to knowing what I wanted.

Saro scratched his beard and I was suddenly dying to know whether his birthmark actually tasted like strawberry.

"If it were your house, what color would you choose?" I asked.

"I prefer natural wood," he said. "All you need to do is prime it with some impregnating oil and it brings the color out." He started looking for a pot of varnish on the shelf.

"Let's leave it natural, then," I answered, grabbing a brush, as happy as when I was little and, together with you, Pà, we painted the chicken coop.

75

Your mother couldn't accept the fact that a girl might like doing boys' work. But at the end of the day, everyone is different and the only person with a yardstick is the Lord. Mena, for example, wanted Lia to do classical ballet, didn't she? And then Lia became passionate about tennis. You can't complain.

Now, see, we're going past the church where you were christened and confirmed and your mother looks down and starts rummaging in her bag as if she is looking for something, but there is nothing to find. Do you think her body language doesn't tell me exactly what she's thinking after all these years?

"I don't like celebrations," you said on the phone afterward. Mena, who heard about it from her mother, told us about the ceremony. At six in the morning, in an empty church, only Nora and Nardina as witnesses. After the priest's blessing, Saro went back to the workshop and you got ready for school. You gave out the flowers in your bouquet to the children in your class and played loves me, loves me not with them. Your mother still hasn't come to terms with it. Why did she have to do it in secret, as if she were stealing the sacrament out of God's hands? And what about her dress, her trousseau?

Amalia sighs and looks out the window again. There's no trace of the wedding, not even a photo. Your mother wasn't there in the front pew crying her eyes out, your brother and sister weren't called as witnesses, there were none of your old school friends, Liliana wasn't there to hold your veil, there was no organ music and no choir, no wafting incense, no altar boys tripping over their cassocks.

I wasn't there to walk you down the aisle and give you away. You gave yourself away. You put yourselves into each other's hands. Right? Wrong? What should a father say? Maybe you needed to distance yourself from everyone, including me, before you could give yourself to a man.

76

We went to Don Ignazio hand in hand, as if we were already husband and wife and were simply informing him of the fact. Nora was crying, maybe because she was counting on me being the last girl in town who was still on the shelf. Nardina had permed her hair at the hairdresser's and had varnished her nails even though at dawn, in a deserted church, nobody would see her. I suppose after a lifetime of being considered unattractive she was used to dressing up for her own benefit. Vito Musumeci's good looks had faded over the years, making him less conspicuous. Time had made them more similar. Just as the dabs of a kneadable eraser smudge the outlines of a drawing, so had age softened her imperfections and dimmed his good looks. They sat on the wooden pew holding hands, indifferent to what the other townspeople thought.

Saro had shaved his beard. I had put a touch of blush on my cheeks to hide my tiredness.

The night before, I couldn't get to sleep. It was hot and, just before dawn, I went out onto the balcony and sat down to absorb the cool air rising from the sea. There was another sound, mingling with the breaking of the waves on the rocks, a regular rhythmic swishing. I leaned over and looked down onto the street. I saw the shape of Carmelina by the front door, holding a broom and sweeping the street in front of our building.

"Donna Carmelina!" I called out to her. "What are you doing up at this time?"

She looked up. The moon shone against the white braid she had wound around her head.

"Sorry, dear, if I woke you," she answered.

"Of course not! I was already up. I couldn't sleep. What about you?"

"I'm cleaning the street," she said in a stage whisper. "For when the bride walks by. The dress must always be immaculate." Later, she came upstairs to do my hair.

Before walking down the aisle, Saro whispered in my ear, "Please tell me before we go whether you're marrying me out of pity." He looked down at his leg. "I don't mind but I just want to know before." "What about you, then?" I asked him. He took my arm and we made our way down the nave: the cripple and the disgrace.

On our wedding night, Saro lay down next to me in my bed and held my hand. I had to familiarize myself with his body and gain confidence, as if he were an animal in the wild. I watched him as he slept, under the shower, getting dressed, and as he carefully shaved around the strawberry birthmark that I had wanted to lick when I was little. Day by day, it felt as though the child Saro had always contained the adult, and that the adult Saro revealed, in a clearly visible silhouette, the child. One night,

I made the first move, as if I had suddenly found a gate open that I thought had been closed.

That's what happens with fear: the gates are there, locked, until we find the courage to go through them.

———

I'm still scared, Pà, when I get to the other side of the piazza and find myself, for the second time in years and years, in front of that door. PASTICCERIA PATERNÒ, the sign says, as it always has. I go up to the counter. There's no one there but I can hear voices in the bakery. I look back and think that I still have time to leave, like a chicken who has lost its sense of direction. Then I hear some steps and a figure appears behind the counter filled with almond cakes.

The shock sets him off kilter for a second, as if he is unable to focus on what is in front of him. The last time he saw me, almost twenty years ago, he had the bravado of a victor—a man, stronger, more powerful, and righteous, the law vindicating him even when he was in the wrong.

He gives me a quick once-over, then looks down at the pastries. I have been waiting for this moment since the day he moved back to Martorana after his father's death. It took time, it took a lot of women who were braver than me, it took a lot more noes, shouted louder than mine, adding their voices to mine. The wait took years made up of days, days made up of hours, hours made up of minutes, and minutes made up of seconds.

77

I t took your phone call, your lunch invitation, and your determination to get us all the way here, street after street, building after building, ascent after ascent. The piazza is exactly the same even with the new stores, the freshly paved road, the junction with the dirt track that used to take us home. The turnoff for the coast road and the new buildings by the sea have always filled me with fear because the sea has no roots.

Cosimino parks the car and we all get out a little stiffly. Amalia pulls down her dress with her hands and looks around. This is your home, you live a life here that we know nothing about, in a modern building that was built no more than ten years ago, in the new part of town. Rather than the loamy scent of earth, there is a brackish smell of salt water. And yet this is where you chose to plant your new roots and bloom.

"Fourth floor," the voice on the intercom answers. "There's an elevator."

"I'll go up on foot," I say, taking the stairs followed by Lia, who is singing something softly in a foreign language.

Saro greets us at the door looking a little bashful, as if he were still the child he once was. He shows us around the house and lets us into your secret life: crockery in pairs, bathrobes hanging side by side, pillows puffed up together.

"You've made yourselves a lovely home," Cosimino declares, Mena nodding in agreement. I know what he's thinking, of course. He's thinking that if you came and lived near us, you'd have far more than two rooms and a corner kitchen. And Saro could leave the carpentry workshop and go into business with him. But you want to stay here; a reed before the wind lives on, and the time has finally come to lift your head.

78

That's what you always used to say, Pà: "a reed before the wind lives on." Well, my moment has come.

"Good morning," I say, without looking down.

He looks confused and picks up the pastry tongs, but his hands betray his nervousness by trembling. He's aged: once dark and curly, he is now graying at the temples and his hairline is receding. I take the liberty to observe him calmly. The corners of his mouth are sagging, the skin under his eyes is puffy, his forehead is furrowed with three deep lines that grew deeper as soon as he spotted me. There is no jasmine smell: he has lost the affectation of the sprig tucked behind his ear. He is like a tree that has dried up. The branches are still strong, though: his muscular arms stick out from his rolled-up sleeves but his paunch pulls at the shirt buttons. When he looks up, I see his eyes are the same but milder. I tune in to my heartbeat and realize I have skipped only half a beat and the rhythm has already returned to normal. I grab my own hand with the other and squeeze twice, to keep myself company.

He is still good-looking, Paternò. Not as handsome as he was twenty years ago, when he cut the air as he passed by, making even saints dizzy with desire. He has the looks of a man who knows how sad it is to win without deserving to and gaining nothing from the victory.

"I'd like a cake for a special celebration. Is there anything ready that I can take?"

Paternò puts the tongs down, sighs, and combs his hair back with his hands. In the left corner of the store there is a refrigerated display stand, which he indicates with his right arm, palm facing up. I walk over to the stand, my sandals gently swooshing against the marble floor. It is owing to a broken heel that we are here today, on opposite sides of the counter. I stand in front of the brightly colored frostings and fillings and my mouth waters just as it used to do when I was little.

"I'd like a cassata for my whole family," I say, pointing at the biggest one of all, covered in marzipan and candied fruit. He looks at the display, then at me, and in no time at all he has walked over and taken the cake out, and is holding it in both hands. The smell of his skin suddenly fills my nostrils but he has turned away and gone back to his place behind the counter. The strength that has been keeping me upright seems to have left me. I feel as if I had run a marathon. My knees are wobbling from the effort as I follow his actions in slow motion: he gets a cardboard box, places it in the middle of the counter, puts the cake inside, closes it meticulously, takes a sheet of wrapping paper with his name printed on it, wraps the box, unwinds a length of gold ribbon from the spool, cuts it with a pair of scissors, ties it in a bow, and curls the ends with the blades. Neutral

gestures that have nothing unseemly about them, hands
with no cruelty in them, the same ones that probably tuck
his daughter up at night. Where has the fury gone? Where
is the contempt and derision? Has the harm he has done
me left him completely unscathed? All the words I wanted
to say drown in my throat. The man I have been fighting
against for so long exists only in my nightmares, and the
man standing before me is not even worthy of my disdain.

Sitting on the stool next to the cash register, I finally
see him for what he is: a tired man who is aging badly, disappointed, like everyone, by how fast it happened. He has
lost out, too. He, too, is a victim: of ignorance, of old ways
of thinking, of machismo to be displayed at all costs, of
laws superseded by time and history but still holding on.
At least they were until yesterday. Maddalena was right, Pà.
Women are not fragile; people who suffer injustice are.

———

I check the price on the tag and put the money down at the
cash register. I pick up the package that his hands have just
touched and am almost at the door when I hear his voice
calling.

"You said you didn't want the cassata that day. Was it
a lie?"

His words stick under my skin like a brittle spine of a sea
urchin and for a second the other him reappears, the one
that filled me with shame with one glance. And yet I know
he can't hurt me because I'm not the same girl I was back

then. His tone is mocking, as it was then, but the question is real. He wants to know, from me, whether he is guilty or not. The conviction he received does not satisfy him. He is asking me to be the judge, twenty years later, standing in his father's pastry shop that is now his.

I go back to the counter. He stands up and stares at me from the other side. This time, he is the weaker party.

"What I want or don't want is nobody's business but mine," I answer, without retreating an inch. The rules of retribution are the most complicated of all: you learn them only once you have already received redress.

"So why did you come here?" he insists, raising his voice, which shakes with apprehension as if he were expecting me to mete out a punishment. "To tell me you were right to refuse everything I offered you? What have you gotten out of it?"

His yelling doesn't scare me: he is no longer my torturer. He is just a man. A man who has not actually understood what he has done wrong. As if I were standing up at school and answering a test, I tell him calmly, spelling out every word because I know the answer by heart.

"I've come to buy with money I have earned from my job what many years ago you wanted to force on me. What have I gotten out of it? The freedom to choose."

He arches his brow and doesn't answer. He looks sincerely surprised, as if he were grappling with something he had never considered before: the possibility of accepting the word *no*.

From the door of the pastry shop, I hear a pattering of feet.

"Good morning, Miss," a high voice pipes up. We both start.

"Hi, Marina," I say with a smile. "Have a nice Sunday!" I bend down to her level and stroke the hair off her face. Then I go out.

I cross the piazza holding the package. Other children, out with their mothers, shout and wave hello. A few old people stop and stare, curious to see me leaving the Paternò pastry shop. A gust of wind clears the hot stale air and I walk more briskly, down the big road, then onto the road that goes down to the sea, when I start running as fast as I can. The rules of running have stayed the same and never change, and I keep going, legs, arms, and heart, breathing through my mouth, my cheeks burning, my unkempt hair flying in the wind, the back of my neck damp with sweat, until I see in the distance the new buildings and Cosimino's car parked close to my house. Carmelina leans out her window.

"They're all up there already," she shouts, smiling.

I hurry toward the front door but she calls again.

"Olì, hold on a second. The postman brought you this." She hands over a letter with no return address. I stick it in my bag and run up the stairs, two at a time, ring the doorbell, and wait for someone to answer. The person who opens the door is you.

79

I open the door and it's you, holding a cake box with the name of the pastry shop on it. Why did you want him to be here with us today? Is it because even the things that hurt us are part of who we are? Is that it? Saro comes and takes the package out of your hands, searching your eyes for an answer. You bat your eyelids and cock your head to one side. He smiles, kisses you on the head, and goes into the kitchen. Out of a bag, you fish a bunch of slightly crushed daisies. I put them in a vase in the sitting room, next to the wildflowers I brought you from my garden.

Your mother throws her arms around your neck and you let her hug you. When she lets go, you say hi to Mena and Cosimino. "What about Lia?" you ask. "Didn't you bring her?" Mena points to the balcony and only then do you see your niece leaning on the railing and looking out at the sea. "Little kids, little problems; big kids, big problems," Mena complains. "You have to believe me, Olì, from one day to the next, she's grown so much I can hardly recognize her. Until a year ago, she was a good little girl, do you remember? Now she doesn't even answer when I talk to her. She asked for that diabolical contraption for her birthday. It's for listening to music and it cost an arm and a leg and of course her father gave in as always. She spends all day in her room with those things in her ears. We used to listen to music together, we practiced our dance steps, and chatted. Things were better in our day. Do you remember what we were like at fifteen?"

You sigh and go out onto the balcony to see your niece. You remember perfectly well what you were like at fifteen. She turns around but she doesn't kiss you. You put a hand on her shoulder and you stay in that position until your mother calls you in because the other guests have arrived.

Fortunata is dressed for a party and she's smiling. Finally, the name we gave her suits her. She and her husband are each holding a child's hand and a third is in the stroller. They have brought two bags full of produce from the factory: jam, olive oil, peeled tomatoes. These are bottled in my section, your sister boasts proudly.

The casual conversation is not for me. All the things I'd like to have said to you, but you've never heard come out of my mouth, must have reached you anyway. I go out onto the balcony and stand next to my granddaughter looking at the sea, which never stops moving. We don't need words, the two of us: she has her music and I have my silence. I wouldn't be surprised if, out of everyone in the family, she turns out to be the one most like me. When Saro says lunch is ready, we both take a last look at the mess of blue waves and white foam and then go into the dining room. You tell us all where to sit: Lia is between her parents, you next to your husband, and me at the other end. You look at us one by one, seated around the table, and smile.

80

I look at you one by one, seated around my table: this is the day of my graduation, my engagement, my first pay packet, and my wedding feast. It is not compensation. It is physical presence after a long absence, speaking after getting past silence, catching breath after running without ever looking back. The table is crowded. Those who are not present are also here: Maddalena, Liliana, Calò, the attorney Sabella, the women on the street who burned their bras, those who now sit in parliament, those who are at home cooking lunch, those who get slapped around and are ashamed of it, those who marry for money, those who call other women disgraces from the safety of their windows, those who have studied a lot and those who still know nothing, and finally, Carmelina, who swept the street in the middle of the night so that I could go into church with an immaculate dress.

Fortunata's kids run around the house; their father, Armando, chases them, threatening punishments, but I let them do it. I don't know whether there will be any other children to fill these rooms. Cosimino and Saro look like two little boys, like when we used to all play together. Armando tries to strike up a conversation with you, Pà, trying to break your silence. He talks about the factory, work shifts, pay differentials. You nod and wait patiently for him to stop. Mamma, Mena, and Fortunata are exchanging the latest gossip.

Lia has found refuge on the balcony again, in the same corner where I often sit. She has stuck her index finger into the cassette and is winding the tape back. "I'm saving the battery," she tells me, even though I haven't asked. I sit next to her and try to start a conversation, "When you were little . . ." but she doesn't let me go on. "Don't talk to me like my mother does. She still treats me like a child and lays down rules for everything. You did what you liked, without caring what anyone thought, you were different. I'd like to run away from everything sometimes: from home, from our town, from Sicily, like you did."

There's a light breeze from the sea and I suddenly feel cold. "You're wrong, Lia. I wanted to be just like my school friends, I would have given anything to be the same as them."

Lia stops winding the tape back, pulls her bangs off her face, and looks at me in shock. She doesn't look like her parents, or any of us. Her beauty is entirely her own. "But you've always been an example for me," she confesses in disappointment. "You rebelled!"

I take the cassette out of her hands and complete the job for her. "Do you know how many times I'd have liked to do this with my life? To wind back the tape and start over differently?"

Lia picks at a spot under her bangs. "Do you mean you regret it?"

"There are some noes that cost nothing, and others that carry a very high price. I paid everything I had for my no, and so did my family. For a long time, I felt alone, judged, mistaken, but now I know I was right and what I did was the right thing to do. But this is my story, and everyone has their own, a bit like your songs." I smile and hand her cassette back. "You, for example, what music do you listen to?"

Lia chews at the nail on her index finger and doesn't answer, as if she were concentrating on another thought. Then she smiles a little, revealing the metal brace on her teeth.

"A friend recorded this for me." She gets the tape, sticks it in the Walkman, pushes a red button, and hands me the headphones.

"And what's this friend like? Do you like him?" I ask, as a romantic song in English starts playing in my ears.

Lia opens her palms and arches her brows. "I don't know if I like him yet. It takes time to know."

"You've gone red, he's your boyfriend!" I tease her.

"Auntie, what are you saying? I'm only fifteen."

———

It is late by the time the door closes and the voices and laughter fade down the stairs. "Come to bed," Saro calls. "We can clear up tomorrow at our leisure."

Everything is topsy-turvy but I don't mind our tidy house being upended for one evening. "I'm coming," I reassure him, then hear his steps going toward the bedroom.

I clear the plates from the table, make a pile, and take them into the kitchen. Then I pick up the glasses and cutlery. I pull the tablecloth toward me and bundle it up into a ball. Don't leave crumbs on the table, or the dead will come and feed, Mother used to say. Better the dead than the living, you would comment, Pà.

When everything is back in its place, I go out onto the balcony and sit in the spot where, until a few hours ago, Lia was sitting. I open the newspaper that I had picked up this morning at the stand and read: "Articles 544 and 587 of the Criminal Code have been repealed: rape marriage and honor killings are now illegal in Italy." A short little article where the stand-out words are: *barbarianism*, *Rocco Code*, *modernization*, *homicide*, *Mezzogiorno*, *rape*, and *marriage*. Then, among the names of the promotors of the law, I see Liliana Calò, member of parliament for the Communist Party.

I lean out over the balcony. The lights are out in Carmelina's house, and I suddenly remember the envelope I slipped into my bag. I go back in, leaving the shutters open so that the sea air floods all the rooms. Saro is already asleep. I turn the light off and go back to the dining room.

On the envelope, my name and address are written in a hand I don't recognize. I pick up the letter opener from my desk and tear the envelope open. There is a white-bordered card with a black-and-white image printed in the middle. In the penumbra it takes a few seconds to focus on what I am looking at: a young girl with eyes as black as olives and unkempt hair, her knees grazed, and a sulky expression. I turn the card around to see what is written: "I kept the promise I made to this girl. Liliana."

I look at the photograph and it is like looking at myself in the mirror. The little girl running as fast as she can without looking back, who knows the secret shapes of the clouds and who looks for answers in daisy petals, is still me.

He loves me, he loves me not.

He loves me, he loves me not.

He loves me.

A NOTE FROM
THE TRANSLATOR

Viola Ardone delicately unpicks the contemporary issue of consent by shifting it back in time and setting the (fact-based) story in Sicily. Sicily is considered traditional even by Italian standards, yet both honor killings and "marry your rapist" reparations were legally sanctioned in *the whole of Italy* until as late as 1981. As a high school history and Italian literature teacher, Ardone recognizes that "other-ing" the time and place of her story makes it easier to address the issue and, perhaps, underscore the fact that we should never take for granted the rights that people like Oliva Denaro and Liliana Calò (in real life, Franca Viola and Maria Angela Bottari) sacrificed so much for.

Some of the translation challenges of the novel are reflected in the resulting historical and geographical specificity. The first words in the novel immediately set the bar high. In Italian, the mother's warning (reflected in a popular song) is *La femmina è una brocca, chi la rompe la piglia*, which I eventually translated as "A girl is a jug, you break her, you take her." Throughout the novel, and in southern Italy in general, the word *femmina*—a member of the female sex—is interchangeable with "girl" or "woman," whereas in English it feels technical, reserved for talking about animals or gender in the abstract. Should I translate *femmina* as "girl" or as "woman"? Oliva was still very young when her mother started warning her of the dangers of the opposite sex. How long can you call a girl a girl, and when does she become a woman? These things depend on context. I went for "girl," in the end, as the mother's pessimistic view is that once you are a "woman" you are somehow already "broken."

The provincial Sicilian town that Oliva's mother finds herself situated in as an "outsider" posed another difficulty. The mother mutters imprecations in a Calabrian dialect nobody understands when she is angry, which is almost always. Her teachings are almost always in the form of sayings, proverbs, or idioms that she repeats incessantly. These are almost impossible to translate fully. Centuries of class barriers, folk wisdom, religion, and agricultural knowledge have crystallized within them and, while every culture has equivalents, they do not always involve the same animals, plants, weather patterns, or customs. In one case, I kept the original concept even though there is no English equivalent—having crickets in your head—because *Pinocchio* familiarized us with the idea of a talking cricket and because I felt the expression's true meaning, "getting strange ideas," lost too much in translation. In the case of the mother's euphemism for menstruation—*il marchese*—I opted to stay close to the original, after discarding a multitude of bizarre expressions in use around the world. The word "marquis," I felt, recognizably conveys the horror (to us) of the idea that menstruation was caused by a male member of the aristocracy, as if he were invoking his right to *jus primae noctis*.

Another sticking point was Oliva's father's level-gazed, "I wouldn't prefer it"—a phrase repeated in different contexts throughout the novel. In Italian, Ardone uses *non lo preferisco*, which is unusual. Nor is it a Sicilian turn of phrase. Italians would normally say *Preferisco di no*, which is how Bartleby the Scrivener's phrase "I would prefer not to" was translated into Italian. I ended up with "I wouldn't prefer it" because it is grammatically incorrect, reflecting the man's illiterate background. At the same time, it denotes a certain pride in being able to make an independent decision and "prefer" one solution over another in a context where there is seemingly no choice. His unwavering support for his daughter, whatever she decides, his insistence that she must be the one to give her consent, even when choosing a cake in the pastry store, is one of the most moving things about the novel, and all these elements are contained in this one phrase.

In the novel, eyes are busy all the time, continuously downcast, throwing glances, rolling, spying, or signaling. Nonverbal communication of this kind is one of the most difficult things to carry across in a translation, as no part of the many-layered significance of a gesture must be taken for granted. My hope is that readers will sense the power of the town's censorious gaze and Oliva's impotence when her looks, words, and actions are deliberately misconstrued.

Receive the intentions and the nonverbal elements of the text without noticing them. That they will feel under their skin the universal force of the message, which is as powerful and relevant today as it was for Oliva Denaro in her specific experience—maybe even more so in a cultural climate that is questioning who owns the decisions regarding our bodies. For our ultimate aim as translators is to be invisible so that the words and their meaning exist in their own right.

—Clarissa Botsford

Here ends Viola Ardone's
The Unbreakable Heart of Oliva Denaro.

The first edition of the book was printed
and bound at Lakeside Book Company
in Harrisonburg, Virginia, April 2023.

A NOTE ON THE TYPE

The text of this novel was set in ITC Legacy Serif, a serif typeface designed in the early 1990s by Ronald Arnholm. This revival set was developed after Arnholm encountered a fifteenth-century printing of Eusebius' *De evangelica praeparatione* during his graduate studies at Yale. Set by the legendary Nicolas Jenson, creator of the Roman typeface, this 1470 volume served as a reference point from which Arnholm crafted his design revival. ITC Legacy Serif reverently captures the original's beauty, delicately rendering increased legibility with dutiful grace.

HARPERVIA

An imprint dedicated to publishing international voices,
offering readers a chance to encounter other lives and other
points of view via the language of the imagination.